Pale Moon Rising

First published in the U.S.A. by St. Martin's Press in 1978
Copyright © 1977 by Rory and Sheila O'Brine
All rights reserved. For information, write:
St. Martin's Press, Inc., 175 Fifth Ave., New York, N.Y. 10010.
Manufactured in the United States of America

Library of Congress Cataloging in Publication Data

O'Brine, Manning, 1913-1977
 Pale moon rising.

  1. World War, 1939-1945 — Fiction.
I. Title.
PZ4.0137Pa   1978   [PR6065.B75]   823'.9'14
ISBN 0-312-59478-X   77-16739

Pale Moon Rising

Manning O'Brine

Pale Moon Rising

St. Martin's Press
New York

First published in the U.S.A. by St. Martin's Press in 1978
St. Martin's Press, Inc., 175 Fifth Ave., New York, N.Y. 10010.
Manufactured in the United States of America

Library of Congress Cataloging in Publication Data

O'Brine, Manning, 1913-1977
  Pale moon rising.

  1. World War, 1939-1945 — Fiction.
I. Title.
PZ4.0137Pa   1978   [PR6065.B75]   823'.9'14
ISBN 0-312-59478-X   77-16739

For

JACK and RUTH

For the memories
that we share

Death and his brother Sleep!
One pale as yonder wan and hornéd moon,
With lips of lurid blue,
The other glowing like the vital morn.
Shelley.

ONE

They grow cabbages there now . . . with ivy and convulvulus knitting random patterns around the rusted skeins of barbed wire. A paint-flaked, worm-ridden notice lies amongst last year's and all the years' compost-making leaves. Generations of cheese-bugs have founded an undisturbed haven beneath it. But if you really care to, you can still decipher the message . . . KEEP OUT.

Two simple words, they made prudent sense at the time. I mean, only bloody fools like me had the urge to get *into* Gibraltar Farm.

Looking back on it, it was one of those things. Things you do on a whim and a prayer and regret afterwards. Though regret is hardly the word. Not when you remember the weeks, months, years of man-hours spent learning, perfecting, operating a trade that offered no more than a six-to-four-on nemesis of death in a dark, disgusting, inglorious way. No, regret is hardly the word; more Jesus-Christ-what-a-stupid-clot-of-a-man-I-was.

And yet . . . I don't know. The thousand-to-one chance of living came up for me. Otherwise I wouldn't be standing here watching the cabbages grow. All the same, I have no wish to be around here at duskfall, November mist rising and mingling with the ghosts of those who knew this place as well, if not better than I did, and lost out. Men and women who left the now weeded-over airstrip of RAF Tempsford, with a parachute on their backs and a looseness in their bowels, waiting to spill out over German-occupied Europe.

Why they did it only they in their secret hearts knew. Hatred, revenge, bravado, patriotism – all were reasons that could have been given but rarely emerged beyond an enigmatic smile. Ask one of them – and I did of several – and it could be summed up in the answer voiced by a fresh-faced boy of twenty. His only qualifications for being there were a

7

rather fractured French and an acute awareness of his failure to become a Spitfire pilot. 'It's a job to be done, isn't it?'

Another said: 'I didn't fancy overmuch being a platoon commander in the bloody infantry, leading thirty reluctant cowards through a mine-field, trip-wires and machine-guns on fixed lines and the odd sodding mortar bomb arriving out of the blue to whip my bollocks away! Oh, no, I'd have been the biggest bloody coward of them all, see, that wouldn't have done, would it, pointed finger of scorn and all that? This way, at least, who's going to know if I turn a paler shade of piss-yellow and crawl up the nearest drain, like?'

That one was a Welshman. The Welsh were always loquacious, a Dylan Thomas baton in every knapsack. Yet not so loquacious I ever knew his true identity. I dubbed him Morgan the Organ and it had nothing to do with his prowess in the choir-loft unless you count the vicar's daughter and *Abed With Me* being his favourite hymn. Not anymore, alas. He died in Block 12, KL-Belsen-I, on the 10th of April, 1945, just five days before the British infantry liberated the place.

Like Taff Morgan, it wasn't the fighting that attracted me. No one in his right mind likes fighting. For the obvious reason – you can get hurt. Even with your enemy disarmed, cowering on the ground. If you are not accustomed to swinging an axe it can take the skin off the inside of the thumb. Very painful. I know, from personal experience, whilst dealing with a member of the Karstjäger SS.

Not the fighting, but the killing. No particular pleasure ... you would hardly use that term when stamping on a cockroach, which is precisely how I saw the German. A filthy pest on the face of Europe. The more I killed, the better, with no trauma of revulsion afterwards, no Macbeth wringing of the hands, no urge to vomit when blood gushed from the mouth of the very first one. They had started something and I was going to finish it ... or die in the attempt.

If that sounds like heroics, forget it. Heroes are made from acts opposed to self-inclinations. Mine never were. They were imbued with a fanaticism which had no roots in love for country or cause. Nor was it born out of hatred. To hate someone demands a measure of respect for that someone. That, above all else, I never had for any German. Deep loathing, yes. Utter contempt, yes. And don't let's start splitting hairs about Nazis and non-Nazis. A nation of bully-boys and baby-butchers, they were with their Führer all the way so long as he was winning. The ratting only came with the turning tide of defeat. And now, thirty years on, looking over the rusted wire at the cabbages, I must refute all I said at the beginning. With hindsight and experience I would do it all over again, but a damn sight more efficiently. I was, in all truth, so green and raw in those far-off days!

TWO

Green and raw I had to be. A student still, just out of my teens, I had got into the British Army under a phoney name, a forged birth certificate, and a cover story with more holes in it than a cobweb and about as substantial.

There was no other way. The country I considered my *patria* had come into the war on the wrong side and a quirk of fate had found me stranded in a neutral country holding the hand of a dying grandmother. I could have stayed on in Eire, I suppose, though God knows why anyone should want to. Not the Irish, that's for sure. They couldn't get out of the place fast enough, even though they were rid of the British. Grandmama used to say it was a great place if you were a priest, a pig, or a publican. She always added she was prejudiced, that's why she stayed there, she felt so much at home. I had no such prejudices about the country. With her death, even Connemara was a nothing.

Thus it was that I went north, across the border to Ulster, to County Antrim, to the Infantry Training Centre at Bally-mena; a new recruit sharing a barrack room with a mixture of Eireann volunteers and East End of London Jewish conscripts. Our squad sergeant was a lovely man. An Orangeman who had served in Palestine and hated the guts of Jews and citizens of Eire alike. Listening to his opening tirade at us

9

Cohens and Kellys left one wondering why we bothered with Nazis whilst we had him for target-practice?

Fate balanced things out with a dyed-in-the-hairshirt saint of a company officer. An actor by trade, a soldier by impulse, and more than something of a psychologist by instinct, he made it his business to understand men, to help them adjust to this new way of life, to treat them as individuals rather than as numbers. Consequently, at the end of a first week of shivering on pre-dawn parade; of blue-fingered fumbling at the parts of a rifle; of running on the spot long past the stage where lungs gave out; of unthought-of muscles stiffened, feet sore and mind sick of phrases such as 'What we are going on with now—' and 'What are youse? I'll tell youse what youse are, a dozy, idle, fockin' shower, move t' th' le-eft in threes, w-a-i-i-I-T for it!' from our oh-so-lovable three-striper; at the end of that first week that lasted a thousand light years, you saw and heard Captain Jack Allen of the gentle smile and soft voice as Christ Walking The Water.

After two weeks, the incredulity became a respect tinged with awe. At the end of three months' preliminary training, it wasn't such a bad war, after all. If all the officers were like this one, you'd take that fatal step forward and volunteer for anything he might ask, be it over the edge where the flat earth ends with a fall into limbo. Oh yes, a shrewd cuss was our Jacko. Those somewhat-vague, slightly myopic blue eyes had all their marbles behind them; he had each and every one of us hook, shit or bust. 'D' Company was The Company.

Even so, he could have come a cropper. For reasons best known to himself, he saw me as Potential Officer material. That put a lance-stripe on the sleeve, white tape at the shoulders, and a dice with the Unknown – an interview with the Inquisitor-General. At that time, in Ulster, it was Carton de Wiart, VC, of 'one eye, one arm one anus' fame. And a one-track mind when it came to ferreting out a candidate's history. 'As far back as the bleeding womb!' – was the dejected observation by the first of our group after emerging from the mental torture-chamber.

That, then, was me for the high jump. My story blown

apart in five seconds flat. I went in wondering whether they shot people who enlisted under false colours or merely hung them by the thumbs. I was still figuring out the likely punishment when I heard the Great Man say: Ah, yes, Captain Allen's protégé, that right? Dam' good chap, Allen, knows how to pick men! You'll make a dam' good officer, I'm sure! Work hard at Sandhurst, you'll like it there, nice place, goodbye!' A firm grip of the hand. The interview was over.

I presume I saluted, made a smart about-turn. I was still in too much of a daze a week after to remember. Five months later, I walked out of the Royal Military College a second-lieutenant.

THREE

Earlier that same year – 1941 – 'X' Troop of the 11th Special Air Service Battalion had made a 'drop' at Tragino, in Southern Italy. The purpose had been to destroy an aqueduct carrying the main water supply for the province of Apulia. It was thought the operation might create alarm and despondency and even hamper Il Duce's war efforts in both the Adriatic and North Africa. Hardly specious reasoning, but it did provide an excuse to try out British paratroops.

About all that can be said for it. Only partially blown, the aqueduct was back in service before the nearest reservoir ran dry, and 'X' Troop were rounded up in a manner bordering on high farce.

It started with a pack of mongrels led by three pointers giving chase. The dogs were followed by a shrill of village children. These, in turn, were pursued by a gabble of anxious mamas screeching at the *bambini* to come back at once, with irate papas with pitchforks demanding the same of the mamas. Very much in the rear, came some circumspect *carabinieri*. Behind them, even more wary *fascisti militia*. To avoid unnecessary bloodshed, the paratroopers surrendered without firing a shot. The only casualty was their interpreter –

11

Fortunato Picchi, ex-Savoy Hotel, London. Failing to live up to his Christian name, he was duly court-martialled and executed for 'aiding the enemy'.

Yet it was this news of Operation Colossus that prompted a decision on my part. Until then, I had seen little hope of reaching Italy for a long time. As an orthodox soldier, at least. And it was the one country where – if I had any value at all – I could best serve the war effort. The Italians, it was evident, had no stomach for this war. Not for the glib reason given by the press and newsreel media – that they were a nation of organ-grinders and ice-cream salesmen incapable of courage. Any student of history would know that Garibaldi had more than nailed that lie less than a century before when leading them to liberation. The basic truth was that no matter what the shouting and wild gesticulation emanating from the balcony in Piazza Venezia, patriotism, *per se,* just wasn't enough. The people needed a reason. And all the reasons were *against* the war. Il Duce's allies – the Germans and the Austrians – were, by tradition, enemies. The concept of anti-semitism and racial persecution was an alien one, even to die-hards of the Fascist regime. The only bond that held the Axis partnership together – apart from personal friendship between Benito and Adolf – was, ironically enough, anti-Bolshevism. And at that particular time, Stalin was the fat cat purring over the cream that was his share of Poland, and supplying the necessary oil for Rommel's gang already on the move into North Africa.

Meanwhile, back at the ranch, across the Atlantic, two words – Pearl Harbour – were still unknown to most Americans, and Roosevelt had yet to make up his mind about Lease-Lend. And Britain soldiered on, alone, fumbling in the dark under a continuous rain of bombs.

But for me, at least, there was a personal glimmer of light. If only they would take me into Special Services, I might get back to Italy sooner rather than later, in some anti-Fascist resistance capacity.

It turned out to be later. Very much later. But that is another story. Thanks to a captain and a general, my luck had held good twice. A good pagan, I believed in the mystic trinity of the Mother Goddess. There was a third person – a man in high places – who might be prepared to help by pulling a few strings.

He did.

And I landed up at Gibraltar Farm.

Following my commission, I was quickly to learn that all officers were not Jack Allens. 'Regulars' still showed a flatulent hostility towards those who had been part-time, week-end Territorials. And the erstwhile members of the Sunday-morning Club at Chelsea Barracks, eyed newcomers like myself with friendly suspicion, ears cocked at accents, sly probing of backgrounds over pink gins in the mess. I played it like a clam, spent most of two months guarding a Martello tower, and waited for my mentor to make the first move.

It came one Friday afternoon. I had applied earlier in the week for a forty-eight hour pass, to be spent with a lady of my acquaintance, mostly in a horozintal posture. I arrived at the Adjutant's office to collect the vital passport to paradise, only to be greeted with a shake of the head and a slightly sadistic smile. He handed me Part II of Battalion Orders, a sealed envelope, and a travel warrant. I had been posted to STS Establishment at a place called Lochailort, twenty-five miles west of Fort William, and I would proceed forthwith.

'On Monday morning?' I asked. Hope springs eternal.

'On Monday morning,' he said, slowly. 'You'll be on a forty miles run-and-march. In full equipment. They call it getting to know the ground. I suggest you conserve your energy for that.' He read his watch. 'You have exactly one hour to pack, say any fond farewells, catch the London train in time for the Euston connection. My regards to Scotland. If you bag a few brace of pheasant the mess will remember you kindly.'

On that happy note, I was dismissed. So was the lady of my acquaintance. If she is still waiting under the clock at Victoria, I trust she will accept this tardy apology. I did telephone some months later, but a male voice answered. If it was Daddy, you never told me he came from Texas . . .

The house at Lochailort was built by Dracula's father, all over with mist and hemmed in by a black cliff topped with trees. The sun never showed itself throughout the twelve weeks. The mist lifted once in a while, to give way to sleeting rain. I 'died' with monotonous regularity four times a day and the only break was Christmas. That was spent in a Force Ten gale off the Shetlands, culminating in a raid on Vaagso in Norway. As an observer I wasn't strictly part of the Commando Force, but no one informed the enemy. A bullet furrowed my scalp, left me bloody and very bowed. 'Ye ken th' harrd wa', sor!' said my sergeant-instructor. 'Kep ye bleedy heid doon th' noo!'

The course came to its end. I was informed I had suffered well enough to pass the agonies on to others as an instructor. An invitation came from a few miles up the glen. Within a spit of Glenfinnan, to be precise. Only it wasn't a spit. It was a cloudburst. Situation normal, they told me, when there's no rain for sixty minutes the natives mutter in their sporrans about the drought. But if I wasn't to stay a Commando, I could opt for somewhere else.

I opted. The 'somewhere else' turned out to be Omagh, where they got the weather before Glenfinnan. The river was in full spate, the parade ground was a paddling-pool. The first person who splashed past me stopped, did a double-take, came back, gave me his hand.

'What are *you* doing here?' said Jack Allen.

'Come to show you how to train soldiers,' I said. Cheeky.

'H'm,' he said, then smiled. 'I've got a fresh intake. Deserters, delinquents, busted NCOs, odds and sods that others don't wish to know. In army terms, a right shower. I'd like to prove the army wrong. Interested?'

'Interested,' I said. 'Where do I start?'

He led me to the office, rapped his cane on an in-tray piled high. 'Do you understand pay-books?' he asked.

14

When I left him two-and-a-half months later, I had learned a lot about understanding men.

Whitehall had suddenly remembered what they had done with me. It wasn't enough, apparently. If I was going into Europe, it seemed, the first essential was to know the British Isles. From Aberdeen to Yealmpton, schools of demolition, sabotage, cyphers, radio, mine-lifting, unarmed combat, pseudo-Gestapo interrogation, rounded off with a specialist 'I' course in the Wirral and parachute jumps at Ringway, near Manchester.

As a result, I could kill a man seventeen different ways, blow a bridge, derail a train, booby-trap a truck, burn out a bunker, 'brew-up' a tank; I could travel seventy miles in twelve hours, by fair means or foul, with only a compass and the North Star to guide me; I could swim fast-flowing rivers, climb cliffs, beach boats silently, cross non-existent bridges when I came to them by means of a toggle-rope; I could take and transmit Morse, fire a rifle from either shoulder with equal accuracy, throw a knife like a circus performer; I could crawl like a snake, lose myself behind a blade of grass, and milk a cow lying flat on my back. What they hadn't taught me was to turn water into wine, make two fishes feed a thousand, and raise Lazarus . . . but that, no doubt, would come with perseverance.

In addition – a hangover from childhood – I could speak six languages. Although two of these – classical Greek and Latin would not stand me in much stead unless I met up with Socrates or got me to a nunnery. Of the other four, my weakest, accent-wise, was French. So, by process of Higher Command logic, it was decided to 'drop' me in France.

'You can refuse, of course,' I was told.

'If I did?'

'The workshops at Inverlair. Very remote, very damp. You could catch a cold.'

'Sneeze myself to death, in fact? France,' I said.

FOUR

'Your code-name will be Moulin-Bas,' they told me, for the fifth time. 'But your identity will be Patrice Morgat, a Breton from St Malo, a student-draughtsman by trade. You can draw, I suppose?'

For the fifth time I told them I could draw, that I could even do mirror-writing with my left hand, like Leonardo da Vinci. It made little or no impression.

'Your immediate task will be to link up with the FTP – Francs-Tireurs et Partisans, under the command of Joseph, at the same time collaborating as required with the CND – Confrérie Notre-Dame, run by Rémy alias Georges Roulier also known as Jean-Luc, within a proposed network known as Fana,' they said.

'Fana,' I said.

'Forget that bit,' they said.

'And all the other bits,' I said. But only under my breath. I was very much the junior officer of the party.

'Any questions?' they said.

'One,' I said, after giving it some thought. 'What about the war?'

'What about it?' they said.

'Killing Germans,' I said.

The two words brought a thin smile to three pairs of lips.

'Ah, *that*,' they said.

And handed me over to Major Why.

Major Why was Brigade of Guards, eight little buttons all in a row. Very thin, very long, he had to stoop a little to see most people about him. I believe he was Major initial Y—, but will always be Why to me. He had the unfortunate – possibly, deliberate – habit of posing questions even when giving an answer.

'Why are we waiting, h'm, h'm?' We stood on the corner of Duke and Wigmore Street, looking for a taxi there wasn't a hell's chance of finding, not with an air-raid in full crump. 'Why, why, why, eh? Don't tell me the answer, I already know, h'm? Because the Yanks have cornered the mart in 'em now that they're *in*, haven't they, dear boy? The first bloody motor-car into Berlin will be a London effing taxi, won't it, eh? With three American airmen and a tart from Rainbow Corner, h'm, h'm?'

'We could walk to sixty-eight, Orchard Court,' I said.

He looked down his nose at me from a great height. 'Ah – heard about The Flat, have we, and the Baker Street Runners?'

'A little bird up at Ringway.'

'Silly little poop should keep her silly big mouth shut, shouldn't she? I suppose you know about Wanborough Manor, too, h'm, h'm?'

I had heard about de Wesselow and the house near the Hog's Back, where they chased you from dawn to dusk, then got you nice and relaxed and pissed at the bar; then chased you all over the surrounding hills for most of the night. I had wondered why I hadn't been sent there. I had, after all, been everywhere else. I said as much.

'A glutton for punishment, aren't we, dear boy? From what they tell me, you could teach 'em a thing or two, h'm, h'm?'

'What about this Buckmaster bird?' I asked.

'Prefer him to us, do you?'

'There is a difference?' He had me doing it now.

A cryptic smile, a tap on the side of the nose. 'Wheels within wheels, old son, what?'

By this time we were walking towards Grosvenor Square. He walked fast for an old man. Old in my eyes, at least. All of forty. I was at some pains to keep up with him. As we turned in the direction of the Park, he peered down at me again, made with a little smile.

'If you don't mind me saying so, you don't look a bit like the type, do you, h'm? Very small hands I noticed, eh? Can

17

you really kill a man with a single chop, or perhaps I shouldn't be asking? Takes all sorts, doesn't it?' He brushed the parachute wings on my sleeve with his cane. 'Got to admit I'm envious of those, though, how d'you fellows do it, h'm, h'm?'

'We jump,' I said.

The house in Queen Anne's Gate was one of the grace-and-favour homes of SIS. Major Why led me straight through into the bathroom. 'The one at Orchard Court is used as a waiting-room,' he said. 'But here we're more practical, we take a bath, don't we, h'm, h'm?'

I wasn't sure about the plural. With him in it as well, I would just about wet a big toe if I clung to the geyser. But it was the royal 'we', as he flapped a hand in urgency. 'Chop-chop, dear boy, mustn't keep the lady waiting, must we?'

That sounded more promising. I had passed a delicious-looking Wren in the passage. Maybe she would teach me the breast stroke. I glanced at the lock that wasn't there on the door.

He read my mind with a bleak smile. 'All hope abandon ye who enter, eh?' And left me.

The soap was wartime French, mostly grit and little lather. An odour of garlic wrapped in moth-balls. I was drying myself on a hand-towel when Major Why returned.

'Hands, feet, inspection, eh?'

'Want me to cough, too?'

He lifted his eyebrows. 'Do I look like a medical wallah? If you need a truss, you've left it a bit late, h'm?'

My hands and feet were very clean. Too clean, apparently. 'Rub a little of this under the nails, mustn't we, eh?'

This was dirt.

'French dirt, of course,' I said, keeping it light.

'But naturally. We keep a jar of it for new customers, but next time you'll have brought your own back with you, yes?'

'My navel,' I said. 'It might be full of good old-fashioned English fluff.'

18

'I'll take your word it isn't, won't I?' He handed me a bundle of clothes, from under-vest to shoes. He gathered up my own, including my best barathea jacket, dropped them into a laundry-slip, snapped a lock on it. 'Dress and join me outside. Our little talk, eh?'

The clothes were well-worn and carried the same perfume as the soap. If I met up with a vampire dressed as a Nazis, he would shrivel on the spot. There was a stain on the shirt that I hoped was red wine, not blood. I examined myself in the cheval mirror. Not exactly *me*, but the fit wasn't bad. One of the shoes was built up inside to give me a limp. Dandy. I knotted the frayed tie, went out to find him.

Major Why was propping himself up behind a miniature bar. He eyed me with approval. 'Pretty. Very pretty, h'm?' He offered me an open cigarette box. Virginian, except for one tucked away in the corner. A Gauloise.

I took it. I was catching on. Another nod of approval. 'No nicotine stains on the fingers, I noticed, eh? Good chap. All your own teeth, no fillings, right? Hair cut by a Frog, yes? No appendix or other scars that could be British, h'm?'

'The love-bite on my left knee is Welsh,' I said. 'Girl named Blodwyn who likes to wander.'

'Don't they all?' he said. And dismissed it. 'Don't have to ask you about knives, forks, spoons, all that palaver, do I?'

I knew my French table manners; moving a spoon towards the chest instead of away; loading a fork like a shovel with the aid of a piece of bread. I shook my head. 'If Hercule Poirot is working for the Gestapo, he won't catch me out.'

'Good show – drink?'

'Scotch, please.'

Pastis he gave me. 'Patrice Morgat doesn't touch the malt, h'm?' He clucked like a stringy hen. 'Not *now*. But we'll save you one for when you come back, eh?'

'That's the second time,' I said.

'What's the second time?'

'You've mentioned my coming back. Do many?'

19

'You really expect me to tell you? It all depends on you, doesn't it?'

The Pastis tasted foul. 'If you say so.'

'But I do, don't I? Plus a trifle, too, on an unpleasant type name of Kramms, h'm?'

'Kramms,' I said.

'Fifth floor, Rue des Saussaies, Paris, eh?'

'Is that where I'm going?'

'Only if you are foolish, allow him to persuade you, h'm? And do try to steer clear of the Avenue Koch. Eighty-two, four, and six – Sturmbannführers Boemelburg, Kieffer, and Schmidt, I believe. Karl Boemelburg is a nancy, might fancy, know what I mean? But if they really class you important enough, there's General Oberg – a four-eyed sod – and a Colonel Doktor Knochen on the Boulevard Suchet, h'm?'

'I'll stick to des Nonnains d'Hyeres,' I said. 'Knock three times and ask for Arlette.'

A spark of lechery showed in his right eye. 'She's good, is she?'

'It's a girls' school. There's sure to be an Arlette amongst them.'

He nodded. 'Pity you won't be in Paris, eh?'

'Where?'

'Remember the maps we gave you to study?'

I remembered. Three of them. Photographed in my head. He produced a copy of one, spread it on the bar.

'This one, in particular?'

I read it upside-down. That was part of the test. Of the three, it was the one I wanted least of all. Pas-de-Calais.

'*Merde,*' I said. With feeling.

He chuckled. 'Oh, ever-so *merde,* old son, eh?'

I didn't see the joke.

FIVE

The car was a plush Daimler, with little curtains screening the windows. The driver was a FANY – the lady, I had

20

been told, we must not keep waiting. Fair of hair and a profile chiselled out of fine porcelain. Delicate, beautiful, English-rose, cool-looking. And likely thrashed around like a mad thing between sheets. A pity I would never find out.

A road to nowhere that I knew of brought us through the gate of RAF Tempsford. Sentries carrying fixed bayonets waved us on, past huts blacked out for the night. From one of them came the sound of music and a laugh. And I still didn't see the joke.

We drove on, across the aerodrome. A huddle of buildings loomed ahead, we stopped at one shaped like a barn.

'Out, dear boy, h'm?'

Gibraltar Farm.

Yet another check, just to be certain. Between Queen Anne's Gate and Tempsford I had not concealed a number eleven bus-ticket under my left armpit, nor a seat-tab from the Odeon, Watford. No toffee papers stuck to the soles of my shoes, no shreds of tobacco hidden in corners of pockets. Only a cheap leather wallet with some of the stitching gone that Major Why had handed me in the car. It held a few grubby francs, an identity card, a *feuille sémestrelle* (in case I wanted to eat), a medical certificate exempting me from military service and explaining the gammy foot. A letter from a girl named Denise, post-marked St Malo six weeks before, all love and kisses, and a photograph. Creased and tattered about the edges, this last-named was evidently Patrice Morgat's most treasured possession.

It wasn't a picture of his silver-haired old Mum nor, I suspected, of the dolly named Denise . . . not unless St Malo had come to Montmartre and the Place Pigalle. The scrubber who met my eye was three-quarter-turned with her right knee coyly raised. Her costume consisted of hig heels and a pair of long, black gloves, and one of those was occupied buffing up her back hair.

'My landlady?' I asked, hopefully.

21

'In Béthune?' said Major Why, busy zipping up my jumping gear.

I let out a strangled squeal that had him stepping back hastily, afraid he had nipped me somewhere awkward.

'Bé-bloody-thune,' I muttered. 'That's nothing but coalmines!'

'But a welcome in the valleys, I shouldn't wonder. h'm?' He had quickly recovered his poise, handed me my rubber helmet, gave it a friendly slap. 'You'll find the picture useful at police checks. Take their eyes off your papers.' Then he went a bit awkward again, passed me something else, also coated with rubber.

'You know about *this*, I imagine?' His voice had gone quiet.

I looked at it, nodded slowly.

A cyanide capsule.

As a conversation stopper it was a killer.

The bomber was a Whitley. The crew were young. Growing old was not part of their destiny. The pilot shook hands, said: 'A nice night, we'll do our best to make you comfortable.' He produced a map and fingered a spot to the left of a junction of three canals. 'This is it, yes?' He looked at me, then at Major Why.

Major Why said: 'Roger, h'm?' and looked at me.

I said: 'And out.'

'In a stick of three. Two conainers and yourself. Oh, and a transmitter. You'll be carrying the transmitter.'

I looked and felt bewildered. He hadn't used a question mark in all that speech. 'Tied to my left goolie, I presume. I need my hands free.'

'Ah, yes . . . you jump with an "A",' he said.

'An "A",' I said.

'Larger than the normal chute. Takes a bit longer to blossom. Sways more, too, they tell me. The transmitter is slung above your head, so watch it. Mustn't have it hit you, knock you cold, must we?'

'Shall I take the pill now and save us all a load of bother?'

I said. '*Sir*,' I added. Christ Almighty, I had heard about the 'A' chute. I had even volunteered twice to have a go with one, to get the feel . . . 'No, old boy, don't bother, it isn't for chaps like you.' Now it suddenly was, on my first operational jump, Jesus have me for a sunbeam!

'You'll get there in one, my dear fellow, sweet as a nut, eh?'

'As the actress said to the bishop . . . h'm?' The last word I was ever to speak to Major Why.

The pilot had promised a comfortable trip. From his point of view, it probably was. Searchlights and shells pooping off around us were all part of his business. I couldn't wait to get out, even with that Sword of Damocles poised over my head.

The despatcher appeared with a mug of coffee. He offered to lace it with rum. I shook my head. Major Why wouldn't like British grog on my breath.

'Never dropped anyone in this part before,' said the despatcher.

'Oh?' I said.

'Always considered too dicey. Night fighters an' that. Merville's just up the road.'

'He can stay there.'

'Merville's an it. An air-base. That's how we're making it.'

'I don't get you,' I said.

'We're sneaking in on the arse of the Luftwaffe. Some lot that had a go at the Midlands, according to Skip.'

'If we're up the arse of the Luftwaffe, how does your Skip explain away the ack-ack fire?' I asked.

'Doesn't have to. It happens both sides. There's always some ground job who gets a bit edgy.' He grinned. 'Chocolate?'

Major Why wouldn't approve. The Nazis would know it was Cadbury's. The hell with Major Why. 'Thanks.' I took a piece, bit into it.

'Nearly there now.' He raised the manhole cover in the deck, showed me the big, dark world down below. Only it wasn't so dark. Three canals reflected mirror-like in the moonlight. Then we banked and began a turn, sending the view in a whirl. When we straightened out again, we had lost height. The canals had widened, had towpaths, the dark dots had become houses. A patch of woodland was climbing joyously to meet us.

A gurgle on the intercom, translated by the despatcher. 'You were expecting a reception committee?' he asked.

An academic question. Both he and the pilot knew I was. The code-name for the operation was *stickleback* but that didn't mean I carried my 'babies' around in my mouth. They should be down there, waiting. But, as the despatcher had rightly said, my DZ was a problem area, thick with enemy. I swallowed the chocolate tried to keep it flippant to disguise the fear in my gut.

'If they're wearing coal-scuttle hats and eagles, don't bother. Turn around and drop me off near Dymchurch. I know a girl there who's much more friendly.'

We went round twice more. A long finger of a searchlight streaking up from nowhere on the second circuit did nothing to allay my unease. It wavered towards us, hung for a moment, then slid from view.

Another gurgle from the intercom.

'Roger, this time,' said the despatcher.

He was right. Down below I saw four torches holding a reversed *L* pattern. The torch on the bottom left-hand edge flashed the letter 'S' in Morse.

Action stations. The red light glowed. The engine-pitch changed to a slow, agonizing vibration. The Whitley, flaps down, lost speed.

Red became green. The despatcher's arm dropped. I was away. Out and falling, so quiet after the thump of the bomber, no more than a thin screech of wind. The umbilical cord of a static line snapped. No going back now. If that's five hundred feet below, I'm Cleopatra's left tit, those woods are too bloody close for comfort . . . then the jerk of a lazy canopy opening, flapping like an over-fed duck. I began to swing, a watch on a chain, but I was the one hypnotized, eyes rolling upwards, conscious of the transmitter in its canister above my head.

Wildly out of control the canopy began to lose shape, spilling out air. A black tree rushed past me, I cannoned off the leafy point of a branch. It snapped and fell with me. I heard a loud squawk that might have been a bird, but was more likely me. Then I hit a mound of leaf mould with my feet, rolled sideways, knees, hip, and shoulder, face slithering in pig shit.

Moulin-Bas had arrived in France.

SIX

'*Une opération arithmétique?*' the voice said.

'*L'amour,*' I said. '*La preuve faite, on passe . . .*'

'*. . . à un autre probleme,*' came the answer.

Love is an arithmetical problem. The proof established, one passes on to another problem. The sort of damfool password some twat would think up in an idle moment.

The voice became a man. If I had been Snow White, he would have said 'Heigh-ho'. He was not much bigger than a gnome and shouldered a spade.

'You all right, then?' he continued, in French, coming out from behind a tree.

'Pants a bit wet. Otherwise, can't grumble.' I started to strip off the jumping overalls. Another gnome appeared beside him. They got to work, one digging, the other gathering up my chute.

'The other two?' I asked. 'The containers?'

'Taken care of,' said the first gnome. 'Do parachutists always jump like that?'

No note of criticism. Only curiosity.

'All the time,' I said. 'Bloody idiots, aren't we?'

A chuckle. 'Follow me when you are ready.'

I removed the helmet, dropped it on the overalls, glanced at the hole the second gnome was spading. It would take the

25

three of us, as well as my gear. I pulled on a greasy beret. 'All yours.'

'Sorry about the pigs,' said the first gnome. 'But they have the run of these woods.' He humped the transmitter canister, set off down a track. At the bottom of the slope was a platform – the French equivalent of a farm-wagon drawn by two horses. It was parked in the shadows of a huge tree. The first gnome slid the canister across the tail of the wagon, turned, said: 'Aristide,' and offered a hand.

I gripped it. 'Moulin-Bas, alias Patrice.'

'Alors, vous voilà!'

I was here, all right . . . but where?

Other gnomes appeared, hefting the two containers. Once they had them on the wagon and straightened up, they were a little taller. I climbed aboard and we trundled away. The track became a muddy lane. After a mile or so, a gate swung wide into a farmyard. A chain rattled furiously, there was a whimpering. But the dog did not bark. Someone had had the sense to muzzle it.

Inside the kitchen, a woman in black offered me her cheek whilst wiping her hands on her pinafore. She was five feet high and might have been my grandmother. She chumped gums in a toothless smile, waved me to the table. Soup and fried eggs. Aristide poured wine from a stone jug. I was suddenly very hungry. I wiped the yolk of a third egg around with a slab of coarse, grey bread, gave a burp of contentment. I became aware of the others watching me. Aristide made introductions: Bernard, Philippe, Claude, Henri, and Raoul, the second gnome.

'And Madame?' I asked.

She swung her head from where she was stirring a pot. Call me the Witch,' she said. 'They all do. Behind my back, of course.'

'She is, too,' murmured the one named Claude. 'All the girls around come here for love potions.' He gave a dirty chuckle.

'They need them with stallions like you?' My gesture embraced the entire company. It brought a dirtier laugh.

26

'And Joseph?' I went on.

The laugh died, strangled with quick glances. You could have heard a bomb drop. A tiny one. Aristide sucked his teeth loudly. 'In the morning. Bed, now.'

A thumb at the door. I rose, followed it, into the loft of a barn. No need for three guesses. They wanted rid of me, to see what toys Santa Claus had brought them in the two containers. Guns, ammunition, grenades, explosives. I hoped they knew how to handle them, dared not ask for fear of offence. Not on such short acquaintance. All I said was: 'Don't start the war without me.'

Aristide grinned green-brown teeth in the lamp-light. *'Ne vous en faites donc pas pour ça!'*

I wasn't a bit worried. I removed three items of personal equipment that Major Why had not dumped in the laundry-skip. A .38 automatic, cocked with one up the spout. A long-bladed Wilkinson knife from its neck holster. A length of cord with a double-knot and a nail in it from around my waist. The genuine Indian rope trick a Thuggee garotte.

I brushed my teeth with a finger. I was ready for bed. I went to sleep amid the sweet scent of cows.

A funny dream. Funny-odd, that is. All mixed up with Jacko Allen, his lovely wife, Ruth Dunning, and a little, fat Jew named Fred who had been in our squad. Fred – in peace-time – was a cabaret act, point numbers at the piano. The last time I had seen Fred he had risen to the heights of sanitary corporal, prodding away at a drain. 'The ups and downs of life, dear,' he had said, in his ever-so-slightly camp voice. 'You're on the upsies, I'm on the downsies, but I'll be in Scotland afore you, though why I should *want* to, *zayt moykhl!* I *died* a *death* at Gleneagles in thirty-eight, my life!'

In this dream, I was down around a U-bend smelling of pigs with Fred poking away at me with what he termed his 'divine' rod. I came out on stage where Ruth was draped on a chaise-longue doing her sketch about Fifi La Tom and the

27

cadets of Saint-Cyr. Jacko was in the wings, hissing at me: 'Stage left, you silly fart?' But Stage Left was Kramms, Kieffer, Boemelburg, and Major Why going 'H'm, h'm?' A loud noise from the orchestra pit like a bellow of pain had me worried . . . I awoke, in a cold sweat, knife in hand, the other groping for the gun.

'Maude is throwing a calf,' said Aristide, from down below. Or maybe it was Raoul.

'He'll know worse before he knows better,' cackled the Witch.

I turned over, went back to sleep.

The creak of a light foot on the ladder aroused me. Sunlight streamed in through gaps in the roof. I rolled on to my belly, looked down. Coming up was a cascade of hair to make the sunlight pale with envy. Shoulders young and smooth, breasts full beneath a tight, white blouse. The hands were small but long-fingered, and one of them carried two mugs, steaming with what I hoped was coffee. I slid the gun and knife away, made a comb of fingers in my own hair, sat up.

The face appeared. Small, oval, with what is politely called a 'strong' nose. Violet eyes, a generous mouth wearing a friendly smile. In my conceit I could say I had met more beautiful women, but none, to that point, more welcome.

'I'm Solange,' she said, as I took the mugs from her. 'You are Patrice, yes?' She swirled a swell of hips gracefully, spread her skirt, sat down on the straw, one foot resting on the ladder. She eyed me candidly as she took back one of the mugs. 'You are very young.'

'And you've made my day, old lady,' I said, in English.

'Comment?'

I tried translating it into idiomatic French. She got the gist, laughed prettily.

'For your information I am twenty-five,' she said. She found and offered me a cigarette. Lit it for me, too. It was English, Virginian. So much for Major Why and head-quarter's cautionary training. 'Thank you for the transmitter,'

28

she added. 'The last one I had was faulty. And spare parts, well . . .' A shrug of the bare shoulders bounced the blouse, completed the sentence.

'How did you let London know?' An instinctive question. I hadn't learned to trust her yet, only fancy her.

'Bob, in Paris, you know?'

I did know. Bob was Rémy's personal radio officer. A legend of sorts in Duke Street. He had been dropped in the previous summer, about the time I was finishing at Sandhurst.

'How is Bob?' I asked.

'In Fresnes, I'm afraid. Arrested a month ago. About the time he made that call for me.'

Check. Bob – Robert Delattre – had been arrested on May 29 . . . one of the snippets I had been told. There was a flap on. An agent known as Capri had been taken earlier that month and was suspected of a mass betrayal. A whole network blown. A wonderful moment to make one's debut in this underground caper.

'And Joseph?' I asked.

'What about him?'

'I got the frozen eye from Aristide and the others when I mentioned the name.'

'He is still in circulation,' said the girl. 'But rather busy.'

'For *rather* read *too* busy for this sector of the Pas-de-Calais?'

She evaded the question diplomatically. 'The Francs-Tireurs work in tight cells. It's the best way – the only way – to survive. Within the cell you are assigned to, you have carte blanche to do as you think fit. Network Fana has been shelved for the time being.'

'Who runs this cell?'

'Maurice. He is very good, has a willing group. But they need arms.'

'I brought them with me.'

'Not nearly enough. He also needs training and guidance, the best targets, you know.'

'How old is Maurice?'

29

The words shaped on her lips. Old enough to be your father. She didn't say them.

I did. 'And I'm so very young,' I added, with something of a sting.

Her hand touched mine, gently. 'I am sure London knows what it is doing.'

'Let's hope Maurice thinks so.'

I killed the cigarette in the dregs of the *ersatz* coffee.

Down in the yard, Aristide was feeding the pigs. 'We named the calf Patrice in your honour,' he said.

Kind of them. In a few months, I might be fatted up enough for the table. A Gestapo table ... Christ, man, forget it, no way to think. Already you've lasted longer than the man they dropped at the last full moon. Mec had arrived a little before dawn on the day Delattre had been arrested. By seven that same evening he had been caught. He had swallowed his capsule and had been carried out feet first. Mec – whom I had known as René-Georges Weill – had been a gutsy officer who had grown tired of sending others and had decided to go himself. The trouble was, he had gone in a frame of mind sure he would never return. Poor devil, there was a moral in it somewhere ...

The Witch gave me breakfast. The same slush that passed for coffee, a loaf of bread, and more butter than most of London saw in a week. Plus a confiture that looked and smelled like beetroot jam. I gave that part of the meal a miss. Solange rejoined me as I washed down the last crumb.

'I have transport into Aire. Want to come with me?'

'Maurice?'

'One of the reasons I am here.'

'To twist my arm nicely?'

She smiled. 'You are a cynic.'

'For one so young, hein? Let's say that idealism flew out of my window at a tender age. Before France, Britain, and the rest thought they could do deals with Hitler. I was only eighteen when I killed my first Nazi.'

'Where? Spain?'

I raised two fingers. 'That to the International Brigade.' I shook my head. 'Heidelberg. Willi Eigenbrodt was celebrating his twenty-first birthday by beating up some old Jew. Later, when he was paralytic drunk, I caught up with him in a dark alley.'

'How did you—?'

'I kicked him to death.' I pushed back the bench, got to my feet. 'As soon as you like.'

The violet eyes met mine in a long look. She went out in front of me, very quiet.

SEVEN

The agricultural scene in the Pas-de-Calais is a bit like Holland without the windmills and the tulips. Aire-sur-la-Lys is old and very much a market town, lying low amid marshes, at the junction of the three canals I had seen the night before. Haig or someone had made his headquarters there in 1917. Twenty-five years on, the putties and trench feet had given way to jackboots and the goose-step. A swastika flaunted itself from the hôtel-de-ville.

Solange parked the produce van near one of the canal bridges, went in search of Maurice. I sat there idly, twiddling thumbs, one eye on a gendarme who had both eyes on me. After a moment or two, he strolled over, looked in.

'No parking here.'

'My very words. But women drivers.' I tried to keep it light.

'Move it!'

'Without a licence? That would be breaking the law.'

'Five minutes then. Or I'll move it myself. With you in it!'

I nodded thanks. He went away. But only to the far side of the bridge. I had no doubt he meant what he said. Five minutes . . . I would have checked it off on my watch, except that it was back at Queen Anne's Gate and they hadn't given me a replacement. Come to that, they hadn't given me the

31

gold cuff-links and silver hip flask that I had heard were standard 'going-away' presents. Maybe they had considered I wouldn't have them long enough, maybe a lot of things . . . I counted off the seconds in my head, growing damp about the collar. Two-seventy, two-seventy-one . . . and the gendarme was thumbing his belt, a sure sign of business.

The door clicked. Solange slid into the seat beside me. I murmured our predicament. She laughed. 'You should have offered him an onion. That's probably all he was after in the first place.'

Onions? *Mine*, I thought. I wiped perspiration from my neckband. We moved away with a stocky man in his middle-forties clambering in behind us. He took my shoulder in a grip that was iron.

'*Ca va. Je suis Maurice.*'

'*Ca va.* But there's no need to take me apart. I'm for real.'

He released me with a rumble of a laugh. 'You'll do, *mon ami.*'

'I'll have to. No hope of a replacement for a month, at least. And he'll probably be still on the teat. The latest intake is code-named Moses-in-the-bulrushes.'

Another belly chuckle. Solange had evidently appraised him of the dirty great chip on my shoulder. He leaned forward, waggled a sausage of a finger under my nose.

'Papers.'

I passed over the wallet, screwed my head to watch him. A lifted eyebrow at the *poule* in the black gloves, but he pounced on the letter from Denise.

'You know this girl?'

I shook my head. 'For my money, she's a little old French lady living near London. Probably writes those letters at so much a hundred words. The Bureau seems to think they add colour.'

'If M'lle Solange will pardon me the expression, the Bureau thinks through its arse. Colour like this is open to be checked upon.' He ripped letter and envelope to shreds, scattered them behind him in the manner of confetti. I was only glad he hadn't expected me to chew it. The paper was thick and

32

coarse. He thumbed the francs in the wallet. 'This all the money you've got?'

'Apart from three hundred thousand wrapped around me like a body-belt . . . yes.' It was a half-million in fact, but Major Why had warned me I might have to account for the petty cash.

'Now we are talking.' Maurice grinned his relief, handed me back the wallet. 'And talking about talking, your accent . . .?'

'Breton, so they tell me.'

'I knew it wasn't French.'

Charming, I thought. *'Entre copains et cochons, l'aimable familiarité est de mise,'* I said.

Between pals and pigs, familiartiy is permissible.

He fell about laughing. If he was that easy to please, Maurice and I would get along very well.

'Ideas?' he said, over lunch. Lunch was raw onions, a slab of soft cheees, some vinegary red wine.

'Three more nights of moon,' I said. 'If Solange can get a message through, they might fix another drop. Explosives, I think, plus fuses.' I had read the list of contents from the containers dropped with me. One had been entirely made up of small arms, enough to turn a handful of civilians into a swagger of Mexican brigands. Without horses for the smart getaway. This was no Viva Zapata kick. I said as much.

'D'accord,' said Maurice. 'But will they play?'

I looked at Solange. 'Make it *"ton fils prodigue est malheureux. Je préfère les fraises fraîches cueillés".'*

She nodded. 'And where would the prodigal son like his fresh strawberries delivered?'

'Preferably somewhere else,' I said, glancing at Maurice. 'Full marks to Aristide and company for last night. But further south if such is practicable.' I started to explain the problems of flying over the Pas-de-Calais.

He waved me down, nodding agreement. 'I know the very spot.' He produced a map, showed it to Solange. 'The church

33

steeples, *here* and *here* will make perfect markers for the run-in.'

He turned to me for confirmation. He need not have bothered. I was supposed to teach him to suck eggs?

'Suggestions for targets?' I said.

'That depends on what you have in mind.' He bit deep into an onion.

I watched the juice dribble down his chin. 'Fighter planes will do for starters,' I said, wiping watery eyes. I hadn't a great deal of hope that we might hit the bomber-wing at Merville. The perimeter would be well-policed and, anyway, the RAF themselves would likely slam at that. Fighters, on the other hand, could be hidden by the half-dozen in a field not much bigger than Goering's girth, with mobile maintenance and a handful of troops to guard them.

'Anti-aircraft sites?' chewed Maurice.

Pas-de-Calais bristled with them. But sites in depth might make them difficult for the score of men Maurice could muster. Against that, we wouldn't need to hump around much in the way of explosives. They would be handy on each site. Yes, a possibility. 'Nice work if we can get it,' I said.

'How well do you ride a bicycle?' he asked.

'Side-saddle not so good, but I once pedalled from the Hook of Holland down to Lindau on the Austrian border.'

'Not quite that far,' he said. 'Tomorrow morning, bright and early? Better you see for yourself. You won't get to know the country from this.' He tapped the map.

Commonsense. 'Where do I spend the night?' I enquired.

'Here, with me.'

Here was a barge moored fifteen kilometres out of Aire.

'And Solange?' I said, instinctively.

She was at the primus, brewing coffee. She raised her head, gave me a quick look with those violet eyes. A faint smile flickered on her lips and was gone. 'I sleep with my transmitter,' she said.

'Less fickle than men, hein?' chuckled Maurice.

'But could get you into worse trouble,' I murmured.

'Peutêtre,' she said.

'Take care,' I said. 'Without you we are a hen without a head.'

'So long as you don't see *me* as the hen,' she said, obliquely.

I got the message. 'Nothing personal, I promise.'

'That's all right, then.' She pushed back her hair, returned to the coffee, smiling to herself now. One cluck from her, she knew, and I'd come running.

EIGHT

Three days of cycling were good for the calf muscles, if nothing else. I returned each evening saddle-sore. Upper cheeks crimson, too, from a warm, late June sun. Each night we listened eagerly, ears tuned for the nonsense message on the BBC French Service that would give us an answer. *Josephine n'a plus rien à sa mettre* – Josephine hasn't a rag to her back. If it went on to say *Chez Maurice, Place de la Justice*, it meant our DZ had met with approval. Then would follow an 'appointment time', to which one added seven hours to fix it precisely. If, instead, we received another follow-on: *Ella a la goût qui retarde* – her taste in clothes is out-of-date, then we would have to wait until the next full moon.

Not a bloody sausage. Josephine could walk the streets like the tart in my wallet for all they cared.

'What now?' said Maurice.

'Give them one more night. Even two. It was short notice. If they have the stuff they may not have a plane available, or vice versa.'

'And if nothing after then?'

'We'll try with what we've got on Target One.'

Target One was a Messerschmitt hide-out some forty kilometres away. Six fighters. Three ready for the air; two in stages of repair; the sixth in a state of cannibalization. A significant fact itself. The Luftwaffe were heavily committed elsewhere, both in pilots and in planes. Small as the target might see, it had a certain proportionate value.

35

The situation was a long, flat meadow for take-off, a copse of trees for camouflage, a barn with outbuildings strung over with netting, and an approach lane that looked innocuous but wasn't. It had alarm wires at intervals for the unwary, ready to send a ting-a-ling around the perimeter and bring a half-platoon of men at the double. Guard-dogs, too. A pair of the perishers, German shepherds, lean and hungry for the throat of an intruder.

Claude – one of the men I had met on my arrival – knew the area better than a boil on his backside. He had pleasured more local girls in that meadow than horse-flies on a cow pat. Before the Luftwaffe moved in, that is to say. He also knew the interior geography of the barn and outbuildings ... no fair-weather sailor on the seas of *l'amour*. He had to be lifted down to reality from a fantasy merry-go-round with a certain Yvette, to explain how we might breach the position yet not raise an alarm.

At this point, he seemed unsure of himself. After several false starts I was prepared to write him off as the usual loud-mouthed Casanova. Then he dredged up a memory that just had to be true. It concerned the same Yvette, a girl *très kinky pour le sport*.

At the far end of the meadow, furthermost from the barn, was a sewage pipe. Large enough to take the two of them. She had insisted they try it out.

'In a sewage pipe?' I said.

'Not for sewage,' Claude explained. 'For drainage, *n'est-ce-pas*? It takes water from the marshy part of the meadow into the ditch beyond.'

'Not my fancy for the jig-a-jig!' chuckled Maurice.

'It was January,' said Claude. 'Snow on the ground and quite dry inside.'

'Except for the icicles on her bum,' I said.

'On mine, actually. She did the honours.'

I looked at Maurice, still chuckling. He shrugged. 'Why not? You might find Yvette up there, waiting for a customer!'

'It'll make a change from riding a bike,' I said.

They had counselled me in London that it would take ten days to a fortnight to settle into a Resistance routine. And the same amount of time again to lauch an operation with any degree of success. A logic lurked behind the caution. It was not enough to know the strength of the enemy. The time was required to sum up one's own force, to sort out the men from the boys, the liabilities from the assets, the basic proficiency or otherwise with weapons.

With the exception of three, Maurice's cell had all done military service of one kind or another. But the weapons provided were British and strangers to most of them. A good example was the Bren gun. It was tailor-made for Resistance work. Reliable, accurate, extremely portable, it could take a lot of rought treatment without complaining. Yet to get the optimum out of it, it needed to be understood. That demanded drill in its working, stripping, cleaning, in knowing its various parts.

As an instructor, I was only as good as my last course. And the one in small arms was a long way back on the list. The fact that I had been a fast learner added to the problem. It brought out an impatience with others less quick on the uptake. Consequently, the first lesson on the Bren, given to the Francs-Tireurs two evenings after my arrival, had been a near-disaster.

That night, back in the farm loft, I recalled Jack Allen's own brand of perseverance with the most backward of recruits. Our ranting sergeant had been going 'spare' . . . 'Youse'll never learn to fire th' fockin' think! Youse 'ud better use it as a fockin' shillelagh, clobber the fockin' Hun over th' head wi' it!'

Jacko had been watching from a distance. He sidled up quietly.

'Squad, 'shun!'

'Stand them at ease, sar'nt.'

We were stood at ease, aware of quizzical eyes ranging over us.

'Who thinks he knows this weapon best?'

A bunch of bashful violets. No hand raised.

37

'Permission to speak, sor! Him's the quickest!' The sergeant's finger jabbed at me.

'H'm. Not quite my question, sar'nt. Choose one of the slower riflemen.'

'Sor! Mendelbaum, one step forward, march!'

Mendelbaum was detached to show the hapless O'Grady under Jacko's gentle supervision. The rest of us moved on to higher things.

'Th' blind leadin' th' fockin' blind!' was the sergeant's under-the-breath comment, producing a titter. A titter wiped off our faces when the other two showed their prowess on the range a few weeks later.

The 'Mendelbaum' in Maurice's group was little Aristide. On the second night of training, he took over the teaching of the Bren. Using the same tactics, Bernard became instructor with the Tommy-gun, Henri dealt with revolvers and automatics, and Maurice was responsible for grenades. I devoted my talents to time-fuses and explosives, but soon found a valuable help-mate in an ex-quarryman known to all as 'Le Claque'.

With no response from London to our call, I was not prepared to wait a further month. There were a number of reasons that prompted the decision. In their counsel, the chairborne warriors did not – or so it seemed to me – take into account the mentality of those in the field, the local FTP. They took the risks, not only to themselves but their families. Especially so if *la Geste* – the Gestapo – moved into the area. In taking such risks, they expected their money's worth. The advent of even a solitary man from the sky was tantamount to a mini-Second Front, his presence synonymous with action.

Maurice, himself, typified his group. He had fought at the Aisne in 1917, at St Quentin, a year later. Both victories, if bloody ones. He had the scars, the medals, and the memories, and felt the bitter shame of 1940 all the more.

A second reason was the uncertainty. There was no guarantee we would get the extra supplies the following month.

38

Short nights of summer limited the hours of operational flying. Prune-spit though we were across the Channel, we were not the sole unit in France dependent on Tempsford. And Squadrons 138 and 161 had just twenty-one operational bombers between them, plus a handful of Lysander pick-up aircraft.

The third reason was personal. Pas-de-Calais, for me, was only testing ground, experience for something much bigger. *Stickleback*, I had been warned, would become *Moray Eel*. Whatever that meant, I knew that sitting on my backside wouldn't help any. Experience comes the hard way, the more I could cram in the better. So – one week after the day of my arrival on Friday the 3rd of July, we hit Target One.

NINE

The previous night – the Thursday – I made a final recce, taking with me the amorous Claude who knew the area, and little Raoul, a man I had discovered could move like a shadow.

Whether he had laid one bird or a hundred in that meadow, it was soon evident that Claude's *modus operandi* must have been akin to that of the bull elephant. One dry twig in a hundred square metres and Claude's foot would surely find it, snap it like a shot from a gun. Bushes were for blundering through, not finding a way around. And he would talk. Albeit in hoarse whispers, but they carried a distance on a quiet night.

Fortunately for us, an air-raid was in progress. A constant hum of 'planes, a continuous crack of gunfire, and searchlights enough to outshine the late-rising moon. Activity, too, in the meadow, as three night-fighters took off, whipping low over the trees, then climbing high with a thin pitch of sound.

Claude pointed out the ditch. I sent Raoul down it to find the pipe and give it the once-over. Fifteen minutes passed on Maurice's luminous watch, during which time Claude produced a cigarette. He would have lit it if I hadn't indicated, by forceful gestures, that the lighted end would be thrust up his left nostril and retrieved via his right ear. He got the general idea and only disturbed a roosting bird.

Raoul returned with a smirk and a nod. The pipe was still in place, but festooned with barbed wire on the outside. *Barbed* wire, I queried, he was sure of that? He looked a little perplexed. Wire was wire was wire, it had to be barbed, otherwise where was the point? No pun intended and none taken. But I was not satisfied. I warned him to cut Claude's throat if that one took as much as a deep breath, and went to see for myself.

A pencil-torch investigation, using my body as a shield. Barbed wire, certainly, but inside the coil was a triple-strand of hairline stuff *sans* spikes. Warning systems, like those in the lane, or booby-trap? I made a careful trace, found what I was looking for . . . a right little bastard, buried in the bank of the ditch. And not one. *Three.* Any or all capable of turning our lot into cats-meat on the spot.

I probed carefully with my knife, found a nipple. Not one of the acrobatic Yvette's, unless she had since become a mine. The nipple gave way to a breast, saucer in size, round in shape, but more lethal than any woman's. No fuse with these buggers, a trickle of the hair wire armed it, and once the tickle was released it was good-night; what was left sailed over the trees in a splatter of blood, brains, and bone-marrow.

It took a sweaty fifty minutes to render them safe, with the added fret that any moment a German shepherd might be licking the salt as it chewed my ear. Twice I had to freeze flat, but each time it was only a human sentry on the other side of the wire making a solo patrol. A further ten minutes were spent checking the inside of the pipe for more surprises. I saw nothing to arouse suspicion, withdrew the way I had come.

I must have looked pale in the light of the moon. Both Raoul and Claude stared at me anxiously. Claude even gave me his cigarette which I allowed him to light.

'You were a long time,' whispered Raoul.

There was no percentages in being modest. The sooner this crew faced up to the full realities the better. 'It could have been never-time,' I said, blowing smoke. 'The bloody thing was mined. Three of them.'

'It's off, then?' muttered Claude.

'It's on . . . they're safe now.' I made a decision. 'I'm spending the next twenty-four hours here, in case the *salauds* check up and find out what I've done.'

'And if they do?' asked Raoul.

'I'll just have to undo them again, won't I? Or find another way in.'

Claude opened his mouth to say something. I put a hand over it. I was in no humour to hear how Yvette or some other slag had got her legs about him through the skylight of the barn. All I desired at that moment was my own company, the privacy maybe to vomit.

Raoul was practical. He came back, handed me an apple, a piece of cold sausage, and a small flask of *marc*. 'Breakfast,' he said. 'I bring the boys here tomorrow, the same time?'

'Make it that copse a hundred metres nearer the road junction. And one hour earlier. And for Christ's sake,' I whispered. 'Tell Maurice not – and I mean *not* – to bring Claude. Find him something else to do. Like stealing a gun from an ack-ack site, preferably while it's still firing. That might cover the noise of his feet.'

He grinned sympathetically. 'Whatever you say, *mon capitaine*.'

No captain yet, I should live that long. I watched them away into the darkness.

What was left of the night passed uneventfully. Major Why had handed me other pills besides the cyanide job; blue benzadrines to keep one going; some white knock-outs that did the trick for six solid hours. In theory, anyway. I fed myself a couple of 'blues', made myself comfortable in the fork of a leafy tree with a reasonable all round view.

The three night-fighters had returned whilst I had been

dealing with the mines. One had lurched in over the trees as if clipped by some on-the-mark rear-gunner. But he had landed clean enough, as had the other two. Engines cut, men from the huts had wheeled the machines away under cover. I had heard laughter and something of a cheer as the pilots had made their way to the barn. One of them had scored a hit, maybe? And somewhere in Britain, within the next twenty-four hours, telegrams to parents or wives stating bald regrets, so-and-so reported missing . . . a sobering thought.

At the darkest hour before dawn, the guard was turned out. A bunch of Claudes, by the sound of them, stamping around, yawning, grunting, to come to a stiff and silent attention before the Duty Officer. He dismissed them, made a tour of the perimeter, on the outside. With him went a *feldwebel* and a soldier with a dog. Approaching the ditch, the dog strained at the leash, scenting some previous alien presence. The handler muttered a command, the dog came to heel. The *feldwebel* sprayed a flashlight around the area of the stack pipe, seemed satisfied. The party moved on. Shortly afterwards I heard the staccato burst of a motor-cycle combination coming to life, to die away down the lane. The Duty Officer had returned to his clean sheets and soft bed somewhere in the nearest village. I screwed around in mine, shut my eyes. Not to sleep, only to rest them.

Dawn came. Birds twittered. A fox hurried home from its nightly prowl. Life went on in the animal world, impervious to the stupidity of men. The sun rose uneasily, pushing back a thin blanket of cloud, red-faced and looking irritable, as if wondering why to bother with an earth in turmoil.

I knew how it must feel; a week in France and I had been forcibly made aware of two things. A unity of purpose where the Germans were concerned had given me heart. An obsession with post-war politics had left me confused. The FTP, I knew, were left-wing motivated, yet of the sixteen men I had met in Maurice's cell there were seven splinter groups, each adamant that their's was the only way when the war was over. It never would be, if they were any barometer for the rest of the country. Only the avowed Communists

42

showed solidarity, perpetually praising the Red Army as if they, alone, were shouldering the burden of battle. I had maintained a discreet silence about my own views until asked – indeed, demanded – as a professional (sic) soldier for my opinion.

'They did a magnificent job stabbing Poland in the back,' I had said, finally. 'And after a desperate struggle they defeated the mighty Finns. Since then, well . . . the Nazis are nearer to Moscow and Leningrad than they are to London. Does that answer your question?'

A sullen silence had greeted my words. Then:

'You talk like a fascist, Patrice.'

'If you believe that, then you equate fascism with truth. The Red Army will be as good as the arms the Americans and British supply them with. That goes for you, too. Preach your philosophies if you must, but for me, at this moment, bullets speak louder than words. It is the only language the Boche knows. Unless you are equally proficient at it, you'll be wiser to shut your traps. So let's get back to the grammar of the gun.'

Had I been insufferably pompous, I wondered? Had I sown an antipathy that would reflect in the coming operation? I bit into Raoul's apple, took a swig of *marc*, felt it smooth the cold creases in my gut. This time tomorrow I would know . . . or not know, if I was dead. In which case, it wouldn't matter one way or the other.

I slithered down from the tree, flexed arms and legs, checked and double-checked the weapon slung under my jacket. A Thompson. Much better than the newly-invented Sten Mark One which could chop a man fingerless if not handled with care. Still in the process of change, the para boys back at Alton Priors were doing their best to discover and remedy faults. Better they find them out than my lot.

Breakfast came and went on the airfield in a clatter of mugs and plates and the tantalizing smell of fresh coffee. None of your *ersatz* slurp for the darlings of the Third Reich. I took another nip of *marc*, a nibble at the fatty sausage.

A truck ground up the lane at eleven, disgorging a fresh

squad of men. Middle-aged, most of them; thirty-fives-to-forties, anyway. Something of a mixed blessing. These would be more awake to their duties, yet maybe not so sure of themselves, needing time to adjust if they were newcomers to the field. Equally, if they had done this job before, they might see it for a 'cushy number', a bloody great bore yet preferable to the Russian or any other front. Fighting was best left to the younger ones, the callow youth from which heroes are made. These Occupation troops had it all going for them, plenty of food, brothels laid on, silk stockings, perfume and butter to take home to Gretchen and Lisl. I thought of the RAF bomber crew who might have 'bought' it last night and the telegrams. With a little luck, a few telegrams would be going the other way tomorrow, across the bloody Rhine.

Back again in the tree, I cat-napped the day, eyes opening at any and every sound that was German-made. A two-man hourly patrol inside the perimeter, smoking the sly cigarette as they went. But no dogs sniffing in the direction of the pipe, no sign that my hour of sweat had been in vain. With the approach of dusk, I eased myself out of the tree, finished off the *marc*, circulated life back into cramped limbs. I had spent many a worse twenty-four hours waiting around in the wetness that was Scotland. Patience, we had been taught, was not a virtue. It is the alternative to a wooden overcoat. Wear it at all times like a string vest.

I moved away carefully to the copse near the road junction, waited some more.

TEN

They came in pairs, at three-hundred-metre intervals, with a third man linking between, in case of alarm. Maurice had devised this system of movement by *velos* – slang for bicycles. Fifteen men in all, and Claude wasn't one of them.

Maurice greeted me with a giant hug, some bread and cheese, and a flask of hot coffee. *Real* coffee, 'a little of the

special saved for an occasion'. It was nice to be An Occasion.
He made me eat and drink before submitting to question and
answer. Raoul, I learnt, had passed on the story of the mines.
It had probably reached a baker's dozen by the time he got
back. I was ten feet tall with the whole band; a Croix de
Guerre for that alone, was the consensus of opinion.

'For a fascist?' I murmured.

'My cell farts with its mouth,' said Maurice. 'I told them
so afterwards. I also told them they need *you* more than you
need them; that if they fail you tonight, you'll leave us!'

'Oh, sure. I've my passage booked on the Dover ferry.'

'They won't let you down, I promise. And Solange sends
her love and this . . .'

An English cigarette. I made a mental note to ask her
where she came by them. 'Claude,' I said, taking Maurice's
light. 'How did you cope?'

He grinned. 'I said you had recommended him as reconnaissance officer, with daytime duties checking out further
targets. He was greatly impressed. We left him treading a
cloud.'

'With those feet, we can expect a wet July,' I said. And
turned to the serious business of the night.

Le Claque and I would each lead a two-man demolition
team. Maurice would go in with us, in command of four
'bombers' armed with grenades. Another four would range
along one side of the airfield ready to give covering fire if I
threw up a red Verey flare. The remaining four would stay
back in the area of the copse in case the Boche tried their
usual ring-around-and-seal-off tactic.

'Leaks all round, then we move off,' I whispered, as we
finished blacking faces and hands. Any beetles in the copse
must have thought The Deluge had arrived. Maurice handed
me the Verey pistol. I put it away in the back of my trousers,
handed the Thompson to Raoul. Then followed him, snaking
along the ditch. Maurice came next then Le Claque and the
others. Last would be Aristide, to drop down with the Bren
towards the top end of the ditch.

Snip-snap went the wire cutters and Raoul was laying it

back gently, curling the thorns clear of flesh or material. I slithered in cautiously, pencil-light checking every inch of the way. Fifteen feet of pipe in all, room to throw an orgy *à la* Yvette. At the far end, more wire, but no tell-tale fine strands to presage disaster.

Light out and wait. The sentry had passed ten minutes before, but listen, check just the same. Nothing. Snip-snap with the cutters; snip-snap, snip-snap; and why the hell hadn't I thought of gloves? Because Major Why hadn't issued me with any . . . I used my beret to bend the wire back. A quick wriggle and I was through, throat dry, heart pounding, lungs gulping air, and more sweat coursing down my face than Lochailort or the baths in Jermyn Street had ever produced. I rolled away quietly to the darker shadow of a tree, started to come up. Then froze at a tinkling sound.

The sentry was watering the bushes. Twelve feet away, his back towards me. My right hand flew to the back of my neck, the knife was out and speeding on its way. It took him clean, beneath the shoulder blade, driving in and almost to the hilt. A cry began to gargle in the throat, but I was coming fast behind the knife, the beret in my left hand moving to smother the mouth. I jerked the knife free, stabbed again, twisting it upwards. Then out and across the jugular as he started to collapse. He slid away, one hand still cuddling his penis.

I picked up his machine-pistol, turned. Maurice was half-way out of the pipe, hands and knees, staring up, eyes like organ-stops.

'Jesus God!' I heard him whisper. 'What a way to go!'

'Jesus nothing' I grated, as he came to his feet. 'One less to string from a lamp-post. No prisoners, *capisc'*?' I thrust the machine-pistol at him, wiped the knife in the grass, put it away.

The Italian word had slipped out, but Maurice didn't appear to have noticed it. He was still eyeing the corpse as he moved aside to make room for Le Claque and the others. Le Claque festooned me with a haversack containing detonators. Jules, my side-kick, was humping the explosives. I

46

waited for Maurice's bombers to emerge from the pipe, then touched their leader on the arm. The veteran of Aisne and St Quentin was quietly spewing his heart up. 'Don't breathe a word of this, hein?' He wiped his mouth on his sleeve.

I squeezed his shoulder. 'You did one for me.'

A lie, of course. That would be the day when I felt anything for a German. But if it helped saying it . . .

The first plane was one hundred metres away, under camouflage netting that swung clear on a simple pulley-and-rope arrangement. One of the two undergoing repair, the fuselage raised on blocks, the undercarriage missing. I stood by and watched Le Claque and Bernard go to work. It had been a delicate decision, not wishing to hurt the quarryman's pride. But he had made the suggestion in the end.

The charges were made of PE – plastic explosive. Very convenient, safe to handle, it could be slapped on where and how you fancied, with a pencil timing device well thrust in and activated. These detonators could be set from five to thirty minutes – in theory. I had used them on the demolitions course and was not too happy with the reality. My hand hovered and stopped Le Claque before he set it going.

I'm doing it wrong? his eyebrows said.

I shook my head, smiled. 'On the way back,' I whispered. 'In case we're held up.'

He nodded understanding. He and Bernard moved on to their next target along the perimeter. Jules and I hurried past them, making for the third plane. It had been moved out of cover at dusk, ready for take-off should there be an alert. Jules placed two charges, one under the engine, another under the tail. I fixed a third for good measure deep in the cockpit, activated all three to blow in thirty minutes. As I swung down to the ground I caught the dim shadows of the other team moving on to the fourth.

I crooked a finger at Jules. We went into a crouch, crabbing across the meadow in short spurts, dropping and crawling, eyes peeled for the second sentry. So far as I could tell from the previous recce, each kept to his own half of the field, meeting up twice only on their two-hour stint. We must now be in the second man's zone. The fifth plane was well out in the open. We came up to it, Jules had his first charge ready, then stopped in the act. I went down, looked past him, under the fuselage.

A pair of jackboots. Splayed legs, part-hidden by the undercarriage. Knife already in my hand as I looked, but it was an awkward one. A deep slash at the artery or a thrust up the anus, but either way he would scream blue murder. That would defeat the exercise. With the Messerschmitt between us, there was no clear field of aim. I would have to take a chance, come up beside him.

He solved the problem for me. He dropped a cigarette butt between his legs, stamped on it, moved away. Right away, towards the far side of the field. I watched him go, nodding at Jules to get on with the work. Engine and tail only, this one, no time for silly buggers in the cockpit, the sentry might just look back.

We slid away at right-angles, heading for the barn. Fifty feet short, I veered across to the far corner. Something that looked promising. Three trucks. One I had noted before – a fire tender. The other two were new arrivals that must have come up after dark, after I had left the tree. One was a fuel-tanker. A glance over the tailboard of the other and I was the original Cheshire Cat. Ammunition. Cannon-shells and stuff.

Jules went in, placed his charges neat and nice. He was learning fast. He gestured at me for a detonator. He wanted one bang he could call his very own. I passed it to him, knowing he could hardly miss. We had placed sufficient to blow the truck all the way home to Karlsruhe where it had come from. I set one under the driving seat, in case some hero tried moving it out in a hurry.

As I came out of the cab, searchlights were suddenly probing the sky. I saw the distant flare of the first shell. Blast 'Bomber' Harris, why couldn't he lay off for one night, for even an hour or so? I slid to Jules who was lagging charges to the tanker. We activated two of them, then I grabbed his arm, jerked my head for him to follow. Any moment the klaxon would fart off and men would pour from the huts. I went fast along the far side, dragging out the Verey pistol as I moved. The hedgerow cast a deep shadow and I was upon the second sentry before either of us realised it.

'Halt!'

'Los! Flieger Alarm!' My free hand waved skywards at the playing searchlights. 'Schnell, du verfluct' Narr! Bewegst!'

The sound of his own language made him hesitate fractionally, lower his machine-pistol. The Verey came up, jumped in my hand as I squeezed the trigger. The cartridge went high, took him square in the eyeball. It must have lodged, for he went backwards and red light, blood, and brains exploded under his helmet. His trigger-finger twitched convulsively, stuttered a burst too close for comfort. Then I was past him, running again, Jules at my heels.

We cut across the field, reached the mouth of the pipe as the klaxon began to cough. Men appeared through partly-curtained doors, orders were shouted. Figures ran to the planes, some climbing in, others removing chocks, propellors poised to swing. It was an alert to 'scramble', not an awareness of our presence. I crossed my fingers, hoped the rest of ours would sense this too, hold their fire . . . we could get the desired effect without a pitched battle.

Maurice loomed up beside me. 'No grenades!' I said. Jules was already down the pipe, backside waggling out of sight. 'Le Claque and Bernard?' I added.

Maurice gestured at the pipe.

'And you three?'

'Outside. I reckoned they could lob their lemons as well from there!'

Sense. Why hadn't I thought of that?

'After you,' he added.

No pointing in arguing etiquette. I went through the pipe with his heavy breathing on my heels. Out in the ditch, I turned, reached back, gave him a hand. Without checking his watch, I reckoned we had five, six, ten minutes at most in which to get clear.

Famous last thoughts. Even as I said *'Allons donc!'* the first of the taxi-ing Messerschmitts went up. It had started its run down the meadow, gathering speed, then suddenly it was a great gout of flame, an out-of-control catherine wheel going arse-over-tip across the grass, whirling around into the path of the second plane . . . then one almighty slam as both disintegrated into a shower of nuts, bolts, and pilot flesh, erupting with a force that flung us back into the ditch. As we lay there, there was a glimpse of the third fighter becoming airborne, screaming clear, only to turn into a flaming cartwheel in the sky.

In the flaring glow, I saw rumps working overtime, going away along the ditch. Maurice and I followed, passing little Aristide, still rock-firm behind his Bren, the barrel aimed at the barn. I jerked a thumb, a gesture to follow. He half-turned his head, grinned a blacked-up face, like a minstrel at the end of the pier.

'I cover,' he mouthed. His eye went back to the sights of the gun.

I raised my head involuntarily, curious to see what he was seeing. The three trucks on the move, the fire tender heading for the inferno in the centre of the meadow. The other two were swinging round for the main gate, scattering men as they went. I watched, fascinated. Suddenly, the top half of the ammunition truck sailed up and over the gate in a blinding flash. A crack of doom shook the ground as the tanker flew in all directions. A chunk of metal sliced through a tree, swished past above us. I could hear the squeals of men in pain, but saw not a sign of one standing.

'Cover what?' I muttered at Aristide. And made to move on.

It was then he let go with a burst. I swung back at him. 'I got one!' he said. 'I got one!'

'De quoi est-il mort?' I asked.

What did he die of? I tossed a clod of earth at the Bren. Aristide stared at me, then understood. We got to our feet and ran.

Blast you, 'Bomber' Harris? No, *bless* you, old cock, we

got three pilots as well, far more important than all the planes.

Back in the barn-loft again, I slept like a babe.

ELEVEN

Saturday evening. The post-mortem. Maurice, Le Claque, and myself.

'You must be well pleased,' said Maurice.

'Not very,' I said. 'Too many mistakes.'

'What kind of mistakes?'

'Sentries, for a start. Twice I was nearly surprised by them. Twice is twice too many. They must be eliminated first.'

'You'll need to teach us your method. We're not apache with the knife. As for the second one, maboul!'

'Crazy, maybe. Panic, even. I fired the Verey on a reflex action. But having done so it should have brought down covering fire. As things turned out, I'm glad it didn't. But *why* didn't it is what I want to know.'

'I think, perhaps, they were not sure.'

'Then they should have been sure! Like they were at getting to hell out of it! The four lining the ditch were there to cover our retreat. Only Aristide stayed at his post.'

'What was there to cover?' shrugged Maurice. 'One helmet and a pair of boots hanging on the wire? That was the most I saw of any Boche as I left.'

'I don't care if it was Mata Hari's shrivelled-up figu, drill is drill, both in attack and withdrawal. It isn't necessary to dwell on that with *you* – an old soldier?'

He scratched his chin. 'Point taken, *mon general*. What else?'

'Explosives,' I said.

Le Claque's turn to look disconsolate. 'I know. We took out only four of the six planes. Bernard and I, we used too much on our second and third targets. Nothing left over for the fourth.'

51

'And your first? The one you were supposed to return to?'

'Bernard wanted to set it off. I thought he had earned the right. He failed to do it properly, but the fault must be mine.'

I thought of Jules wanting *his* own 'bang'. I was equally at fault, but had got away with it.

'It happens,' I said, magnanimously. 'But you put a finger on the real error. Too much explosive. We used more than two-thirds of our stock.'

Maurice grinned. 'It belled the cat, sure enough! My head is still ringing!'

'The cat will clang louder when la Geste get around to it. If they haven't done so already.'

The grin faded. He spat on the barn floor.

'That won't stop them, either,' I said. 'It means the next job will be that much harder.'

'Not if we're quick of the mark, keep them on the hop.'

'Hop is the operative word . . . for us.'

'What d'you mean?'

'Disperse.'

He stared at me. 'Disperse *la cellule*? You must be mad, when we're the talk of the country!'

'Talk of Aire-sur-la-Lys, possibly,' I countered. 'And that's the last thing we want.'

'But the people – everyone – they're proud of what we did!'

'Shit-scared, too. If the town suddenly fills up with SS, there'll be a lot of laundry hanging on the line.'

Maurice dismissed it with a gesture. 'It took place forty kilometres from here. Why should they pick on Aire?'

'The talk,' said Le Claque. 'Patrice is right. There is too much of it. The Boches are not fools. They must have informers.'

But Maurice wasn't listening. 'Disperse the cell?' he repeated, anger rising. 'Is that what the British do every time they win a battle? Or is that an embarrassing question? They have not won so many of late, *non?*'

Back again to the Red Army argument. I had no intention of being drawn into that a second time. I tried quiet reason.

'A temporary break-up, no more. Live to fight another day has its merits.'

A slow, sorrowful shake of the head. 'You shock me, Patrice. You are not the same man of a few hours ago. In one short week, the name of Moulin-Bas has become a legend in these parts. This very moment, instead of sitting here, listening to defeatist talk, I could gather another ten, twenty men behind you – just like that!' He swept a handful of straw into his fist.

'You want a group that size?' I asked. 'Remember it is only as strong as the weakest link. The first rule of the FTP, yes?'

He shrugged. 'So we make another cell in Merck Saint Liévin or Béthune or wherever. You organize, put steel into the backbone as you have done here. From these cells will come other cells, and soon the Boche cannot cope. If every cell did the same as we did last night, every night, they would be another Dunkerque. With the British coming back this time and the Tête Carrées on their way out.'

'The Squareheads have square arses,' I said. 'They won't be so easy to shift.'

'But the Second Front?' asked Le Claque. 'It must come soon now the Americans are in?'

I had seen the first contingent of GIs arriving at Londonderry. Well-equipped, but still untrained. Greener even than I was.

'It takes time to create an army,' I hedged.

'Out of a bunch of cowboys, yes,' was Maurice's sneer.

'And we're a rabble of Mexican Petes,' I reminded him. 'On velos. With no Sierra Madre to retire to when the going gets rough. And it is going to, take my word for it.'

'Of course!' Maurice's sneer was now directed at me. 'You have been in France a week and know what we have known for two years. Two long, stinking, pig-swilling years, *mon fils!* It is easy enough for those Frenchmen who skipped to England when the battle was lost, *le grand* Charles and his crowd! They can sit in country mansions and talk the patriotic *baragouin!* Dogs may bark but that won't keep

53

France alive! France is people, *us,* doing our living under the heel of the arrogant *salauds* from across the Rhine!'

And some doing the dying, I thought, remembering Mec and others like him. I remembered, also, the butter, cheese, eggs placed before me in the past eight days, more than I had seen in eight months in Britain. I thought of tracts of London laid waste by bombs and incendiary, of holes in the ground that had once been Plymouth and Coventry. True, it wasn't the same as being occupied, of seeing a crooked cross flaunting from the local town hall; of rifle-butts on front doors and children weeping for fathers dragged away; of knowing a friend suddenly classified by a yellow Star of David and to be avoided as a leper with a bell. It was none of those things, but let not Europe imagine it was a bloody picnic, an everyday Hampstead Heath Bank Holiday across the Channel. But I was not in France to argue the toss. No Nazarene, me, astride an ass preaching the gospel of goodwill to all men. Maurice was right, in one sense. I was here to harrass, to make life untenable for the conqueror. The only caution I had right to counsel was against an attitude I had been warned I would find prevalent amongst some elements of every resistance group . . . *Ca ne risque rien.* There's no risk. The cocksure excuse of the lazy, the one who can't be bothered with humdrum detail. A detail, all too often, the difference between life and death. Which brought me to another matter of concern.

'Solange,' I said.

'What about her?'

'She has the one transmitter. In theory, she should have several, spread around, so that she can move from one to another as much as possible.'

'Whose fault is that?' Maurice threw his hands in the air, annoyed at the change of subject.

'Forget whose fault, face the reality!'

An elaborate shrug. 'She had the Renault van—'

'—with the set hidden under cabbages and early beans. It isn't good enough.'

'She knows the risk.'

54

'Does she? Do *you?*'

'What is that supposed to mean?' He was on the defensive.

'It means an ambulance we passed in St Omer four days back.'

'So we passed a Boche ambulance . . .?'

'Carrying some Nazi with a dose of clap?' I felt like adding 'caught from a French whore' but thought better of it. 'No. More likely a flap of ears under headphones. Mobile direction-finders that can pin-point a transmitter within a few square kilometres.'

'She is never in any one place long enough. And the old Renault has a fair lick of speed—'

'—on charcoal and wood chippings—?'

'—on any fuel! Can you do better?' The words came in a bluster. I sensed the unease.

'So all they get are four fixes in four days in four different spots from here to St Pol. And what are the SD or the Abwehr doing in their front-wheel-drive Citroëns? They are moving to these spots, checking and double-checking through informers and collaborators, and coming up with the coincidence of a strange and distinctive market van driven by a blonde girl without dirt under the fingernails from handling freshly-pulled spinach. So a description is circulated and sooner rather than later she is in the nearest *boîte* with *no* fingernails, only bleeding stumps. That – or even the threat of it – could turn her against us.'

A quick exchange of glances. 'She would never betray us.'

'You can say that for sure? Even about yourselves?' I looked from one to the other. 'Tough, dedicated men, both. That I grant you. But I don't know your family backgrounds and better that I don't. Married men, I would imagine, with kids. If they took your youngest, began knocking its teeth out with a hammer, with you looking on, forced so to do, to listen to the screams, what then? Would you still keep your own mouths shut?'

'You have a vivid imagination,' muttered Maurice, sullenly.

'And – if you will forgive me – a wider knowledge of fact. This pretty, smooth-faced boy who has known the soft life of safe old England for the past two years, also knows the bastards from student days. The Hitler-Jugend, for example, graduating into the ranks of the Totenkopf. Not just drums and banners and right arms raised for their Führer. There are other rituals to test their courage and devotion. One such proof is removing a live rat from a cage and biting its head off. You think *that* is vivid imagination? On my grand-mother's grave, it isn't! Why, in the name of Christ, d'you think I'm in this war? Because Winston Churchill planted a Union Jack in my head? Never in a million years! I don't give a tinker's fart for patriotism, for Britain, France, any country. Nor any more for politics – left, right, or centre. I'm in it because I refuse to accept a short-arsed, loud-mouthed shit of an Austrian telling *me* what *I* shall do; deciding whether *I* shall be permitted to breed children to some crackpot Aryan-purity-of-race formula or finish up a eunuch-slave in a Krupps factory! I like to think I would die rather than submit to such a future. Yet, come the crunch, if I am the one taken instead of Solange or *you* or *you*, I'm not so bloody sure I wouldn't squeal, because I don't know how much I could take. That's your Moulin-Bas, your over-night legend of the Pas-de-Calais, your testicled Joan of Arc!'

I ran out of breath.

Unnecessarily so.

I might just as well have saved it.

TWELVE

Claude was to blame. Two evenings later, he came pedalling back like a yellow-jerseyed leader in the Tour de France, scattering hens and pigs as he came through the farm gate.

'I've got it!'

Maurice asked what.

Claude's eyes settled on me. 'Raoul said something about an anti-aircraft gun, *mon capitaine*. That you would be pleased if I . . .'

'Christ Jesus, you haven't . . .?'

'Not a gun, no. That would be impossible. But a shell . . .'
He wiped sweaty fingers down his jacket. 'Not with me
naturally. I had to leave it in a wood near Hazebrouck. It was
a bit heavy.'

A bit heavy. Fifty pounds of HE in a metal casing, complete with clock mechanism, fuse and detonator, guaranteed
to wing upwards at high velocity and fragment into a hundred
flying fish of death.

'How?' My voice was suddenly hoarse, as with a heavy
cold.

'Easy, really.' A modest grin diffused over his moon-like
face. 'I was riding past this place with the onions and there
were these Stols, two of them—'

'Whoa,' I said. 'Stols?'

'Schloks, Boches, you know.'

'Onions,' I said.

'Ah, that is my cover. You being a Breton gave me the
idea. Bretons sell onions, n'est-ce-pas? Strings of them on the
handlebars and in the knapsack on my back, the salauds never
give me a second look except to buy . . . anyway, these two
were unloading a truck, piling the shells on the grass verge.
I knew they were anti-aircraft because the gun was in the field
the other side of the ditch and there was a chain of men
moving them to the site—'

'Get on with it,' muttered Maurice.

Claude looked pained. 'The details of reconnaissance are
important, non? Carefulness is the essence, *mon vieux!*'

Coming from Claude that was priceless. I grinned. 'We
understand.'

'So,' he went on. 'One of the Stols waved me down, said
they wanted onions. They took all I had in the knapsack but
short-paid me on the deal, telling me to come back later for
the rest of the money. Their idea of a joke, of course.'

'Of course.'

'But I went back. The same two were still there, stripped
to the waist and taking the sun. Sleepy, I thought, after their
midday meal. I knew this because the chain of men had

stopped working and were back at the gun site around the field-kitchen and . . .'

'Don't bother with the menu,' snarled Maurice. 'It was pork stew and sauerkraut!'

Claude ignored him. 'I leaned my bike against their truck, dropped the knapsack over this shell on top of the pile nearest the tailboard, casual-like, but out of sight of the field, then went along and asked for the francs owing. One waved me away. The other told me if I didn't disappear they would have me fired from the gun. A big joke. They both laughed their pig heads off. I went back behind the truck, picked up the knapsack with the shell in it, slung it across the handle-bars and rode away.'

'Just like that?' I said.

'*Exactement.*' Face dead-pan. Like the story of the stack pipe, it was crazy enough to be true.

'And then . . .?'

'I came to this belt of trees. The knapsack was back on my shoulders now and weighing heavy and there was the chance some other Stol might stop me to buy onions . . . in fact, they did, *after* I had dumped the shell, my last two strings.'

Maurice rolled his eyes. '*Tu deviens marteau!* What do we do with an anti-aircraft shell?'

Claude turned to me in appeal. 'We are short of explosive, non? I thought there must be some way we could remove it from the case and use it. If I had had a screwdriver with me, I would have tried myself.'

Something walked over my grave. The thought of Claude with a screwdriver. He would have been in smaller pieces than his onions, spread over most of Hazebrouck. I forced a grin of approval, shook his hand. 'We can do much better than that.' I glanced at Le Claque. 'If you can handle it like the new-born babe it is, get it to our weaponry class, we'll have a new lesson.'

A simple lesson. A screwdriver – in any other hands but Claude's – applied to the base of the shell. Screw-heads turned, work the base off gently. Drop it, and here endeth the lesson. Report back for duty with halo and harp. The base removed, examine the inside of the casing. A wheel and a spindle, connected by a pair of screws. Undo the screws, turn the spindle to the right as far as it will go, then ever-so-carefully lever the spring away from the time mechanism. Replace the base as before.

All set. Hand the shell back to the Boche, for him to load it into the breech, and get your arse out, fast, before he tugs the lanyard . . .

'What happens?' asked the ever-curious Philippe.

'You tell him,' I said to Le Claque.

The quarryman hesitated for a moment, then: 'When the gun fires, the detonator is struck. This explodes the charge that sends the shell out of the gun. The time mechanism sets off the main charge when it is in the air. Now, after what Patrice has done, there is no time lag between the first and the main charges. The shell will explode in the breech, the hot air or gas will not get away fast enough, and the gun will blow back in the faces of the crew.' He looked at me.

I nodded. 'That's it, near enough. Treat a number of shells in a similar fashion on as many sites as we can reach and quite a few gunners will gain their wings in an unusual manner.'

'When do we start?' Maurice was eager.

I was less enthusiastic. 'When every man jack knows the drill backwards, forwards, and in his sleep. Not before.'

The shell was screwed and unscrewed twenty times that night. Claude alone never handled it. Nor showed any desire. He was, it seemed, learning his limitations.

There began another series of recces. Gun sites in open country were to be avoided like the plague. Shelter was required, as close to the guns as possible, both for reconnaissance and strike. It was a much more complicated business than a piddling little meadow with a handful of half-asleep guards. An ack-ack complex comes close to being self-

59

supporting; guns and gunners; transport and drivers, signals and signallers; plus all the odd sods doing the donkey work, from cookhouse to latrines.

Once decided upon, the target had to be stop-watched around the clock, checking *modus operandi* – guard changes, stand-downs, 'alert' drill, gun and ammunition inspections, who was there, why, and at what time. Nothing left to chance. Only in comic-strips can a party of raiders stroll in, wreck the joint, stroll out again, with a final stutter from a Sten and a 'Have this one on me, mate!' Try it, if you want, but be ready to inform the next of kin.

Six did watch-duty. Two on four off – Maurice, Raoul, Jules, Aristide, Philippe, and myself. We found two likely sites, both near trees with reasonable approach ground. One had a set-up of six guns; the other, only three, though further positions were being prepared. I reasoned prudence. Three out of three made better arithmetic than nought out of six. No fight with Maurice over this. He had won the dispute of dispersal and could afford to give ground on a tactical point.

Solange got a message out asking was there a chance of aircraft swanning over the area in the near future and if not, could it be so arranged? The message started and finished with a code-name *Joke Cigar*. Four night later, some bright 'I' boy sent us a reply. *Joke Cigars were popular with Punch. He gave 17 away with the first issue. Jane Austen smoked another the day she died.* Some random figures followed.

All clever stuff. I was presumed to have an Old Moore's Almanac stuffed up my left nostril to help me work it out. Solange proved the bright one. She informed me that the author of *Pride and Prejudice* had spun off this mortal coil on July 18, 1817. By simple guesswork it was assumed that the magazine *Punch* had made its debut on July 17. *Ergo,* we could expect some bait to be dangled in the sky on one of those two nights, weather permitting. The random figures unscrambled as 1.30. a.m.

'What night do we strike?' asked Maurice.

'The nearer the time the better,' I said. 'The dapper little ponce in command may change his routine and call for a spit-and-polish shell inspection. He looks the type who would whitewash the coal if he was stationed in Béthune. And there is always the bright eye in every battery who does the job thoroughly. One hurried screwdriver scratch that shouldn't be there, one not-so-tight screw head, and our work will have been a waste of time. The sixteenth, probably.'

The seventeenth itself would be cutting it too fine. It would be just our luck for the 'bait' to turn up before we had finished fixing the 'hooks'.

'Tonight would have been nice,' he said, somewhat ruefully.

I understood why. It was the fourteenth. Bastille Day.

'Another reason why not, I'm afraid. They will be especially on their guard. There were more motorized SS on the roads today than I've seen since a Nuremberg rally.'

His glance was almost one of suspicion. 'You have been to one of those?'

My smile was bland. 'Out of curiosity. I was sixteen at the time and knew then it would come to this eventually. You might say I was picking out targets. I have a good memory for faces. One day – who knows? – I could be lucky.'

'This is something of a vendetta with you, isn't it?'

'You could call it that. In an impersonal way.'

'*Very* personal, I would have thought. Solange told me . . .' He looked troubled.

'About Heidelberg?'

A nod. 'When I heard it, I took it for bravado, an attempt to impress. But having seen you with that knife . . .' He took a long, deep breath, expelled it slowly. 'It was not *what* you did that made me vomit. It was the manner in which you did it. So cold-blooded, efficient. Inhuman, almost.'

'It's that kind of war, *mon vieux*. I fight on their terms. No quarter, no pity.'

'So long as you don't finish up like them.'

'Filled with hate?' I shook my head. 'They hate because they are so unsure of themselves.'

'You are not?'

'*Aquila non capit muscas*. A family motto. The eagle does not stoop to flies. I hope I can live up to it.'

An arm slid about my shoulders, gripped hard. 'You are a good lad, Patrice. I would be proud to call you my son. Don't let anyone stop you doing what you want to do. But, above all, don't let them stop you becoming an old man.'

He let me go, turned away sharply. There was a tilt to his head that hinted at tears. I felt a lump form in my throat.

'*De toi à moi*,' I murmured. '*Il faut s'y mettre.*'

Between us, we'll have to see to it . . . rash, brash words.

THIRTEEN

Nineteen months of strenuous training – from the parade ground at Ballymena to the para-jumps at Ringway – had failed to raise as much as a blister. Nineteen days in the field and I was suddenly in physical trouble.

The cause was the built-in limp supplied gratuitously by some clever dick at Headquarters. If I had been given a fortnight to practise with it, break it in, things might have been different. But it gave them sadistic pleasure to spring surprises, part of the exercise, old boy, teach you to adapt fast.

Codswallop. The message needs time to get through to the left metatarsal and extensor tendons. Net result: all the makings of a dropped arch plus a neurotic gastrocnemius. Come the morning of the 15th of July, I had a natural hobble of my own.

One of the group, Henri, was a cobbler. He was able to remove the offending lift from the shoe and promised to make me a new pair for Sundays, holidays, and picking-up-by-Gestapo wear. Solange, meanwhile, arrived at the farm late that afternoon, and took charge of the leg. Long fingers probed sympathetically, massaging muscles back into shape from the knee downwards. The Witch brought us supper, with a carafe of wine and a wink.

'He wouldn't let *me* do that,' she cackled. 'And me a nurse in my time!'

'Is that why Napoleon retreated to Moscow?' I murmured. Solange snorted, dug fingers deeper, made me squirm.

'*From* Moscow . . . get your history right! And don't be unkind to the old. You'll be that way yourself one day!'

Shades of Maurice . . . I nearly repeated the words I had used the previous day, but stopped myself in time. I'm not superstitious, but better not tempt fate too often.

We finished supper, lit her cigarettes, lay down in the loft, side by side. What qualifications she had as a masseuse I had no idea, but the morale value was unquestionably high. We lay silent until the cigarettes were finished. Then she came up on one elbow, stubbed hers, kissed me shyly on the cheek. I killed my own, found her hand. She allowed me to hold it, but returned to her former position before I got the wrong idea.

'Why?' I asked, in English.

She answered in the same tongue. 'Because you have been so busy since you arrived, yet have found time for me.'

'Not as much as I would have liked.' I tickled her palm with a finger. She slipped her hand free, slapped mine.

'Not *that* way!' I mean concern for my safety. The RD people.'

Maurice had not entirely ignored my warning, apparently.

'I had a fright yesterday evening,' she went on. 'Soon after I closed down the set. I was staying with a schoolmistress near Estrée. A nice old thing, but deaf as a post. She talks so loud the children could take lessons from the other end of the village.' She gave a nervous little laugh. 'Where was I?'

'Having a fright,' I said, soberly. I caught the hand again, held it gently.

'Oh, yes . . . there was this man. He was walking by, wearing a topcoat with the collar turned up. And a hat pulled down over the ears. Strange, I thought, for the middle of summer. Rather sinister.'

My hand tightened about hers. She turned her head.

'It means something?' she whispered.

'Or nothing. It could have been an Algerian feeling the cold. Or what the well-dressed man is wearing in Paris . . .'

'Don't joke, Patrice.' I felt her shiver. I stroked her wrist. I had no wish to frighten her more, but clearly someone should have taught her about the birds and the bees.

'A small receiver strapped on the chest, headphones plugged in under the hat. I did the same thing myself at Wareham, playing tag with a radio-operator. The final refinement after the mobiles have a fix.'

'They trained you very thoroughly,' she said, after a moment.

'The British never do things by halves. Usually it's three-quarters, leaving the final quarter out on a limb to fend for itself. They call it initiative. It's supposed to give us the edge over the Germans who are so thorough they scratch their parts by numbers.'

A long silence followed. I played soft piano up to her elbow, trying to ease the tension from her. Without much success. Her problem wasn't muscular.

'Where is this Wareham?' she asked, finally.

'County of Dorset. On a river called the Puddle. It waters a number of villages known as Affpuddle, Bryantspuddle, Tolpuddle . . .'

'I have heard of Tolpuddle.'

'They make martyrs there,' I said. 'Or did, a century back. Now Hitler has taken over, put the thing on an assembly line. In places called Dachau and Mauthausen, to name a couple.'

'Is there such a place known as Buchenwald?'

'I wouldn't be at all surprised.'

Her head moved, came into the crook of my arm. 'Oh, Patrice . . . I'm so scared.'

'Better than being complacent.' I slid the arm under and about her. 'I didn't mean to frighten you for pleasure, Solange.'

'Keziah . . .' she whispered.

'Keziah?'

'My real name.'

'Daugher of Job, isn't it? In all the land no woman so fair. It suits you.' I brushed her hair with my mouth.

'Why – why do they hate us – the Jews – so much?'

'Legend has it you crucified a false prophet. A safe tack for the Nazis to work upon. The German nation are so Christian.'

'You are not?'

'No. I'm a Mab.'

'What's a Mab?'

'Marian Altar Baptismal. It was done within the Church in the old days to keep our ancestors from the stake. The ritual still persists, with the child's future placed under the protection of the Virgin Mary. Only she isn't seen that way – not as the Mother of God. Rather as the Mother Goddess, the old religion. Four thousand years older than the Christian thing. Older even than the Jewish faith. By two hundred and forty-three years, give or take a full moon.'

She raised her head a fraction, to see if I was serious. And saw I was. 'That is called witchcraft, yes?'

'You've been nursing my cloven hoof. You should know.'

'I meant no offence . . .'

'If you had, you'd be a toad by now. I'm quick on the spells.'

'Spells?'

'*Le maléfice, charme.*' I wiggled fingers in her face. 'You think I'm so very young. In truth, I'm older than Methuselah—'

I stopped talking as her lips met mine. They were soft and warm and could have been clinging. But she pulled them away abruptly, buried them in my shoulder. 'That was a mistake.'

'We all make them. To err is human.' I tried to raise her chin with a forefinger.

It burrowed deeper, the voice became muffled. '*You* are not human, if I'm to believe you.'

'Like Zeus, I can change shape. Watch out next time you take a bathe in the canal. I'll be the third swan on the left. I'll have you hatching eggs like the lovely Leda.'

65

'Idiot!' A touch of the giggles back in the voice.

I glanced at the roof. The light was fading, if the gaps were anything to judge by. Curfew time, soon, by Maurice's watch. The words dragged out of me with reluctance. 'Getting late . . . your schoolmarm will be chewing her moutstache.'

'I don't sleep there. Not tonight. She knows that.' She turned her head a fraction, made a pillow of my shoulder.

'Ah,' I said.

'Why "ah"?'

'Where then? Not with your transmitter. I forbid that.'

Her head came up. She looked down at me. 'You *forbid?*'

'Insist, then.'

'There could be another message . . .'

'There could be a man in the moon. But there is no step-ladder long enough for you to find out.'

'What does that mean?'

'Nothing special. A saying of my grandmama's when I was being particularly difficult to get to bed.'

A wisp of a smile. 'That is what you are trying to do with me, no?'

I ran a finger the length of her nose, gave the tip a little flick. 'You, my dear Keziah, are as safe as you want to be.'

'H'm . . .' Not suspicious. More weighing the words in the balance as a compliment or otherwise.

'On that score,' I went on. 'My grandmama said something else – when I was much older, of course.'

'*Very* much older, without a doubt! What did she say?'

'That two hooks-and-eyes and four pins were enough to defend a girl's virtue, and she invariably had more than that most of the time.'

'Your grandmama was an old cheat! She stole that saying from Marcel Pays!'

'I wouldn't be a bit surprised. A very erudite kleptomaniac, my granny.' I did the finger thing down the nose again. This time she lifted her head, snapped with her teeth, catching it and nipping hard.

'Jesus!' I muttered. 'You've got pins and some!'

'No, no . . .' She took the bruised finger in hers, kissed it better. She gave me a long look, pushed back her hair, bent over me. 'Not really, *chéri. Aucun d'épingles* . . . no pins. Not for you.'

We never noticed the night crawl in beside us.

FOURTEEN

Thursday, July 16th. The Francs-Tireurs moved in twos and threes throughout the day. Those who went first – Maurice's party – scouted the approaches. Any unexpected activity, any signs of more-than-usual uniforms, any plain-clothes men in Citroëns, all were noted and a farm gate or telegraph pole was tagged with a twist of wire and a torn rag. It meant 'take an alternative route, this way is dicey'. Arrival points at our rendezvous area were marked gypsy fashion – stones set in a casual but agreed pattern, a strip of bark torn from a tree, a screw of corrugated paper caught on a bramble. The *velos* were parked in pairs, over a wide area, carefully screened, and each arrival was expected to know where he had left it. Come dusk, he would have gone through a drill of withdrawal, covering the ground from the area adjoining the gun-site. It was of equal importance to steal away with certainty after the task was done, as the doing of it.

I left the farm with a final hug and a kiss from Solange. And something of a conscience. My attitude towards sex was a trifle old-fashioned. Old-fashioned in the sense that no matter the physical urge, lust alone wasn't enough. Old-fashioned in the sense that women commanded respect and were not objects to be remembered for their bodily attributes alone. If that sounds priggish, it isn't meant to be. Two years of primarily masculine company, twenty-four hours a day, had blunted moral sensitivity to a degree. Girls like the one I had stood up at Victoria were all too often ships in the night, passing momentarily. Like oneself, they sought comfort, consolation, love, relaxation – call it what you will – on the long dark, lonely, restless sea that was war. Some had known the deep emotional tangle of loving and losing and had no desire to embark on a voyage of serious commitment again; not, at any rate, before the final All Clear sounded and they could be reasonably sure of their man.

Solange was one of those. Her husband had been a flier with the French Air Force. Only weeks after their marriage, he had been one of the few to take the air against the thousand Luftwaffe in support of von Kleist's crossing of the Meuse. May 13, 1940 . . . missing, believed killed. Never a word since. That hoped-for, part-printed card form a POW camp had failed to materialize. And without the comfort of his seed within her, burgeoning into a child to offer a lifetime remembrance of a brief moment of happiness. Never a man since, she had whispered, and I had the arrogance to believe her. Maybe arrogance is the wrong word. I felt humility mingled with esteem as I pedalled away with a wave of the hand. I was not in love with her, but I would never ever forget her.

Twenty minutes later, I did. I came round a corner too fast for discretion, missed a car by a coat of paint and a prayer, wobbled wildly and skidded into a ditch.

The ditch was dry. My mouth was drier. The car was a Citroën and had stopped. The man at the wheel had got out and now stood over me. He wore a black, belted raincoat and a soft hat and he didn't need to open his mouth to tell me he was German. When he did, he put together a string of obscenities that had their origins in a Viennese *vogelnester,* a kind of licensed brothel. For my money and experience, the worst of the Nazis were like their leader, Austrian-born. For calculated cruelty, sadism, and such, they had their Prussian and Saxon counterparts in the category of tame mice. Bavarians came closer to the Austrians as out-and-out bastards and Munich, after all, was where the movement originated. Generalisations, in theory, may be wrong; but, in fact, it would not be unfair to say that the softer the glove of accent within the Reich the harder the knuckle-duster hidden beneath.

I got to my feet warily. He shot out a hand, palm upwards.

Papers, the gesture said. I found my wallet, made to open it. It was snatched from my hands. He went through the contents, taking his time.

By now, a second man in a belted raincoat had joined him. An older man, with a beaky nose and brown eyes. A frosted brown that left a chill wherever they landed. The contents of the wallet were passed to him with a sneer from the first man, finger-tapping the photograph of the naked *poule*.

'Thinking of *that* instead of looking where you were going?' he said, in something that passed for French. 'Where *are* you going, hein?'

Where was I going? I heard my voice mumble 'St Omer'.

'Why St Omer?' The question came fast, rapped out by the older man.

'Hoping to find work.'

'What kind of work? This card says you are a draughtsman. What is there in St Omer for a draughtsman?'

'Nothing that I know of,' I said, eyes to the ground.

'Look at me when you speak!'

'Nothing,' I repeated, looking up at him. 'Nowhere. That is the problem. But I know something about mustard . . .' I allowed the words to end lamely.

'Mustard!' said the first man.

'A factory there, m'sieu. They make it for the German Army. I heard they were short of hands, there might be a vacancy . . .'

'Mustard!' went on the first man. 'The height to which these French pigs rise at a time like this! Mustard!' The word spat down between my feet.

'Go on riding like you were and you'll find something hotter than mustard!' snapped the elder man. He scattered the wallet and its contents on the verge. I hesitated. 'Pick them up!' he added, with a gesture.

I bent down, scrabbling hastily, all thumbs, knowing what to expect, and getting it. A sharp toe in the coccyx sprawled me back in the ditch. Anticipation had saved me some of the hurt, but I let out the squeal I knew they were hoping for. Fingers itched to search out the knife from the neck holster, swing and plant it deep into a gut. But I clutched my precious papers instead, rolling over on to my back, knees curled tight, hands covering head to protect it from a second swing of the boot.

The first one pissed on me. The older one laughed his contempt. Then both turned back to the Citroën. Doors slammed, it moved off. I waited a long half-second before raising my head.

La Geste had gone. Gestapo, I was sure, they had to be. I ignored the sickening pain in the spine, the urine on my hands and face. I stuffed my papers away hastily, got the bicycle back on the road. Spokes had snapped in the front wheel and the handlebars were out of true; yet I put a pair of kilometres behind me before stopping to straighten them out. With those bastards, you never knew. They were in no great hurry, otherwise they wouldn't have stopped. Idle German hands liked something to play with. They might change their minds and come back for me . . .

I reached the rendezvous point fifty minutes later. Maurice came to meet me, looking anxious. I pointed to the slightly buckled wheel and let it rest at that. 'What's new here?' I asked.

'Plenty,' he said. 'The guns have been on an alert most of the morning. No firing. But some were banging off, way up the coast. I never knew the British did daylight raids.'

Neither did I, I had to admit. But everything had to start sometime. Short nights and little moon was as good a time as any. And today, of all days, was the best possible for us.

We went forward, crawled to our point of vantage – a slight rise of wooded ground overlooking the site. Maurice had not exaggerated. The guns were manned, the crews in full battle-gear. They would be hot, miserable, short of temper in the humid haze of this July day that carried no consoling breeze. A long period of stand-to and they would turn into their cots ready to drop, eyes rimmed red from searching the sky for the lost sheep wandering off course on its way home from wherever. There could be a few. If Harris had put the RAF up in daylight, it had to be a big one.

Maurice handed me binoculars. I took a closer look, eyed the nearest gun, checking the line of approach. Work was proceeding on one of the new pits, a fresh pile of sandbags since forty-eight hours before. Good. More cover for us. I ranged over the shells stacked neatly beside the gun, pyramid fashion. Top one missing meant the gun was ready to fire. We must check on the 'unload' when it came.

The same went for guns two and three. I brought the glasses round to bear on the rest of the site. Cookhouse tent, field-kitchens, a fat little Schlok in a dirty singlet stoking one of them. They would have their *Krenfleisch mit Knödelen und Apfel Strudel* if it choked them. It would make our task much easier if it did. I had had a fleeting thought at one time how I might slip across to the cookhouse and deposit my knock-out drops into the pots. A wistful pipe-dream, no more. Errol Flynn would have achieved it with ease and a gay laugh. I was no Flynn. I hadn't even got a pencil moustache.

On to the officer's caravan and the signal section; to the transport under its screens, to the main ammunition dump itself. It would have been nice to have got those, too, by way of an encore, but don't stretch your luck, feller . . .

'Satisfied?' asked Maurice, as I handed him back the binoculars.

'As can be,' I muttered, eyes on the roll of wire between us and our target. It brought out a trickle of sweat.

FIFTEEN

Wire encompassed the whole perimeter. Double-concertina, heavily barbed, it was much too close to the manned areas of the site for anything but a suicidal approach from open ground. Only here, amid the trees, was it set back at a distance.

The first recce – a week before – had been approached

with caution. Trained to expect the worst. I had feared the area would be booby-trapped.

We had found none.

Moving on to the top of the rise, I had felt sure there would be a man-made clearing, allowing a field of fire for a Spandau machine-gun.

No clearing. No Spandau. No indication that one might be moved up after dark. Only the wire, and beyond it, the trees thinning out on a downward slope for fifty metres or so. There, where the undergrowth gave way to grass, stood the one visible sign of defence – a half-track with a 20-mm Oerliken-type gun mounted upon it.

It was too good to be true. The spider inviting the fly.

My eyes had searched the ground immediately ahead. The wire, it appeared, had been laid by a poltergeist. Not a jack-boot print in the loam. Here and there, a scattering of leaves, mostly withered products of the previous fall. But not all. Some were recent, green, especially the larger ferns. I was no Red Indian with buffalo squirt on my moccasins, but I knew my *Scouting for Boys*. Baden-Powell would have been proud of me.

I made a gap in the wire with the cutters, went through cautiously. Six feet inside the wire and under the second fern I found what I was looking for. Three prongs thrusting up through a scatter of earth.

An S mine. Step on it and there's a flash. A metal ball flies waist high and bursts, spraying shot in all directions. Capable of killing or wounding more than the one who steps on it. Quite a number if they were bunched close after coming through the gap in the wire. And those it didn't get would be minced by the 20-mm gun once the alarm was raised.

I moved back, closed the gap in the wire, rejoined Maurice and Jules, the other members of the recce party.

'*Merde,*' was Maurice's comment. 'If it's like that the whole length of the wire—'

'It would be too easy,' I said. 'Lifting a pair to create a gap is relatively simple.'

'You mean it is mined all the way down?'

I shrugged.

'It's off, then,' he said, flatly.

'Not necessarily. They will have been sewn thicker close to the wire. The further in, the easier it should be.'

'You can be sure of that?'

'A hunch. Yet not entirely without logic.' I showed him the fern I had lifted. 'This is still showing sap. Forty-eight hours, at the most, since it was broken. That's how long the mines and the wire have been laid.'

'What does that prove?'

'A rush job, a precautionary measure. Possibly as a result of our raid on the airfield. That being so, the object is to deter Francs-Tireurs, not to combat an Allied invasion. If every ack-ack site in the Pas-de-Calais is to be protected it would take far too many mines to do it in depth.'

'You could be right,' he conceded.

I could be wrong. But there was only one way to find out. 'I can try to find a safe route,' I said. 'Marking it as I go.'

'Beforehand, you mean?'

'There is reasonable cover as far as that U-shaped tree.' I pointed it out. Thirty metres, at a guess. Rather more than halfway to the last of the trees. 'Beyond that point it will have to be on the night and fingers crossed.' Legs, too, or risk becoming a soprano.

'How will you mark?' asked Jules.

'Sticks with a dab of white paint would help.'

'Wouldn't luminous paint be better?'

Bright boy. Worthy of an upraised thumb. 'You can do?'

He nodded. 'Leave it to me, Patrice.'

I had left it to him. He had provided the goods. And twenty-four hours later I had safely reached the U-tree. My hunch had been right, it seemed. Fewer S mines and less care taken to conceal them. Very much a rush job, the final twenty metres would not be too difficult. I had dared to take a snake's eye view of it from the tree. It was as well I did. It knocked my complacency for a loop.

73

Sunlight dappling the trees had glinted on trip-wires criss-crossing the ferns. Pressure on any one would jerk the pins from a pair of grenades. To cover the shortage of mines, the last section was booby-trapped.

And all I could do was sweat it out . . .

Stand-down for the Germans came at dusk. Equipment shed, they got into line for supper, took it away to tents. A tray went to the officer's caravan, complete with white cloth and cruet. I chewed on a piece of cold stringy hare, wiped greasy fingers in the grass and dwelt on the cadet mess at Sandhurst and the passing of the port. Jules handed me a pint bottle of *marc*, wiping the neck with a dirty thumb. A gesture that assured me I would not catch his gingivitus, I need only worry about amoebic dysentery. I would have preferred a cigarette, but Solange wasn't there to provide and, anyway, we had agreed on No Smoking in the forward area.

We watched the sentries being posted. Six in all. One to each gun, a fourth to cover transport and ammunition dump. The fifth to guard the caravan whilst the sixth climbed on to the half-track. The guard-commander returned to his tent with a flashlight and a book. And their reliefs hovered near the cookhouse, scrounging coffee and any food left over from supper. One by one, they, too, retired to the guard tent. Nothing new in the routine. It had been observed for a succession of nights and notes compared.

I handed the *marc* on to Aristide, wiping the neck with due ritual, and moved back to find Le Claque, a late arrival.

He looked gloomy. '*La Geste* are in Aire.'

As if I didn't know. I described the two I had met on the road.

'The same,' he nodded. 'Does it mean they're on to us?'

'You yourself mentioned the talk around the town. It could be a routine enquiry, a house-to-house check to see who should be at home after curfew.'

'Tonight?' he said, quickly.

I shook my head, more in hope than conviction. 'The

74

salauds love their paper work, making lists, starting files. Praise the Lord for German bureaucracy and a thing known as the *Reichssicherheitshauptamt* register.'

'I hope you're right,' he muttered. 'But I brought the rest of our stock with me, just in case.'

I sighed relief. It had been one of the things on my mind all day. I had even considered postponing the operation until the next night in order to shift the stuff to a safe place. Until Maurice had pointed out that the next night might be too late . . .

'I'm aware the seventeenth is cutting it fine—' I had started to say.

'Tonight *is* the seventeenth,' he said.

'The sixteenth, surely?'

'Not after midnight. At one-thirty, the time the bombers are due to appear, it will be the seventeenth!'

He was right, of course. A simple error that could prove a costly one, it was indicative of the situation. I was trying to do too much in too short a time, a one-man band that could end in a balls-up.

'I got your message,' I heard Le Claque saying.

'Message?'

'Maurice passed it on to Etienne. He came back to give me a hand. We disposed of the containers in the AA canal, along with Claude's shell. The spare arms and ammunition are buried in the beet-sugar field beside it. And Solange's transmitter is in a cachette under the floorboards of Gautier's bakery, sealed and wrapped against the rats.' His usually sombre face showed the glint of a smile. 'You think of everything, don't you, Patrice?'

Yes, I do, don't I . . . When Maurice does my thinking for me!

'*Un homme incroyable!*' Maurice appeared at my elbow. 'That's why we are proud of him!'

I turned my head to say something. He grinned, pushed a cigarette between my open lips. Then winked. '*De toi à moi, non?*' He lit the cigarette for me. 'Forget everything but the job in hand, *mon fils*. A clear head is needed for those twenty metres beyond the U-tree.' He tapped his watch on my wrist. 'Relax for an hour. Not easy for you, I know. I wish Solange was here to help you.'

I threw him a quick glance on that, but his smile was innocent.

'I must check the men,' I muttered.

'I know the drill,' he said. 'Permit me to do something, hein?'

'Sorry,' I said, humbly. And felt it.

SIXTEEN

The markers were three feet apart, glow-worms to follow, the last man past to reverse for the return journey. The ground beneath us was clean, scarcely a leaf or a twig that had not been lifted aside by Raoul, who had helped in laying the path to the U-tree.

Over the days, I had developed a special *rapport* with this little man. He had confided in me his own hopes and fears, his personal animosity for the enemy. Head lad at a racing stables at Neuilly, he had been there two days after the Occupation when an SS detachment had moved in. Their officer had produced a list or owners who patronized the stables. Two were Jewish. All bloodstock belonging to them had been destroyed, the pretext given as meat for German guard dogs. One was a foal that Raoul had brought into the world less than a month before . . . 'a difficult birth, *mon capitaine,* even the *vétérinaire* had been at the point of giving up poor Poulainette'. Poulainette was Raoul's cross and he had borne it back to his home town of Aire with vengeance in his heart.

The U-tree reached safely, I glanced back. The eleven-man

caterpillar was intact, head to ankles. From my angle of view, it was impossible to tell whether Henri, the last man, had turned the markers correctly at 180 degrees. If he had boobed . . . Christ, man, forget it! Keep your mind on the job ahead, Maurice was so right.

I came up into a crouch, touched Raoul's head. The signal telling him I was about to embark on the final twenty metres. If anything went amiss, he had my Thompson with its double magazine of forty rounds. Soft-nose bullets, each cut hot-cross-bun fashion by me for maximum effect. Maximum effect meant it hit and spread and if it did find a way out the other side, you could thrust a fist through the hole and waggle it about. Not Geneva Convention, but that was for politicians and moralists and 'decent chaps' who still saw war as some kind of game. I hadn't seen any of those around to tell me 'yea' or 'nay' since I had jumped into France. Raoul's task was to take out the sentry on the half-track and anyone else who responded to the alarm whilst the ten men behind him made their retreat. He came to his knees wearing a tight grin, slipped the safety-catch, poised the barrel in the low fork of the tree.

I went down, inched my way forward. One metre. Nothing. Place a marker. Two metres. Ditto. Another marker. Three metres. The same. Now stop, concentrate thought. You're supposed to have a photographic mind, remember? Kim's Game, they trained you at it. A few minutes alone, left in a room, and you should know every stick of furniture, where it was, cat scratches and all, the titles of the books on the shelves, even the dead fly on the floor under the window. Compared with *that*, what is twenty metres of booby-trapped ground when you've had several hours to memorize, even map it out on a rough plan? Nothing . . . except the dead fly under the window can't make a bloody bird's nest of your guts high up in a tree.

A half-metre ahead was the first trip-wire, calf-muscle high off the ground. Not high enough to wriggle under unless you knew how; yet higher than most would lift their feet when

77

stepping stealthily. A wire as taut as a virgin's thighs with none of the promised delight between.

Think, think, three hand-spans to the left, a clump of ferns. That's where the charmer is. Ease over slowly, peel back the fronds like they were a pair of drawers, take care not to snap the elastic. What was it the sergeant-instructor said? If it had hair on it you'd find it quick enough.

You find it, immobilize it, but you don't bloody move it, there's likely another at the *other* end of the wire . . . by that rotten stump of a tree, yes? Yes, and worse. *Two* of the bastards, linked together. Clever sods they might be at that School of Mines, but not so clever they grafted you a third hand . . . whoa, Mohammed, wipe the sweat from your eyes, dry your fingers on your front, take a deep breath and count up to five . . . the fellers who laid this trap never set it for a feather touch or it could have gone off in their own faces. So, count another five, grasp the nettle firmly or something, render it safe. Simple, isn't it? Now you can snip the wire neatly, in the knowledge that if you've made a mistake you won't know much about it beyond the blue flash.

No blue flash. Red spots under the eyelids, salt-dry the mouth, heart yammering against tonsils. Swallow it and move on, you're not out of the wood yet.

To the right, this time. A way around the next trap. Five metres to mark but watch it, there might just be the odd S mine lying around. There is. Badly laid, though. Hardly laid at all. Easier to lift and shift, over there by that tree root.

What was that? A movement amid the ferns, the faintest of rustles. Hand to neck, knife in hand, swift. But the movement was swifter, blurred, a flash of ghost-white. And a bob-tail twisted in the air, touched down a foot from my nose; then up, down, up, down, swerving a zig-zag route, all the way to the open ground before swinging back and across, out of sight.

Jesus join a girls' school, a rabbit in a mine-field! I sheathed the knife, grinned ruefully. Probably wearing a gold albert and muttering I'm late, I'm late . . . very *late* if it had tripped a wire! The grin vanished, the sweat came, cold and clammy.

Where there was one, there could be a score, all flashing away, and all my care would be for nothing. One explosion and the shit would fly, from the half-track and from Raoul with yours truly middle-for-diddle . . . calm it, boy, mark and move. Right hand forward, make an arc, search and find or not find. Swing the left slowly, a body's width, check, mark again. Ten metres covered, ten to go. Left, now, well clear of that cat's cradle of wires, but not too far over, is that something under your touch waiting to give you a stump in place of fingers and a thumb? No more Chopin, Gershwin if it is, nor even Czerny or Chopsticks, not that you were *that* good at the keyboard, anyway. Your last maestro had put it succinctly: 'As a musician your place is in the Opera House, painting scenery.' No, it isn't a mine, nor a booby-trap, just a hard, sharp stone, forego the urge to toss it aside, it might do what the rabbit failed. Just mark it and ease on, eyes to the ground, don't distract them with distance still to be covered, you'll get there yet, even if it takes from now until the Peace Conference.

So long as it's not Hitler in the chair, of course. Given that state of affairs, Christ help you, you'll still go on crawling, from the Pas-de-Calais all the way to the Unter den Linden, how about that . . . a bomb between your teeth, ready to stuff it up his brown-shirted arse, hero lunatic stupid fucking clot that you are . . .

Suddenly I was out of the trees and in the long grass, not twenty feet from the wheels of the half-track.

SEVENTEEN

Away from the trees the night air was fresh, almost chill. It dried the sweat on my brow, teased the neck of my jacket. The sentry was perched on the side of the vehicle, head turned away, shoulders hunched, rifle slung.

I wriggled forward, breath coming lightly, came to my feet.

79

'*Ich liebe dich*,' I murmured, in sibilant whisper.

The head came up, the shoulders swung round. The knife flew deep into the throat. He pitched forward and down, hit the ground with his face. I dropped a knee on the spine, grasped the helmet by the rim, jerked it up and back. The neck snapped, the point of the knife protruded clear as the hilt took the weight. I rolled him over, retrieved it, twisting it to make sure.

A gurgle of blood, a final belch of used air. Dead as mutton. I dropped flat, peered about me.

No shadows pounding across the site, no click of rifles in the dark. Against the blackness of the trees, death had come unseen. I rolled him away, under the half-track, out of sight, out of mind, thoughts already on the next.

A glance over my shoulder. The caterpillar was on its way down. Raoul joined me, followed by Le Claque, moisture beading his upper lip as he nodded assurance. Aristide next, making a thumb, rising to hands and knees like some pygmy prehistoric creature with the Bren strapped to his back. Bernard, at his heels, unbuckled the straps swiftly. Jules lowered the gun to the ground. The Lovat Scout at Lochailort would have been proud of them – drill and co-ordination without fuss, in the minimum of time.

Maurice, from the long grass, made a signal. Finger and thumb raised in a circle. Cover party in position, go, man, go.

I looked at my five, nodded.

We went.

Time was the essence. The sentries did two hours on, and the last change had been as we went through the wire. Thirty-five minutes of those two hours had passed, galloping away into oblivion whilst I fumbled those twenty metres.

Stage Two was the gun guards. Work for Raoul and myself. We went ahead of the other four. Cover in plenty to begin with – the trees behind, the sandbags ahead. After that, it was only ammunition piles and the guns themselves.

I came round one ammunition pyramid and there was the

80

first gun guard, rifle slung, having that quick cigarette they all seem to need after the first half-hour. With his back to me, it was too easy. So easy I made a mistake, jarring my wrist as the knife struck bone. My free hand went round the neck, caught the sling of the rifle. A knee up hard between his legs, he arched backwards, the cigarette skittering down his front in a shower of sparks. Knife out as he began to fall, I lowered him gently and stamped on his throat.

Gun Number One . . . over to you, Bernard and Jules.

On to Gun Number Two.

The bugger wasn't there.

Had he heard something? Was he in a crouch, sights aligned? I went into an automatic roll, under the ack-ack mounting, came up the other side.

He was squatting on his haunches, helmet off, a slab of *strudel* in his hand. I murmured the love bit again, but the eyes were already bulging. He coughed cake and keeled sidsways, another knife hilt-deep behind his right ear. Raoul's hand stabbing. 'One for Poulainette,' he spat, thrusting again to make sure. A spike knife, the kind used for removing stones from horses' hooves. I had seen it before when asked pertinent questions on how to use it to effect. He had learnt the lesson well.

Gun Two, ready for Le Claque and Aristide.

We moved on. Gun Three sentry was the tricky one. At the far edge of the perimeter and more exposed. And alert, too, not like the others. Slim, boyish, one from the Hitler-Jugend, perhaps? Acting as though it was summer camp at Bad Tolz, dreaming maybe of Baldur von Shirach crawling out of the nearest bog to turn out the guard.

Too lively by half, all that stamping up and down. Yet not without advantages. Ceremonial may keep the circulation going, but a moving man doesn't see so well. We crabbed, crawled, dropped low behind a pile of sacks left there to take earth from the new pit adjoining. I spread two fingers wide over the knife, showed them to Raoul. Part company. You right, me left. Then the back of one hand. Take him in the rear, no heroics, we're not cowboys quick on the draw.

Raoul lowered his head and was gone, lost in the dark

before I could blink. If all jockeys moved as fast, there'd be no need for horses. I went my way, came in under the long barrel of the gun.

The youth was moving away from me. Too far for an accurate throw. Another four paces, he started to turn. Head high, shoulders braced, a proud little rooster, he'd break into the goose-step any moment. But no Raoul.

Then he was there, suddenly, two skips and a jump, spike knife plunging. It was almost ballet the way the youth stiffened, went up on his toes, offering me his diaphragm and liver. I went in, every ounce behind me. The knees buckled, my hands took his mouth and eyes, swinging him past me and down. A heel on the neck pressed the face into the ground.

Raoul came in again, knife raised. I caught his arm, turned it, shook my head. If the thing under my foot wasn't already dead, it would drown any second from blood and liver fluid flooding the lungs.

A final twitch, a nerve spasm. I turned it over with my toe, collected my knife. Not pretty, anymore. Wide eyes glazed, a dribble of slime and blood from nose and mouth, the acrid stench of a shock-stimulated bowel movement. Nineteen, if a day, he had got his wish – to die for his beloved Führer. *Sieg Heil!* I thought I glimpsed just a flicker of compassion in Raoul's look. My wrist went under his nose, I tapped the watch. Forget the Requiem Mass, the gesture said, we have work to do.

Forty-seven minutes gone. Seventy-three to go. Sixty of them to carry out Stage Three. Out with the screwdriver whilst Raoul and the Thompson kept watch. Bernard, at Gun One, should have managed two shells by now, be at his third; Le Claque would be in much the same position at Gun Two. Practice makes perfect, but when it comes to the real thing, fingers are apt to turn into a bunch of bananas. I seemed to be doing everything twice over. Yet the watch told me differently. I completed my quota with minutes to spare. Screwdriver away, on to the final task – a throwaway to put the enemy off the scent as to what we had really accomplished.

I moulded a slab of the yellow mess that was plastic explosive near the breech of the gun, planted a pencil detonator, activated it to the maximum. If it blew before they found it, excellent; the rigged shells would serve the replacement. If it blew in the face of a gunner in the act of removal, better still. Like the fighter pilots at the airfield, trained men took longer to come by than hardware. If, on the other hand, it was cleared in time, they would congratulate themselves on foiling a sabotage attempt and look no further. A reasonable supposition, anyway.

I tugged Raoul's right ear-lobe. Ready to go. He was away in a streak for the pile of sacks, then down to cover my move to Gun Two. Le Claque and Aristide had already left. A quick shuffle around the piles of shells, a look at the gun itself. A perfectionist, our Le Claque. Two charges, one at the breech, the other under the gun pivot. I activated both detonators to the maximum as Raoul slithered past to cover my next move.

Bernard, too, had left two charges. But one slab of PE was at the bottom of a shell-pile, the bloody fool. I made to remove it, then changed my mind. Not such a bad idea, drawing their attention to the ammunition. The inference being that this was the only method we knew. Full marks, Bernard! No sodding marks, Bernard! In scuffing around at the base of the pile I found something else . . . a *screwdriver*. Jesus wept!

I stopped only to place my second charge of PE on the half-track, then we were all back through the trees, markers lifted, under the wire and heading for bicycles and departure. All away except Maurice and a man named Léon who had volunteered to hold a watching brief.

I was at the point of mounting when I heard the shrill alarm of a whistle. I turned back, curiosity overcoming discipline. As well I did. Maurice and Léon were both so absorbed with what was going on I got within feet of them before they knew it. Both jumped. Léon pulled a long face.

83

He had a reputation as a poacher, ears in his feet as well as his head.

Abject apology. 'I know . . . I should have been facing the other way, guarding Maurice.'

'And you, Patrice, should have been a kilometre past,' muttered Maurice, eyes still glued to the gun-site.

'Reprimand noted. All going?' I asked.

'They've found two of the sentries . . . see for yourself.'

I saw. The boy on Three and the one who had coughed cake. The site was becoming a scene of panic, a confusion of whistles and bellowed orders; of half-dressed men tumbling out of tents, tripping over equipment, heads turned skywards thinking it was a raid, not really knowing whether they were coming or going. More like a farmyard of decapitated hens than the efficient military machine the brass-hats in Britain saw with such hush and awe.

A few weeks out of Sandhurst, I had attended a junior officer's lecture given by the then Area Commander, a certain Montgomery. It had been a great gas about 'Jerry' – a term utterly odious to me – it reeked of respect, almost of affection. It was intended, one could only presume, as a warning against complacency. We must apply the same determination, skills, mental and physical fitness, and guts if we were to win. We, as subalterns, must set the example, instil those qualities in our men. 'Do that, by golly, and we'll knock 'em for six!'

My own response had been an under-the-breath 'Balls!' I did not underrate the enemy. I knew it would take superior fire-power and a lot of dead men before the Nazis gave up. But there was much too much piss and wind talked about the disciplined might of the Master Race. Up until now – July 1942 – their mettle had still to be tested. Their victories had been little more than a ceremonial goose-step behind a tank-crunch through rubble created by Stukas. The qualities of brute force, total lack of humanity. But nothing of that thing called guts. Militarism, in my book, would never be synonymous with courage. It spelled ruthlessness, brutality, arrogance. I was not the least bit interested in 'knocking 'em for six'. I wanted them six feet under. To achieve that, I was prepared to match them in ruthlessness, in brutality, if necessary; to prick that bubble of arrogance and deflate them to the shivering cowards I believed them to be; to show that Herrenvolk could die as easily as we ordinary mortals.

As if to prove my point, four climbed on to the half-track. In time for it to fling them away. My last charge had been deliberately short.

'Duck!' I yelled, as blast and bodies whipped into the trees.

'Time to go home,' I added, as the booby-traps began to explode.

'What about the Royal Air Force?' demanded Max, several kilometres and a half-hour later.

His watch read one-forty-five. I pulled a face. 'Taking a lead from your late emperor,' I said. 'Not tonight, Josephine.'

EIGHTEEN

Not that night. Nor the next night was the promise kept. By a quirk of irony it took a solitary Whitley, belatedly answering our *Josephine* request, to bring the guns into action. On Friday the 24th.

None of us saw it, but everyone between Gravelines and Aire must have heard it – the chain reaction of sound that followed a series of lurid flashes in the sky. Not merely the guns exploding, but shell after shell detonating as the initial blasts flung them aside, until, finally, what must have been the main ammunition dump went up, ripping the site apart. It seemed to go on and on, blood-redding the clouds that had slipped the moon. Then they were lost in a climbing, spreading pall of smoke.

'Bon Dieu!' gasped Maurice.

'If you wish to give him the credit,' I said, switching my eyes to seek the aircraft whose drone could now be heard overhead. 'Pin a Legion d'Honneur under his beard.'

'You know what I mean!'

'I know what *it* means. After tonight, the Pas-de-Calais will be no place for a non-Aryan mouse!'

I caught a glimpse of the Whitley, began stuttering Morse with a torch. One short, three long. It banked sharply. I repeated the signal. The plane straightened out, swooped in. Dark blobs dropped away, blossomed into parachutes. Six in all. As the Whitley began to climb, I saluted it with a short-long-short.

Maurice gestured at the falling containers. 'You talk dispersal nonsense again, when we're in business? *Démerdes-toi, mon cocu!*'

The rude suggestion brought forth a sour grin from me. 'I won't be alone in that.'

We were still collecting the 'drop' when the second plane appeared. It came in low over the trees, spitting tracer, stitching a furrow through the flax. The field was ripe for harvest, the tall plants making us a near-blind target. No casualties, but one canopy was torn from the fingers of Leon and Victor as they were preparing to bundle it. The Messerschmitt rolled away, went into a climb and turn. No time to ponder whether it would make a second run or seek out the Whitley heading for home. 'Forget the 'chutes!' I yelled. 'Containers only, then out!'

They had landed diagonally across the field. Three near the top end, not far from the wagon, two close to the trees at the bottom. The sixth was in the centre, where Léon and Victor were. They could have scuttled for cover, but ran, instead, to help Philippe and Etienne. Between them, they scrambled the container into a ditch as the fighter returned. This time, Aristide, our cover man, blasted back with his Bren, ripping off a whole magazine. I reached him as he reloaded.

'I clipped his tail!' he boasted. 'Did you see that?'

I had seen nothing but a worm's eye view of flax being tossed in all directions by cannon-shells. '*Félicitations,*' I muttered. 'Let's get the hell out of here!'

'But—'

'No buts. If you got him, he won't be back. If you grazed him, he will. Like a wounded rhino and twice as mean. And he may summon friends. *Ca suffit, non?*'

More than enough. Aristide was quick-witted, knew what I meant. He shouldered the Bren, headed for the point where the track became a lane. I moved to the wagon. Raoul's hands and whispers were calming one of the horses, wild-eyed and restive. The top three containers were already loaded, pushed under bundles of flax. The bottom two would be collected on the way out. But the sixth was still in the ditch, two hundred metres in the opposite direction.

'Can we get the wagon down to it?' I asked.

Raoul thrust out his lower lip. 'We *can*. But it is in the open. If that Luftwaffe Schlok comes back . . .'

No need to finish the sentence. My eyes and ears were straining for the sound.

All I got was shouting and cursing from the vicinity of the ditch. The four there had been joined by the six who had loaded the nearer containers. Haste, anxiety, and too many hands brewed a noisy broth.

Rauol rolled his eyes in despair. *'Ils jacassent comme des réveille-matins!'*

Worse than alarm-clocks. And the essence of this work was silence. 'Let's take a chance,' I said.

He got behind the reins, set the horses moving. Out of the deep tree-shadows, into a moon riding clear of cloud. I clambered up on the tail, raised the Thompson, aimed it vaguely in the direction the Messerschmitt might come. A futile gesture. It could tear us to a shambles, men and beasts, before I could get a round off.

We reached the ditch, creaked to a halt. The shouting and argument went on. I called for silence, got none. I fired a shot above their heads. It was like the crack of a whip. Heads turned, mouths fell gaped.

'Coqs qui chantent, ânes qui braient – n'as-tu pas de chat qui miale?' I spat at Maurice.

He made a violent gesture at the others. Mouths closed in stupid, self-conscious grins. Hands raised the sixth container up beside me. Raoul had the wagon turning almost before they had put it down. We bumped back to the shelter of the trees, turned down to collect the remainder. The Messerschmitt had not come back. Maybe Aristide had not boasted, after all.

He came to meet us, arms waving. I jumped down, ran to him. He was now tugging his left ear. I stopped, listened. A night bird in the trees, twittering, serenading the moon. And something else. A thin, staccato sound beyond the trees. A motorcycle, maybe a combination. Outriders for a convoy? Not in a lane that went nowhere of importance. More likely a mobile patrol, following-up on the Messerschmitt. It was logic that the enemy must cotton on to this moonlight 'dropping' eventually. I had made the point to London in Solange's last transmission. It had been ignored.

I half-turned, but Raoul had heard the sound, too. He and Aristide were already removing the horses. I went on down to the gate at the end of the track.

It was shut but not locked. The dangle of chain and rusted padlock had been open when we arrived. It looked as if it had been that way for years. I hoped not. I wanted it closed. Not to delay so much as to deceive. A wagon without horses behind a locked gate, apparently loaded with flax, might give the impression of a farmer who had stopped work at sundown, obeying the new curfew. With luck, it would warrant no more than a cursory glance.

I brought pressure to bear on the padlock. No shifting it. The sound of the motor-cycle grew nearer, more strident. From where I stood I could see a bend in the lane. When it came round that, I would be in view. I strained harder. The padlock began to grate. Quite suddenly, the resistance went. It snapped home. It took the top of a forefinger with it, jerked back the nail.

I gasped, stuffed the injured hand between thighs. Most men do it without knowing why. It was hardly the time to contemplate Freudian thought. A jingle of harness behind me announced the horses were away, into the trees where

Raoul could lose them. Better lose yourself, cocky, or you'll suffer more than a split fingernail.

Aristide had left his Bren near the gate. I picked it up, ran back to the wagon, passed it to him. He was strewing the flax more thoroughly, but it wouldn't stand up to close inspection. As he burrowed under with the Bren, Maurice loomed up beside me.

'Your cocks and asses are bedded down,' he growled. He made a gesture at the hedgerow opposite the trees. 'And the cat that miaows . . .?'

'*This.*' I raised the Thompson. 'Until then, nothing, *capisc'?*'

Again that Italian word had slipped out. I would have to watch it.

'*Capito, pis-pis.*' Then he was gone.

So he had noticed. 'Pis-pis' was a French derogative for an Italian. He had said worse in moments of anger. I dropped down, under the wagon, a more urgent problem to worry about.

A motor-cycle combination had shuddered to a halt beyond the gate.

NINETEEN

Both men dismounted. One raised a boot, jarred the gate with his heel. It protested, but the padlock held. The second man muttered something, then braced himself. He swung up, over, and down on our side.

'*Vorsicht!*' said the first man.

The other shrugged, slipped a Schmeisser from his shoulder, pushed it out in front, hand on trigger. He remained still for a long moment, eyes searching the track, roving over the wagon. Then began the crunch towards us. Only to stop again, swinging the Schmeisser to his right.

The whinny of a horse, from the pasture that bordered the trees, where a second hedgerow began. He moved to it, poked

89

a hole with the machine-pistol, peered through. The whinny became a snort, a thump of hooves. Raoul, I suspected, had shed the tackle of the nervous horse and got it into the meadow against the risk that it might give us away. The man crouched there for most of a minute before withdrawing the Schmeisser. As he straightened up a Porsche *Kubelwagen* drew up at the gate. A figure leaned out of the front seat.

'*Was ist?*'

The first outrider sprang to attention. '*Diesem Tor ist vergeschlossen, Herr Hauptsturmführer!*'

SS. Not Wehrmacht. The officer climbed out, came to the gate, peered over. 'Anything up there?' he called, in German.

'A farm wagon, *Herr Hauptsturmführer!*'

'I can see that, idiot! Look beyond it!'

'*Jawohl!*'

The man on our side crunched closer, moving around the wagon. All I could see now were jackboots and thighs. He stopped. I held my breath. A faint rustle above me. Then he stepped aside, closer to the hedge. His left hand lowered into view, straggling some stalks of flax. But the angle of his stance was heartening. He was clearly surveying the track behind us. He wouldn't much like what he saw. It was narrow and heavily rutted, unsuitable for motor traffic. And he and some other suckers would have to manhandle the wagon out of the way before they could pass. He turned about, made his report.

'*Macht nichts!*' said the officer, who was studying a map with the aid of a flashlight. '*Fahren Sie geradeaus!*'

The first outrider clicked heels, swung into the saddle. His companion left us at a trot, vaulted the gate to show how clever he was, climbed into the sidecar. The motor-cycle kicked into life, roared away down the lane.

The officer had moved out of sight. Now he came back to the Porsche, got in. It began to follow the combination. Behind it came and went two open trucks, with troops seated back to back. By a stroke of luck, I saw someone in the second truck give a wave of derision.

A wave that was not meant for us. It had to be for someone

or more left behind, part of a cordon being thrown around the area. I wriggled out from under, came up at the tail of the wagon, hissed at Aristide. 'Stay put! Schloks still around!'

A thumb cocked up through the flax. I swung away to the patch of shadow where Maurice had disappeared, brought the Thompson across my chest, took it in both hands, moved it up and down and down . . . a signal that meant heads down, mouths shut, no stir, not so much as a whisper of a fart.

Maurice showed. A grenade in his hand. I shook my head, jerked a thumb towards the lane.

'What then?' he breathed.

'Léon,' I mouthed. If anyone could move as silently as Raoul, it had to be the poacher.

Maurice opened his mouth to say something. I gestured no time to discuss it. He hesitated, then faded back into the dark. A whisper down the line, a faint scuffle, and Léon joined me. A .45 Colt in his fist, hammer cocked. Christ Almighty! Tonight was lunatic night with a vengeance!

I eased the gun from his fingers, made it safe. I murmured some instructions in his ear. His response was shifty, hesitating. His eyes dropped to the Colt. I shook my head firmly. 'Cherches-tu!' I added, like talking to a favourite dog, hung my tongue out.

An uncertain smile flitted his mouth. His eyes went upwards at the moon. It was about to go coy behind a lace handkerchief of cloud. A small handkerchief that would not last long.

The moon went. So did he, across and into the trees that fringed away to the lane. I tucked the Colt in the back of my trousers, went after him.

The cardinal rule in any unexpected tactical situation is speed of assessment. To be followed by one of three decisions – right, wrong, or no. The first two may prove to be the toss of a coin, but the third courts disaster. He who hesitates carves his own headstone – or so I had been told more than once.

My assessment had been made before I came from under the wagon. Point One. The SS column had been alerted to parachutes falling. But the lack of suspicion concerning our wagon suggested they were thinking in terms of men rather than containers. Point Two. The low-flying fighter had had difficulty in marking the DZ with pinpoint accuracy, so a tight cordon was out. The *modus operandi,* therefore, was to flush out and drive towards men dropped at intervals. Point Three. The first of these nets was outside the gate. Some minutes had elapsed between Aristide hearing the column and its arrival. Distance could be covered in that time, and I had not heard it stop.

So much for the enemy. From our point of view, we were still too close to the DZ to be healthy. On the other hand, relative safety was only one kilometre along the lane. Another track turning off to a disused gravel pit where the containers were to be hidden.

The decision, right or wrong, was to eliminate the catch-point in the lane and make a run for sanctuary. But, in my hurry, I had repeated an earlier mistake. Doing things myself, without explaining it to Maurice.

I stopped, made to turn back. And found Maurice's garlic breath on my cheek. He had three men with him – Philippe, Victor, and a heavily-built youth known as Albert. 'Glad you got my signal to follow,' I muttered, covering up.

His response was a sly grin. He listened to my outline, nodded. 'So?'

Léon was weaving towards us before I could answer. He had found them, sprawled in the ditch, at the bend of the lane, covering the gate. Two men and a machine-gun.

Good dog. No bone to offer. I gave him back his revolver. And fresh instructions to move a hundred metres to the rear of the gun, give us three minutes, then crash around like several men making a break from the trees. Enough to distract, to turn the gun away so that we could take it from the rear.

'Does that matter?' muttered Albert. A new recruit, he had been with the group less than a week. From what I had seen

92

and heard of him in training sessions, he was more muscle and mouth than brains. His next words were a fair example. 'A grenade would be simpler.'

'And noisier,' hissed Maurice. 'You want the rest of the column about our ears?'

'Patrice knows what he is doing,' Léon murmured, with a grin. He was beginning to enjoy it. 'And afterwards?'

'Scout the route ahead in case there are others,' I said.

He touched his beret with a finger. '*A bientôt!*' And was away.

I looked hard at Maurice. In front of the Alberts of this world I wanted the decision to come from him. My way of apology for the previous error.

He read it as such. 'You, Philippe, and Albert, take the gun. We'll see to the rest.' He gestured at Victor. They faded back into the darkness.

For this kind of job I would have preferred Raoul. But that would have wasted precious time and, anyway, he was needed with the horses. Philippe was the one with red stars in front of his eyes who had called me a fascist. Difference of opinion apart, he was willing to learn. In addition, he had a Walthur pistol, complete with silencer and luminous sights, which should be useful. Albert . . . well, plainly Maurice wanted him put to the test, to learn his reaction to action. I wasn't very happy about the way he was clutching his grenade. The knuckles showed white with tension.

I motioned him to put it away.

'I have no other weapon,' he objected.

'You can have the gun when Philippe and I get it! Follow, but keep your distance.'

They wore Waffen SS collar patches. Insignia of the *Leibstandarte* – Adolf Hitler's Own – the elite, so-called, the creation of a pig-butcher named Sepp Dietrich. The same shit I had been swarming on Bastille Day. Back from the Russian front, so rumour had it. Veterans of a long and bloody campaign . . . against helpless women and children, if their normal role was anything to go by. With the moon behind another patch of cloud, we got within twenty feet of them. They lay below us, crouched behind a tripod-mounted Spandau, one of them nursing the ammunition belt.

It was then I saw the third man. He was a short distance beyond them, up on the same bank as we were, partially obscured by a tree. In the act of removing his helmet, his blond hair gave him away. The field wireless slung about his shoulders made his function equally clear. And accorded him priority.

I froze Philippe with a touch, began a detour. The man was so intent listening to his set, I got as close as ten feet before I paused. Then only to lower the Thompson and leave both hands free. Not a job for the knife. That pack on his back offered too much protection. I fingered my waist, slipped free the garotte . . .

Twigs snapped. A jerking knee clipped the helmet that lay on the ground. It clattered away down the bank. Sounds that brought a quick whisper from the ditch.

'*Bist Du, Franz?*'

Franz was in no state to answer. His mouth was open, his tongue was lolling, his fingers scrabbling. Then they went limp, fell away. I tightened the cord, spoke for him.

'*Mein fehler. Es tut mir leid.*'

No time to stop and see if my whispered reply was accepted. No time to get back to Philippe and Albert. Léon had started his action. After the quiet, it came like a stampede of elephants. Or our Claude treading careful. The voice in the ditch muttered '*Dort!*' and I heard the quick scuffle as they brought the Spandau around.

The crashing grew louder. Too close to the road, I feared. In his enthusiasm, he might even show himself. I grabbed up the Thompson, went low along the bank, making for a position directly above the Spandau.

It was then I saw the grenade hit the lane. It skittered away to the far side, rolled into the opposite ditch before tearing itself asunder in black smoke. That was enough for the

94

Spandau. A yellow stream of tracer spewed out, smashed its way into the trees where Léon was. I crashed forward to the edge of the bank. The Thompson began to jump, to judder, to slice back and forth at point-blank range. Then only the echo of shot as both stopped firing. Mine for one reason only. In that moment of rage I had emptied the whole magazine.

I put in a fresh clip automatically, became aware of Philippe and Albert moving up on either side of me. Philippe was waving his Walthur, looking for something to shoot at. I rounded on him in fury. 'Go knock the lock off the gate! *Vite!*'

He jumped the ditch and ran. I turned to Albert, jabbed the Thompson at his pocket. Nothing more solid than clothing and flesh. He it was who had thrown the grenade. The eyes confirmed it. A flash of defiance. What are you going to do about it? they said.

He never knew how close he came to a bullet. Instead, he got a heel down hard on the instep, then raking up the shin. A sharp hook sprawled him down into the ditch. The defiance became a squeal – 'Don't shoot, don't shoot!'

'The Boches can do that,' I spat. 'You let me know where we are! Now get the gun and prepare to use it. *Amène-toi!*'

He scrambled to his feet, made to ease the Spandau from under the SS men. A gingerly attempt, squeamish of becoming bloodied. I dropped down beside him, swung the butt of the Thompson, clappered the helmet of the dead gunner. The whole top half of him slithered sideways, leaving the legs behind. Thirty-nine rounds delivered from six feet had ripped the pair of them apart. I rolled the other head away, jerked the gun clear, along with the ammunition belt, and thrust it at Albert's feet.

He wasn't interested. He was beginning to retch and cry in the same spasm. 'I can't,' he finally got out. 'I can't touch it!'

'You can, and you bloody will. You take it to a point beyond the gate and you'll fire it at the first Boche who appears. And you'll go on firing until the wagon is clear! *J'emmerde de te et le tien!*' I was suddenly conscious of someone tugging at my arm. It was Maurice. I shrugged free. 'Get that great lump of dog-shit out of my sight! He isn't fit to join the fucking Hitler Jugend!'

I stormed away up the road to find Léon.

I found Léon.

Dead. Half-flung, half-crumpled in a heap amid the trees. The Colt revolver was still in his hand, uncocked. *A bientôt* had been his last words. Said with the salute of a finger.

A bientôt, Léon, *mon ami*, my first casualty of war. You died because I tried to be clever. For all that I hate his guts, Albert was right. A grenade would have been simpler.

I turned away, scouted ahead to the gravel-pit. I saw no enemy, no other catch-points. The wagon was off the lane and out of sight minutes before the mobile column returned. All they collected was the body of the dead poacher.

The next day, Léon was listed as a 'captured British parachutist'. Posters appeared everywhere, warning the populace of the penalties for harbouring 'criminal terrorists'. There were threats of hostages being taken. The whole area was crawling with *Feldgendarmerie* and SD police.

We were on the run ...

TWENTY

Being on the run in reality differs greatly from the simulation that is part of training. Then my set piece had been a mock demolition of the railway workshops at Swindon, followed by an 'escape' across the length of Wiltshire, through Cranborne Chase, down into Doone-cum-Hardy country. Basically a matter of fieldcraft, of not putting up a pheasant or a hare that would reveal one's presence to sharp-eyed 'hunters'. Sanctuary was a country pub near Cerne Abbas, seventy-two hours later, a hot meal in front of a log fire with drinks all round ... 'Fair show, old chap, gave us a dam' good run for our money! Not so sure about the ethics of you lifting the clothes from that Land Army bint for a disguise! Still, if she gave up her whipcords willingly, all's fair in love and war, I suppose, yok, yok!'

In the Pas-de-Calais, sanctuary was lying low, obeying the curfew, sweating it out until the heat cooled off. For most of Maurice's cell it was reverting to everyday occupations and avoiding open contact with one another. The only obvious sore thumbs in the area were Solange and myself. She was no more a *gonzesse* from nearby Armentières than I was a Breton drawing-board diva. I said as much to her the following Thursday morning. We had been cooped up for most of a week in separate hideouts until finally, in a clog of claustrophobia, I had used the services of the Witch to arrange this meeting.

'What do you suggest?' she asked. I marvelled at her apparent calm compared with my own edginess. Apart from a certain pallor in the face she seemed none the worse for her self-confinement.

'Moving on to a healthier climate, starting again.'

'Can we do that? It sounds like desertion.'

'Not if I ordered you to go.'

'Ordered me?' She looked down her nose at that. 'On what authority? London hasn't said anything. Not that I expect them to after your last message . . .'

That had been immediately after the stores drop. We had made a specific request for explosives. They had sent us rifles, stens, ammunition, empty magazines, and field dressings in five of the containers. The sixth might have been taken as a joke if we hadn't just lost Léon in our efforts to collect it . . . a small amount of PE without detonators, a few Mills grenades, and some mines made to look like horse dung. The rest had been so-called comforts – cigarettes, chocolate, tinned fruit, bully beef, milk powder, all wrapped carefully in several pairs of WAAF issue knickers. The final straw had been the three packets of sanitary towels.

My reply had been bluer than the knickers. The last item was much too late comma we were all bloody pregnant full stop why hadn't they sent us french letters question mark. Solange had despatched it under some protest, not so much objecting to the content as to the reaction with which it would be received.

I had said a rude word about London then. I said a ruder one now, muttering something about authority resting here in the field. She came back at me sharpish. 'I send your messages, but I don't take your orders. My rank in the Corps Auxilaire Féminin is equal to yours—'

'—and senior in length of service,' I mimicked. 'If anyone gives orders, it should be you, yes?'

'Why not? Just because I'm a woman—'

'Oh, dear Christ! Emily Pankhurst!'

'Oh, dear Christ! Male chauvinism!' she retorted.

At the tender age of twenty-two, I was not inclined to argue with women. Grandmama's advice on handling difficult ones was to put them over the knee and slap their backsides. Do it gently and they'll enjoy it, but be careful to choose the time and the place. I didn't think a riverside cafe on the Lys at noon qualified. I tried another tack. Sweet reason.

'Look at it my way,' I pleaded. 'Even Maurice is agreed we can't operate at the moment. And London will be moving me soon, anyway—'

'How can you know that?'

'I *do*, chérie. It's part of my brief. All I want is to anticipate that order. And if you go with me, they may think twice before dropping me a new wireless operator.'

That raised her eyebrows. 'Would they? Drop another, I mean.'

'If I'm away from the Pas-de-Calais, of course.'

'She might be very pretty . . .'

'She might be a bloody male!'

'Oh, dear! That would never do, would it?'

She gave a little giggle. I didn't find it funny. It was a sure-fire certainty if London had the remotest suspicion that we had broken the Golden Rule. Two days before leaving Tempsford, I had been lectured by a thin-lipped half-colonel. Given a dog collar he would have made a lovely Jesuit. Sex,

98

outside of its lawful purpose of procreation was not becoming to an officer and a gentleman. Sex, on duty, was a mortal sin. And I would be on duty twenty-four hours of the day once in the field. I would face great temptation. Every woman in Europe between sixteen and sixty, I gathered, was a potential Eve with an apple poised to push under my cherubic nose. One nibble and I would be on the Road to Perdition, facing a firing squad or worse.

Solange had received similar advice about men from a Mother Superior in the CAF. Between us, we had conjured up visions of the various punishments . . . a courts-martial for being partial, sex-communication meant ex-communication. Where authority was concerned we were in agreement on one point, it would have to forget about Belts, Chastity, Agents, For The Use Of. Except that we both knew it wouldn't.

The giggle as she saw the expression on my face. 'You really want me with you, Patrice?'

I nodded slowly. 'Feelings apart, I doubt they could find me a better operator. I shall also need a courier. A chore you did for several months.'

'I didn't like it,' she shivered.

That I could understand. In many ways it was more hazardous than working a transmitter. *Moray Eel* was not likely to be a rosy assignment. 'It's for you to decide,' I said, lamely.

Her answer was not immediate. She ordered another 'wheat' coffee from the child-waitress, smoked a cigarette. I sensed it was not so much the danger that worried her as the idea of bucking authority. When the coffee came, she stirred it slowly, sipped it, pulled a face. Finally, she said: 'Where have you in mind?'

'South, for a start. Champagne country.' That much I knew from one of the maps I had memorised.

'Nice,' she smiled. 'I know it well.'

'That's it, then.'

'I mean I knew it as a child. Not with the Resistance. I don't even know the name of the Network—'

'A pox on the Network!' I said, testily.

She lost her smile, stubbed her cigarette in a gesture of disapproval.

'Sorry,' I apologised. 'But it's no concern of ours.'

'But we will be of theirs, surely?'

'Not if I can help it!'

'There you go again, being a law unto yourself! You are not God Almighty, Patrice, you can't avoid standard procedure—'

'Any more than you can avoid being a bureaucrat!'

A stupid thing to say. All it achieved was to bring her to her feet, eyes blazing. 'Pardon?'

'Granted! I muttered, as she walked to her bicycle. She mounted slowly, giving me the chance to go after her. I didn't take it. I ordered a drink instead, watched her pedal away.

It was old ground between us – this question of procedures, code-names, networks, the mystique and abracadabra of much cloak and all too little dagger. It was there, I knew, in the sacred name of Security and had its values. Only a idiot would deny that. But it was, I believed, carried to an obsessional length, smacking of the dead hand of officialdom, of pigeon-holed 'bumpf' fluttering from In-trays to Pending on a cabal of desks.

I had been warned by my mentor that this would be my most difficult problem. 'Churchill gave the order to set Europe ablaze,' he had said, in a moment of candour. 'But there are far too many playing with matches in the wrong places. Politicians dabbling as staff officers, staff officers dabbling at politics, more concerned with bombs under their own coat-tails than where they are needed most. I tell you this, young Pat, for your own good. No matter how well you are trained to cope with the enemy, the frustration that will confront you from your own side must be learnt the hard way. It is a matter of self-discipline. Whether you like it or not, you'll have to live with it.'

'I'll manage,' had been my response. Now, after a month in the field, I wasn't so sure. I had made mistakes, the worst

of which was expecting too much from others . . . the very
thing I had been warned about. Albert was a case in point.
I had reacted to his weakness with a show of utter intolerance
and, on reflection, an obvious immaturity. That I was aware
of it might prove to be a saving grace. Yet I still raged in-
wardly about the faceless ones in London. One asked for
one thing and got something else. One made practical suggestions, only to find them ignored. One waited for messages
that often never came. Instead, one decoded trivia, demanding
compliance with schedules impossible to keep, or for matter
that could only be described as non-information.

It seemed to me we were no longer flesh-and-blood people,
but little flags planted on large maps by barathea-uniformed,
Sam Browne-belted base wallahs, fresh from the bath tub and
sipping before-dinner sherries . . .

'. . . ah, Moulin-Bas, somewhere in the Pas-de-Calais, isn't
he? Bit quick off the mark with his bangs, eh, what, doesn't
smell of proper reconnaissance. I know, Commando school
and all that, all right for those who like balls and brawn, but
one expects a certain finesse in our game. Bolshy, too, his last
message was positively flippant. They tell me his French is
patois stuff, second person singular, and a weird accent. I
actually heard it on the grapers that his preference was
Eyetie country! *Who*, in God's name, recommended
him? . . . oh, *he* did, h'm, that makes a difference. I mean,
He with a capital aitch, officially retired but still sitteth on
the right ear of Winston . . . ah, well, if His little sod in Aire
goes on being stroppy, we'll have to give him a gong and a
third pip. *That* always calms them down, better than bromide
in their tea . . .'

The very next night they made it two 'gongs' – one British,
one French – as well as a captaincy. And wasted perilous
'air' time passing the news via Solange.

I was back in the barn, having made arrangements to move
on with or without her. I had just coded a final message re-
questing a new operator when she came running in. She

101

pushed me down into the hay, hugged and kissed her congratulations.

'Now I *must* take your orders, *mon capitaine!*'

I got my breath back, wriggled from under. 'What orders?'

'These!' She thrust a single sheet of paper in my hand. Operation *Moray Eel*. I had fretted over it for a week. Now I had it, I didn't like the look of it one little bit.

TWENTY-ONE

Operation Instruction No: D13   From: GSI/VIb/SIS

Dater: 42-VII-31

Operation: MORAY EEL

Field Name: MOULIN-BAS

Information:

50 Five Zero co-ord 21 two one north 34 three four east stop Paix stop OS mine refinery chemlab rail stop supplying AK Rommel Mobiles stop employs F and E-EU force labour stop defences AA/S/MG/HV/FG/SS batt strength stop

Intention: Priority One Destruct

Administration: Self-contained

Finance: As supplied

   Method: Contact LENA V Stores stop extra if required Code ECHIDNA stop Personnel as available MAX Douai stop extra permission granted use MAURICE stop

Communications: W/T SOLANGE Code Pds KEYWORD no change stop Bluff & True Checks Omit TdT as agreed plus emergency 7/8 seven over eight local stop P/B None stop E/R via MUSSEL stop

Conclusion: Debrief DOVER SOLE stop

Transmission ENDS

TWENTY-TWO

Much has been written about SOE – Special Operations Executive – and the men and women who served their various sections during the war. The same is true of the Gaullist equivalent, BCRA – *Bureau Central de contre-espionnage, de Renseignments et d'Action*, and the American OSS – Office of Strategic Services. The work of D Branch, SIS – Secret Intelligence Service – has remained, all too long, under a shroud of secrecy.

D Branch sometimes known as Section D were, in fact, the vanguard in guerilla activity and sabotage. In March, 1938, eighteen months before the outbreak of hostilities, they were planning against the eventuality. To anyone who could read, the German *anschluss* with Austria in the spring of that year must inevitably lead to the rape of Czechoslovakia and an onslaught on Poland. Both were marked down in *Mein Kampf* as countries holding 'defenceless German minorities,' to be swept aside in the cause of 'unification of race within a Greater Germany.'

So, whilst politicians played the proverbial ostrich, waved umbrellas and bits of paper and brayed about 'peace in our time', D went ahead, studied the situation in detail and worked on HE and incendiary devices. War came like a damp squib to the West, a long autumn and winter of do-nothing behind the Maginot Line. D, again, knew better. They prepared a partial collapse of France by setting up a string of sabotage dumps from Strasbourg to Rouen. When the final capitulation came in June, 1940, key men had been left behind to carry on the fight. But their numbers were small, the links tenuous, if they existed, and any immediate hope of augmenting supplies was virtually nil.

Further plans had to be formulated. These were put forward by a 'sister' body, MI Research, to create an overall directorate to handle Irregular Activities. And from this, SOE was born, with a minister in charge and Sir Robert Vansittart to assist and advise him.

Vansittart knew Europe better than most and had seen his premonitions vindicated by events abroad. Now he witnessed it happen on the home front. At the crucial moment when unity was paramount, it was to be proven non-existent. The whole concept became subject to shabby internal intrigues and squabbles over who did what, where, and why. Service chiefs were not in favour of this 'Fourth Arm.' They saw it as hiving-off their own authority, becoming a rival in the field of supply. A further complication was the growing animosity between SOE and de Gaulle. F Section of SOE were accused of seducing potential agents away from BCRA. An impasse was reached when all contact was severed. To bridge the gap, a RF section was formed with headquarters a convenient spit from either Duke or Baker Street. Aptly enough, One Dorset Square had been the administrative home of a circus in times of peace. Now it became the abode of tight-rope walkers endeavouring to maintain a balance between the two. But with little success at desk-strata. Sectional jealously became a virus, an endemic disease that reached plague level. Nor was it improved by yet a fourth section – EU/P. Comprised almost entirely of Poles in exile, it sought to concentrate on the half-million compatriots who were living in and around Lille and St Etienne. If there was one point where the others found agreement it was on the impossibility of working with EU/P.

A disillusioned Vansittart and the professionals of SIS viewed the confusion wrought by people they regarded as amateurs. There was a not unnatural resentment that their cherished Section had become D for Disappearance, lost in a welter of acrimony and flagrant bureaucracy. And, being professionals, they set about resuscitating it as D for Destruction.

How the others felt about it, can only be conjecture. SOE had all the hallmarks of a very exclusive club and those I had met at Ringway had offered me a raised eyebrow. No matter how similar our training, we were seen as 'spies' where they were 'agents'; we 'killed' where they 'disposed of the enemy;

we 'liquidated' where they 'accidented' traitors . . . a question of semantics, of terminology, yet it stressed the difference. The Gaullists, on the other hand, were so obsessed with the *perfide Albion* of SOE, they were prepared to co-operate providing we did not employ Frenchmen. The Poles were of a like mind, so long as we did not use Poles.

In all, it was an Alice-in-Wonderland world with everyone trying to emulate the Duchess by minding their own business. Co-operation where given, was done so begrudgingly. And where France was concerned it was to grow worse rather than better with the entry of the Americans and their peculiar preference for Giraud rather than de Gaulle. In mid-1942, the only thing the various groups had in common – throat-cutting and the enemy apart – was their dependence on 138 and 161 Squadrons, RAF, based at Tempsford and Tangmere.

So far, my venture in the Pas-de-Calais had crossed no wires. BCRA and SOE were suffering troubles enough of their own. The treachery of *Capri* had hit the Gaullists badly. The machinations of a double-agent, Mathilde-Lily Carré – The Cat – had dealt a similar body blow at *Autogiro*, a main SOE network. She had also betrayed a EU/P set-up, *Interallié*.

Yet as if to prove the point made before, I had gone in under false pretenses. My code-name had been a compliment to one of BCRA's top men – Jean Moulin – whose aim was to bring the FTP under the banner of the Free French. Hence my liaison with Maurice's cell. But having got the co-operation of Duke Street, SIS had no intention of allowing it to become a permanent arrangement. I had been given a double 'brief', to make use of the Francs-Tireurs in order to gain the necessary experience before moving on to something more specific – *Moray Eel*.

Again, *Moray Eel*, did not fit into the operational pattern of either F or RF sections of SOE. With them, sabotage was only part of a plan that embraced a long-term policy – the organizing and training resistance nests for tactical deployment come the Second Front. A task that called for men and women of the quality of Yeo-Thomas, Heslop, Cowburn, de Baissac; Bloch, Borrel, Gianello, Szabo; the many who would go back again and again . . . compared with these, I was in a different class. Mine was a relatively simple, one-off task, a set target on a date to be fixed, then out.

Now, as luck would have it, some last-minute deal had been arranged between Duke Street and Queen Anne's Gate, precluding a complete severance with Maurice's cell. In addition to the services of Solange, I could - if necessity demanded it and they were willing - call on those I had helped to train. This brought a sense of relief not born entirely out of sentiment. A case of 'the devil one knows' when one is ignorant of the help that lay ahead. I was certain of one thing - wherever it came from - it would have to be good or D would end up as Disaster.

TWENTY-THREE

Oil shale, to the uninitiated, is a substance mined from a sedimentary deposit rich in organic matter. Under optimum conditions, the process yields 65 per cent oil, 10 per cent gas, and 35 per cent residual products. The oil can amount to fifty gallons or more per ton, of virtually any grade of petroleum. The gases produced are methane, ethane, propane, butane; hydrogen, ethylene, propylene, butene, and hydrogen sulphide, as well as carbon monoxide and dioxide. The crude oil, under distillation, yields naphtha which, in turn, contains napthenes, paraffins, olefins, and aromatics. And if that isn't stink enough, the sulphurous content produces ammonium sulphate fertilizer of up to 100 pounds per ton of shale. Anything left over can be breathed in by an ungrateful populace who do not appreciate how lucky they are to be alive.

In France, many thousands of these folk lived at Aniche, Corbehem, Dorignies, and Sin-le-Noble, suburbs of Douai, the capital of an *arrondissement* in the department of Nord, some twenty miles south of Lille on the line to Cambrai. As well as being a world of mines, it had an oil refinery, chemical works, iron and engineering shops, an arsenal and a cannon foundry. Put that lot together with a school of instruction in brewing and the smell was only exceeded by the noise, which had the added advantage of a glass-bottle factory and railway sidings clanking day and night. Extra-curriculum in August, '42, was a ring of ack-ack batteries, searchlights, and a full complement of mobile SS and *Feldgendarmerie,* barbed wire, control towers, and machine-gun posts. Plus a high-voltage fence around some of the more vital areas in case an idiot flea should get past the rest. I was the idiot flea with instructions to leave the Paix complex a dirty great hole in the ground.

Why not leave it to Bomber Command? A simple answer. Bombers made dirtier, greater holes than saboteurs, but not necessarily better ones. A small charge placed in a vital spot can inflict more damage than a rain of bombs from the sky. Less wasteful in terms of lives, both civilian and RAF crews. Where the latter were concerned, it was illogical to risk a hundred highly-trained men where one might succeed. And it has yet to be proved that the civilians in enemy-occupied countries died one whit happier in the knowledge that the bombs were British.

This, in turn, posed another problem for saboteurs on the ground. Paix worked the clock round, night and day, employing Frenchmen and a force of slave labour imported from Eastern Europe. Whilst there was no mention in my brief to spare them, it was tacitly understood one should if one could. But only so far as it did not interfere with Priority One – total destruction. Every litre of oil processed was keeping the Afrika Korps on the move and without it Adolf's favourite general – Erwin Rommel – would grind to a halt.

A piece of information to be taken with a pinch of salt, but if it was only 5 per cent true, then bravo for me, move over Montgomery . . . when you've finished swinging your bat at El Alamein or wherever, I'll slip in a wicked ball, short-fused and shoulder-high, at a moment when the umpires are not looking. Not the kind of tactics the Eighth Army Commander would approve of against 'Jerry' – which was as good a reason I could think of for doing it . . .

First, however, we had to collect stores. It would have been so much easier had they been dropped on that Friday night instead of the stuff I had complained about. But making it easy was not part of the plan. Its originators had already conceived the brilliant idea of using *Lena*. *Lena* stood for *Laissé en arrière*, the dumps left behind in 1940. But *Lena V* was at Epernay, one hundred miles south as the crow flies or two hundred and fifty on the vulture circle that took in Amiens and Paris.

The journey by train offered scant appeal. Not so much the actual travelling as the stations. The Gestapo virtually camped at the ticket-barriers, with nothing better to do than pick their teeth and any unfortunate they fancied out of the throng. My *affiche* – permit to travel long distances – was a forgery. A reasonable facsimile against Solange's genuine one, it was foolish to risk it if a more suitable method could be found.

This I had already done through Maurice. A man named Emile ran a garage at Bruay, near Béthune. By doing odd jobs for the Germans, such as servicing their coveted Citroëns, he had permission to run a gazogène truck. With further permission to travel as far afield as Soissons where his wife and children had been evacuated. Soissons was two-thirds of the way to Epernay, across country avoiding the Route National. Emile was willing to do it for a fee, but I suspected more as a safeguard against the day the Germans departed. He might find himself accused of being a collaborator. A polite blackmail, it was a necessary part of clandestine activity.

Four of us were travelling. Le Claque and Raoul had volunteered to join Solange and myself. Le Clague's knowledge of explosives would be invaluable and I welcomed his decision without questioning why. Raoul had insisted from

108

the moment he heard I was leaving – 'There may be horses where you are going, you'll need a head-lad. Also, I wish to christen Poulainette.' Poulainette was his name for one of the useful items in that last drop – a Wilkinson knife like my own.

The journey went without hitch, except for an occasional need to climb out and walk at the steeper hills in order for the truck to surmount the rise. As a precaution it had been loaded with Pas-de-Calais produce and vegetables, but the only Germans we saw were at Peronne and Ham, guarding the canal locks. They waved us on with a jeer, a whistle at Solange up front with Emile. She wore a kerchief and peasant black, making herself as unattractive as possible with a dirt-smudged face and grimy hands. I had offered to blacken out her teeth but she had drawn the line at that. The sun was warm, the wheels billowed dust, the charcoal smuts from the engine all took their toll. When we had reached the wooded hills near Soissons she was looking more like the Witch than the girl who had climbed to the loft that first morning.

'You're no beauty, either!' had been her response to that. 'Even worse, you *smell!* Dedans! When *did* you last have a bath?'

Queen Anne's Gate, June 26th. Thirty-eight days past. Many a strip-wash since, at the pump in the farmyard with the old woman cackling from the window, offering to towel me down . . . but the luxury of a tub of hot water . . . that was a dream of yesteryear.

'We'll share one together at Epernay,' I murmured. 'Lena is sure to have one. He may even top it up with champagne!'

'*Tu l'as dit!* You would, too, if I gave you the chance!'

'Worse could happen to both of us,' I said. Then wished I hadn't.

Her manner changed. A quick look of fear came to the dark eyes. 'I am afraid for you, chéri. This mission – the more I think about it . . .'

'Don't be a nit,' I said. 'Nip behind a bush and spend a penny. You'll feel all the better for it!'

That brought the colour back into her cheeks. *'Ouo-dá! Nous ferons route ensemble!'*

I grinned. 'I'd love to hold your hand, darling, but I'm supposed to be pushing the truck!'

Emile's family were on a farm at Fére-en-Tardenois, another eighteen miles further on from Soissons and that much closer to Epernay. I did not have to suggest he took us on the extra distance. He did it himself for obvious reasons. Four strangers dumped in a village might cause comment. One couldn't be sure who had a ready tongue.

That suited us. The trip had cost ten thousand francs – about fifty pounds in sterling – and was cheap at the price. Of the money I had been dropped with, I had passed two-thirds on to Maurice for use in his cell. The remainder I had now spread amongst the four of us, but mostly in Solange's bra where it was less likely to be turned out if we had met with a random police check. She had submitted to this with justifiable ill-grace, mostly because the banknotes had been rubbed in dirt to make them less conspicuous in the using.

Approaching Epernay, we all cleaned ourselves up. It was a Sunday, and Sunday evening habits in a French provincial town still remained, war or no war. Emile dropped us off as near to the centre as he deemed safe and was gone almost before we could pick up our bags. An unseemly haste that Raoul and Le Claque countered by waves and thanks and goodbyes.

It worked. The only uniform in sight was a gendarme caressing a pimple on his face. He went on caressing it, ignoring us after the first glance. We stood for a moment as if chatting, then shook hands, went our agreed ways. Le Claque and Raoul headed for the nearest bar and something to drink, taking with them the two largest suitcases. One of these held Solange's transmitter. It sounds hairy, but it was

110

the best ploy. The bar was close by a bus-stop and there were other cases around, making for safety in numbers.

Solange and I made for the old quarter of the town, a maze of narrow, irregular streets. After ten minutes we were back roughly where we had started, but rather nearer to the gendarme and his pimple.

'Shall I?' she asked, as we exchanged glances.

'Your accent has to be better than mine,' I said.

'I would hope so,' she smiled. 'My first-ever kiss came from a boy at Choilly. If there's one dialect I should know it is Côte des Blancs.'

'Sounds like a promising language,' I muttered.

She made me a tongue, turned and approached the gendarme. He lost interest in his pimple, gave it all to her, eyes lingering overtly on her bosom. Two hundred thousand francs had given it somewhat startling proportions. There was gold in them there hills, if he only but knew. Suddenly, the attention became animated. He produced a book from his tunic, they studied it together. A street plan of some sort. His free hand went into a series of gestures, finally coming to a reluctant rest at the peak of his cap. There followed a slight bow and a lecherous approbation of her *derriere* as she made her way back.

'Fourth to the right, third to the left. But I was careful not to ask for the correct street,' she whispered.

'That helps us?'

'But, of course. Security, *n'est-ce-pas?* He might think about it afterwards.'

'But—'

'I said I wasn't sure of the street name, except that I knew it was in the old part of the town. Then I saw it on his map and gave him the name of a street turning off from it. I did wise, no?'

'Cunning these Chinese!'

'Comment?'

'Never mind. He was too busy dating your bustle to remember.'

'*Toupet!* The dirty beast!'

111

'I don't know . . . I would. Did, in fact, the first time I saw you.'

'That's different.'

The inscrutable logic of women.

We went and found *Lena*.

TWENTY-FOUR

There were certain rules about calling on strangers. It was usual to telephone them first, slipping a password into the initial enquiry, such as 'I am friend of cousin Lena, is it convenient to call?' If the answer was 'No, I am sorry,' it meant the coast was clear. If it was 'Please do, you are very welcome' one would be wise to read it as 'get the hell out of it I have the Nazis on my neck'. A simple, inverse system that probably worked but without *Lena's* telephone number we could hardly put it to the test.

The house was near the top of a twisty street, close to the railway and the river. I left Solange to admire the view, knocked at the door. After a long wait and a twitch of curtains, it opened. A small, grey-haired woman peered at me from the passage beyond.

'*Qui êtes-vous?*'

'A friend of cousin Lena. May I come in?'

'We have no cousin Lena, m'sieu. You have the wrong house.'

'Cousin Lena is Uncle Robert's child,' I said. 'The fifth one. He was here in nineteen-forty. Easter Sunday. He brought presents.'

She hesitated, made a half-hearted effort to close the door. Not easy with my foot in the way.

A man's voice came from the gloom behind her. '*Qu-est-ce qui se passe?*'

She moved aside. The man wore a neatly-curled moustache and eyes like busy cockroaches run over me. I repeated my piece. He sucked his teeth, then: 'You are?'

112

'Patrice. A nephew by marriage. From St Malo, in Brittany.'

'So?' A thin smile showed under the moustache. 'It would explain the accent. Bretons speak strange French. Almost like *Britons*, hein?' He used the English word in emphasis.

I shrugged. 'Better than some salauds in France today.'

The smile widened. So did the door. I made to remove my beret, step across the threshold.

'What of your companion?' he asked. 'The one at the corner, is she not?'

The cockroaches were sharp this evening.

'Solange, isn't it?' he went on. 'A pretty name for a pretty girl. Leave her there and one of the salauds you mentioned might pick her up!' He took my hand in a firm grip. 'If you cannot trust me, cousin, God knows who you can!' He released the hand, made a gesture.

I went to Solange, took her arm. The choice was Hobson's. If the real *Lena* had been blown and I had been speaking to an *Abwehr* plant, we wouldn't get very far. I had spotted a telephone in the passage. We turned, went back to the house.

The woman was nervous but more friendly. 'You must both be starving. I'll get you something to eat.'

'I would like a good wash,' said Solange.

'Of course. Come with me.' She headed for the stairs. 'A bath, if you prefer. Do make yourself at home.'

Solange caught my eye, gave a little laugh. I handed her the larger of our two suitcases, sighed. She laughed the more, followed the woman upstairs.

'My sister made a joke?' asked the man. He led me into a small parlour which was all over with anti-macassars. A stuffed owl fixed me with a beady eye.

'Solange thinks I need a bath,' I said. 'She is probably right.' I hesitated to sit amidst the immaculation.

'You fancy to share, hein?' One of the cockroaches disappeared behind a drooped lid. 'Myself, I could not care. But my sister, she is – how do you say – straight of the lace?'

The last four words in English.

'*Le sentier austère de la vertu?*' I said, doggedly.

He tapped the side of his nose. 'I mean what I mean, young

113

man.' He found a bottle and glasses, poured two drinks. 'If you *are* the nephew of Robert, you speak English of a kind. Let us not beat the bushes, yes?' He handed me the drink. The bottle said it was *Eau de Vie de Marc*.

I sipped before answering. No rot-gut. Matured, with a taste of the soil. 'Vive la France,' I said.

'Vive de Gaulle!' He waved at a chair. 'Sit, sit! My sister is clean to a stage of insanity but she is no dragon.'

I sat, glancing at Maurice's watch as I did so. His going-away present. It told me that Raoul and Le Claque had been separated from us for forty-five minutes. If one of us did not join them within the hour, they would make their way here. Fifteen minutes to make up my mind if the man in front of me was the genuine *Lena* or not. I watched him watching me, reading my mind.

'You still want me to prove myself?' he said. 'The mole on my left arse, perhaps? Or will a message broadcast last night help you to decide?' He took a tin from his hip pocket. Tobacco, papers, three home-made cigarettes. He picked out one, passed it across. 'Not for smoking . . . not in *this* room. Open it up.'

I split the cigarette, found a second paper, folded small. I spread it, read: *Hélène L'Etoile ne fera plus dodo jusqu'a Solange et Patrice sont chez elle.* That was it, in the colloquial idiom of all my messages. Hélène L'Etoile will sleep no more until Solange and Patrice are at her place. I passed it back to him.

'I should have asked for Hélène, not Lena,' I said. 'My error.'

He put the tin away. 'Mine was greater. I should have made *you* convince *me*. Drink up and have another.'

I drained my glass, rose, moved to the window. I took Solange's kerchief from inside my jacket, pushed it in front of the curtain. 'You have no objections?' I said.

'Who are we expecting?'

'Friends. It will tell them the house is safe.'

'You have decided in our favour then?'

'Apologies,' I said. 'Treading eggs is part of my trade.'

'Of all of us, these times.' His smile was sly, his glance away at the part-open door. Who was lurking outside – the sister with a carving-knife? He handed me the refill. I took a drink, still wary. She came in, carrying a bath towel, laid it on the back of a chair. 'For you, m'sieu . . . your wife said you would like to follow her.'

I choked a little over the *marc*. 'Er – merci . . .'

'At the top of the stairs, straight ahead.' She went out, shut the door behind her.

The sly smile became a chuckle. 'As well you are married,' he said. 'We have only the one spare room.'

'You are very kind.'

'*Pas du tout*. How about your friends?'

'Two of them. Do you know of someone reliable?'

'Madame Jonquet. In the next street at the bottom end. She only talks with God.'

'She can trust him?'

'You don't?'

'Let's say I'm a trifle anti-social.' I was also feeling tired. The journey, the edginess of the past week, the strain of making new contacts, the gnaw of doubt concerning my own ability. 'Forgive me, m'sieu—'

'The name is Felix . . . go take your bath. I'll attend to your friends.'

I left the drink, picked up the towel and suitcase, climbed the stairs. A faint splash of water came as I tapped on the door.

'*Qui est?*'

'It had better be me . . . *wife.*'

The splash became a flurry. Then the key turned. As I went in, she was skipping away, groping for a towel. Some of my fatigue faded at the view. I flicked her rump a back-hander. She squeaked, turned, lost the towel in her hurry.

'Oo-la-la . . . you're showing your marriage licence,' I said.

She went all September Morn. 'It was *her* idea!' she whispered.

'Which you didn't discourage.'

115

There was a wicked look in those violet eyes. 'Neither will you when you see the bed!'

'A bed,' I said. 'Whatever will they think of next?'

TWENTY-FIVE

Like Maurice, Felix was a veteran of the first war, of Chemin-des-Dames and the second battle of the Marne. Four thousand enemy guns on a forty-mile front, a three-and-a-half hour bombardment including poison gas. Forty-seven divisions of field-grey flung at them day after day for weeks stretching into months. The whole thing not a phosgene cough from where we were sitting . . . I learnt this over breakfast the next morning, the old soldier impressing the young one that he knew what it was about. I gave it a polite ear and crocodile murmurs of sympathy, but the arrogance of youth saw that holocaust as bad chess played by idiot commanders, their moves recorded by a million crosses in a field of poppies. The game finally won, the peace had been thrown away. Instead of destroying Germany they had allowed the bastards to rise again.

'Your generation won't make that mistake?' said Felix.

'If they hand it back to the politicians . . . yes.'

'You would leave it to the generals?'

'Christ, no! They are all of a breed, no matter what side!'

'What is your solution then?'

I pulled a face. 'Let's put away the crystal ball, get on with the job in hand. Lena Five,' I prompted him.

The *cache installé* had been stored in the heart of the miles of tunnels that honeycombed the area. Caves used for fermenting stocks of champagne. But the previous January, *Lena IV*, at Vitry le François, had been unearthed by the Germans. Only weeks later, at Nouvion le Vineux, near Laon, *Lena VI* had gone the same way. With Epernay and

116

its tunnels situated equidistant between the two, the methodical-minded *Herrenvolk* had reacted accordingly, searching again and again. It had ended in a stupid, drunken frenzy of vengeance, the destruction of a whole year's harvest when nothing was found. Felix and his friends had anticipated the action, removed the *cache*.

'Where?' I asked.

'You will never believe . . . no more than those salauds would.'

'Try me.'

'Belleau Wood.'

'Should that mean something?'

'If you were an American.'

'I am not. So what?'

'It is an official cemetery of *our* war.'

I stared at him blankly.

'My colleague in Lena Five, Jean-Paul tends the graves. He can come and go as he wills . . .'

'. . . you shifted the stuff there?'

He nodded slowly, rolled a cigarette. 'You are not shocked?'

'Should I be?'

'I don't know. Some would see it as an insult, an act of desecration.' He lipped the paper carefully, smoothed it down with a thumb. 'Myself – I think they would not mind. The dead, that is. I served alongside many of them, sharing a drink and a cigarette. They helped France then, in life. Why not again, in death?' The cigarette flamed and crackled to a match.

'God bless America,' I murmured. And meant it. To have endured the lunacy of trench warfare and contained one's sanity, must have demanded above all else a sense of humour. I liked to think the tenants of Belleau Wood would be chuckling at this. 'When can we go?'

'To see . . . or to lift?'

'Both, naturally.'

'A Mercier truck goes out to Château Thierry in about an hour. We can put *velos* on it and cycle from there. I have

117

passes and machines for you and your two friends. I did not think you would want one for Solange.'

'She has other things to do.'

'*Mais, oui, naturallement* . . .' Said simply, with a shrug, he still managed to put over a *double-entendre*. And the implications in his smile were obvious. She was a soldier's comfort and I was a lucky young devil.

The bed had been a rewarding experience. I wasn't disposed to argue with him.

Cemeteries do not rate amongst my favourite places. War cemeteries even less, with their rows of regimented dead. Standing at the site of Belleau Wood, I thought if it should happen to me, then lay me where I drop, by some casual roadside, to be forgotten or remembered by some kindly soul with a thought for the dark days. The remarkable thing was how Jean-Paul had inserted new 'graves' without disturbing the pattern of orderliness. No bones had been disturbed, no grave defiled. *Requiescat in pace.* Yet a quarter of a ton of stones had been distributed in five places, each with a marker, a tribute to an unknown American soldier. Four, in all, had carried out the 'burials'. Four would be enough to commit the resurrection, with a fifth acting as a look-out.

The nearest enemy post of any size was a *Wehrmacht* reserve depot between Le Ferté-sous-Jouarre and Meaux, and they had their eyes permanently turned towards the flesh-pots of Paris, a tantalizing ninety minutes away. However, according to Jean-Paul, the odd transport did pass this way to and from Reims. During the day, they stopped, occasionally, visited the cemetery. Camera-clicking officers, as a rule, who had not seen enough of death in this war, and had to root around the past. But at night it was only convoys on the move.

Night, then, was the time to play Burke and Hare. With the moon in its last quarter, it would be dark enough around eleven o'clock. In the meantime, there were problems to be discussed. Cartage was one. Temporary re-storage was another. Felix offered solutions to both. Framed Alpine ruck-sacks, Norwegian pattern (how he came by them, I had no idea, but after Belleau Wood itself one ceased to wonder) would help in the removal. With each grave holding one hundredweight of stores, packed in four separate containers for convenience, it would be no hardship to shift them by *velos* to a disused wine tunnel thirty kilometres away. Two trips a night for two nights would do it.

There were two problems we had no control over. One, the curse of any clandestine activity, the barking of dogs. Farm dogs, in particular, bayed at every shadow, every un-wary footstep, and topped the list of collaborators. Fortu-nately, the enemy took little notice of any but their own Dobermans or German Shepherds.

The second concern was the weather. The days of sun-shine had given way to cloud, a threat of impending storm. Thunder and lightning might keep the dogs quiet, but we could not trample around the cemetery in rain, leaving tell-tale signs behind us. Some sightseeing officer could just be sharp-eyed enough to notice and wonder, and Belleau Wood would be swarming with men and shovels.

Point taken. Pray for many things. No passing convoy, no dogs that bark, no surely Charon to haunt us. But, above all else, no rain.

Twenty minutes to midnight, everything going smoothly. Raoul as the look-out, Felix and Jean-Paul opening the first grave, Le Claque and I standing by to lift the contents. With the turf-line cut in daylight, it only requires fingers under a metal panel and the whole thing lifts – chalk, soil, and grass, five feet by two, a knack to it but easy if you know how. And these two veterans do. Gently, ever so gently, the only sound a quick hiss of breath expelled. Moving now, a fractional tilt, but enough for a rattle of errant chalk to escape into the hole below. A few pebbles, no more, but each is a clapper of hell.

A dog barks. A second takes it up. A third, and a fourth. Sweat streams my face and all I'm doing is holding a pencil torch, waiting to shine it down. The barking changes to howls, the kind that herald Hallowe'en, maybe we've opened a genuine grave by mistake . . . for Chrissakes, you and your imagination! Switch on the light, take a look . . .

Nothing but boxes. Sweet metal boxes, black and shiny in a coat of grease, marked with luminous symbols – A, D, G, and X – telling their contents at a glance. Swing them up, one at a time, feed them into the rucksacks, they don't swallow them whole, but never mind, fix that afterwards . . . and what's that on my face? And *that*, and *that*? Oh, Jesus, *no* . . . rain. Great gobs of it, coughed and spat by the blacker than black cloud above. A blue-white flash rips the night apart, the dogs go silent in a crash of thunder, and Peter is pulling the Great Chain In The Sky, a bloody great flush over Belleau Wood. All we need now is Nazis and, sure enough, Raoul is at our elbows, whispering of lights moving along the road.

He grabs a rucksack, Le Claque does the same, and both move for the trees. With Jean-Paul and Felix working to get the top back into position, it's for me to hump a rucksack on each shoulder, sixty pounds of dead weight including the boxes. No Atlas, I, a dozen steps and I'm close to kneeling but not in prayer, swaying, teetering. A smell of something dead, coming from one of the rucksacks swinging round under my nose. If it's what I think it is, nitrogen dioxide, we'll be airborne any moment, including the long-since dead of Belleau Wood! Lower it carefully, stumble away with the one to join Le Claque and Raoul, only to turn and see Felix lifting the stinker and coming towards us . . .

'Put it down!' I hiss. 'But gentle with it!'

'What is wrong?'

'Use your nose! Decomposition! A fart is all it needs to set it off!'

To prove me wrong, another clap of thunder like the end of the world and we are still whole. Whoever is up there has decreed we shall drown for our sins. The torrent becomes a deluge.

Raoul touches my arm, gestures at the rucksack, then at

the road. Dump it where it'll do some good. I move away, take a look. Trucks rumbling by in a swish of wet tyres, nose to tail, much too close, it wasn't on. Nothing was *bloody* on, including Moray Eel, unless London pulled their finger out, gave us a practical drop. *Je m'en fiche* . . . I wipe rain from my face with a sleeve, return to the others.

'It's not all bad, Patrice . . .'

Le Claque, the raving lunatic has the box out of the rucksack, under a tree, the lid raised. A flicker of hope, a lunatic but also a quarryman, he *should* know.

'You're sure?'

'I'll have to check it under better conditions . . .'

'In a diving bell, of course!'

'It'll ease off in a minute,' says Felix.

It does. Into a steady downpour.

A sorrowful shake of the head from Jean-Paul. That's it. No more grave-robbing tonight. Load up and move once the road is clear, the last tail-light gone. With Le Claque carrying the dicey one if he's that confident.

Four a.m. 'How did it go?' Solange was drying me off with a towel, everything dancing under the black wisp she called a nightdress.

'You there in that thing would have been the touch-paper!'

'Bad, was it?'

'A right cock-up!'

'*Qu'est-ce que c'est cock-up?*'

An innocent question. I found myself grinning. 'There are a number of ways of explaining, chérie.'

'Oh, yes?'

'Oh, yes!'

I took her hand, led her to bed.

Every storm has a silver lining . . .

TWENTY-SIX

Le Claque had been right. Only a small proportion of the *cache* was unstable. After lifting the other four graves, we had one hundred kilos of varied quality – from a *brisant* stiff jelly mix of collodion nitro-cellulose dissolved in nitroglycerin, to a more sober amatol of French manufacture. Primers and detonators in plenty, including some early pencil-type activators. In addition, there were hand-grenades, .45 revolvers, and two Thompsons with vintage circular magazines, reminiscent of Chicago in Capone's day.

The decomposing explosive was found a suitable home. A goods-train going east, carrying machine-tools and cellophane fibranes. Products from Déville-les-Rouèn and Mantes, they became debris between Châlons and St. Dizier and the following day three groups of Résistance were squabbling over the credit for it.

Situation normal. France was as splintered in its action as it was politically. A sad and bitter truth of democracy that worked to the advantage of the Third Reich. But for one operation, at least, I hoped to weld a few together – Maurice's FTP, Felix's *Ceux de la Libération,* and the unknown Max at Douai itself.

In theory, that is. In fact, only four men in Epernay had known about Lena Five – those who had helped in the re-burial. Two had since left the area to work in the non-Occupied Zone. The third – Jean-Paul – was willing but suffered from asthma. Douai would kill him quicker than any German. That left us with one – Felix.

'It is out of the question to approach the local group,' he said. 'They would argue that the stores were theirs to use, having complained all too long about being forgotten men. If they knew I'd been sitting on the *cache* all this time, they'd crucify me!'

'You wouldn't make a good Christ with a waxed moustache,' I agreed. And sent a message to London. More information regarding Max and his potential strength.

The reply was swift but not very helpful. Max worked for *La Voix du Nord*, a Résistance newspaper, handling distribution from a house in Aniche. No mention of an action group or its numbers. But they did give us a date, twice repeated, so there was no mistake. The job was to be done on August 16.

This tag line came as a bombshell. Unless there was some overall strategic reason, it was for those on the spot to make such a decision. It was already the 5th and I had been thinking in terms of the end of the month and the wane of the moon. Now I would have to get skates on.

Solange and I left the next afternoon. Felix got us on a Mercier truck travelling to Paris, a delivery of champagne to *Wehrmacht* HQ. She was listed as tally-clerk and I as one of two unloaders. The other was the driver and in the know up to a certain point. He had, it seemed, moved a number of people 'on the run' by this same method, and there was no better pass to get through check-points *en route*.

Even so, the journey started with a shock. We picked up the vehicle at 75, Avenue de Champagne, only to find two *Feldgendarmerie* climbing in with us, one in the cab alongside Solange and the driver, the other in the rear with me and the suitcase containing the transmitter. Big men, both, armed with machine-pistols and wearing metal plaques across their chests denoting their function in life. Escort and guard duties in the main, they were not the brightest examples of the New Order, which was as well. My companion had a smattering of pidgin French and, in a moment of magnanimity, he offered me a cigarette. The reason for the generosity was soon obvious. It was American, a packet taken from the pilot of a shot-down bomber, he informed me, then showed me a watch that had come from the same source. '*Americans, ne pas bon, nichts gut*,' he kept muttering. '*Trop mou, trop mou.*'

123

Maybe, I thought, smoking the cigarette, maybe the Yanks are as soft as you say, but they'll grow tough with their first baptism. Like their fathers in Belleau Wood they'll learn the hard way but learn it fast, then Christ help sods like you . . .

Coming into Paris, his mood grew jovial. He had a forty-eight-hour pass and several ladies in the capital would benefit by it. Obscene gestures demonstrated in what manner. He, Ludwig, was a *liebmeister*, did I know any addresses where he might offer instruction? I gave a subservient smile and a house in Montparnasse – a place with a reputation for slags and a high incidence of VD. For this courtesy on my part, he pressed on me the remainder of the packet of Camels.

Unloading the truck was no great chore. The second *Feldgendarme* was keen to impress Solange with his own physique. He removed four cases to my one. After we drove away, she told me he had made a date. She had given him an address at Sèvres, in the suburbs, with instruction how to get there. She was staying with an aunt who had a spare bedroom especially for Germans. The aunt, the bedroom, the address – needless to say – did not exist.

Between us, our two guards might wish they'd never met us.

The train was crowded and slow. At each stop more climbed aboard and before we reached Lens, even the lavatories were occupied. We left it there with only a few minutes to curfew, a scatter of passengers under a drizzle of rain. Solange knew a 'safe' house close by the station. Safe, that is, if it showed a china dog in the window.

There was. We were in. Madame Vermalen fussed over us, a hen with chicks, cooking omelettes and giving up her double-bed. A miner's widow, she took in lodgers to help out her pension. She had none at this moment and told us why. On the 25th of July, the day after I had killed the three SS men, twenty-eight civilians had been taken, tried, and shot by order of the *Oberfeldkommandatur* 870, in Lille. She produced a copy of the underground newspaper *Combat*, listing

124

the names and addresses. Mostly mine-workers, two had lodged here and a third – Albert Vermalen – was related to her by marriage. The charges had been acts of sabotage and illegal possession of arms.

We retired upstairs in a mood of gloom. I undressed, got into bed. But Solange made no move to do the same. She sat at the window, smoking, staring out. It was foolish to come here, she kept repeating, it wasn't safe. I tried to reason with her.

'No Germans have been here for a fortnight. La Veuve Vermalen said so . . .'

'They could have the house under observation.'

'She has kept her ears and eyes open. The dog would not have been in the window if she had had doubts.'

'Supposing she is—'

'—working for them, under threat? I've thought of that. Why, then, put us on our guard by showing us the newspaper?'

'We could have known, read about it ourselves, If she hadn't mentioned it, we would have been suspicious, no?'

'If we had known we would never have come here, *mon ange*.'

Mon ange Solange, my favourite expression for her. She turned her head from the window, looked across the darkened room.

'I suppose not . . .'

'I *know* not. Now stop trying to curdle my blood. The only place for Poe is under the bed. I prefer Ethel M. Dell *in* it.' I patted the mattress beside me.

'If you say so, chéri.' She started to undress, then stopped suddenly. I felt her eyes on me.

'She is very nice?'

'Huh?'

'This woman who is so magnifique en lit. Much better than me?'

'What are you nattering about?'

'I do not natter, whatever that is. Perhaps your Ethel Emdell does, that is why you prefer her!'

125

'*That* Ethel!'

'Ah, there is more than one?'

The tension, despondency, fear, all dissolved in helpless laughter. Not for Solange. She struck a pose in her bra and pants.

'I am not amused!'

Neither was Queen Victoria. But to have said it would have confused the issue further. I stifled the giggles, reached out and caught her hand. 'Please . . . listen. I don't know the lady or anything about her, beyond the fact that she writes love stories. That's what I meant when I said—'

'I know what you said! You prefer a book to me! *C'en est fait! Filez!*'

She tried to wrest her hand free. I hung on. How does one explain except by action? I pulled her down beside me. After a while, she stopped struggling. Then:

'You swear you know no Ethel?'

'Only one.' Stupid clot, telling a woman the truth. She began to wriggle away.

'One,' I repeated, holding her firmly. 'A school mistress. *School,* not mine. And always perpendicular. In my presence, anyway. What she may have done behind the bicycle-shed was her affair. Now let's forget her and take care of ourselves, oui?'

She gave a little sigh, slid her arms about me. '*Mais oui,*' she whispered. '*Ce n'est pas de refus le plus beau!*'

Finally, we drifted into sleep. On my part, an uneasy one, filled with premonition. The tension was with me again. Solange awoke at dawn, crept into my arms.

'Come with me to Aire, chéri.'

'I have to go to Douai.'

'Not today. You could see Maurice first.'

'It's already the seventh. I have only nine days.'

'Will one make all that difference?'

'You know it will. And if I'm to be my own courier, I should have left you at Epernay. You would have liked that?'

'No. But I don't like leaving you now.'

'I'm not wild about it. But we did make a pact, remember?'

'That first night, in the barn . . . I know. And I've kept my part of it. I have not tried to tie you down, make promises.'

I kissed her gently. 'You've been wonderful, *mon ange*. Without you I'd have long since gone out of my tiny mind.'

'You mean that . . . not just words?'

'Mean it.'

'But there have been other girls, non?'

'None like you.'

'No one special?'

'All were special at the time. That's the way I'm made. I'm no casual bed-flitter, I've told you.'

'The one in your wallet . . .'

'What about her?'

'Please, Patrice, I didn't mean to pry. But when Felix needed your identity card for the Mercier pass, you asked me to get it and—'

'—you saw it and decided it must be my wife or fiancée posing stark naked so her man wouldn't forget—'

'—no, no, nothing like that . . . but, well, you do carry it with you everywhere—'

'—because London imagines a man needs the personal touch. Like the letter Maurice tore up the first day we met, remember? The photograph was someone else's idea. I've never met the lady. I never will. I have no wish to. Satisfied?'

'Yes-es. But I wish it was one of me . . .'

'If La Veuve Vermalen has a camera, I'll take one. In the same pose. Only we won't bother with the gloves.'

'Don't joke. I have a pass photograph I can give you.'

'No.'

'Why not?'

'You know damn well why not. If I'm picked up, it could be your death warrant. You must see that.'

'I only see this horrible war and the things it does to people.'

'It brought us together.'

'In a little while it also separates us.'

'Not for always.'
'You can be sure of that?'
I made no answer.
It was the best way.
It was the truth.

TWENTY-SEVEN

Goodbyes were said in the bedroom, although our ways
parted in the main square of the town. We left the house
separately and I caught a final glimpse of her at the bus-stop,
cases in hand, amongst a jostle of people and luggage. Her
pale face turned momentarily in my direction as the Hénin
Liétard bus arrived first and I fought for a place aboard. I
tried to view her again from inside but a large woman smelling of stale sweat and onions thrust between me and the
window. No matter, *mon ange*, see you in Arras, when the
job is done . . . a Lysander pick-up for both of us, back to
England, to Tangmere, Sussex-by-the-sea, thirty days hath
September, we'll spend it together, somewhere quiet, nothing
to do but eat, sleep, and be happy. Then a desk job for you,
teaching W/T to others, no better piano-player on the Morse
key, a marvel with your speed and accuracy, I'll pull strings in
high places, see you safe. I might even do something utterly
foolish like falling in love, that's why I didn't take the picture
you offered me, not for the official reason, but I couldn't say
so, it would have only made the parting worse.

I blew my nose, moved my backside into a less precarious
hold on the fraction of seat left by the large woman, peered
past her, out of a window as if tight shut against the depths
of winter instead of a humid, leaden, August day. If Lens had
been depressing, the new scenery was more so. Slag heaps,
mineshaft winders, chimney stacks, rusted pipes. Here and
there, heaps of rubble and blackened shells of building like
rotten teeth; little rows of grey-black terraced houses with
grey-black people gossiping or queueing for rations; young-

old women fretful with children, the odd one breast-feeding a mite under a shawl; others swollen and heavy, that pleasure still to come . . . mile upon mile upon mile of a coal-grimed, soot-laden stretch of elastic that passes for living, with no more than an occasional glimpse of grass, green, defiant, proud.

At Hénin Liétard, I changed buses, glad to see the back of the large woman, but not pleased to have papers checked by a gendarme. The first time they had been under real scrutiny since the Gestapo at Aire. A Frenchman now, if *he* questioned me at length . . . forget your accent, it has improved beyond belief in six weeks, thanks to Solange, a quick ear, and the need to make yourself understood by Maurice's group. All the same, I felt the prickle of sweat.

Without reason. The eye was lack-lustre, going through the motions, more concerned with corners of suitcases bumping his legs. An umbrella strapped to one swung between us, the ferrule aimed at his groin. He thrust my papers back, turned on the umbrella's owner with a snarl of rebuke. He met his match in a virago with a swift tongue that said what it thought of the law and unnecessary harrassment of innocent citizens, if it had nothing better to do than lick the arse of the Boches then the nearest lavatory was the place to do it; the start of a slanging match with others joining in. I was away, on the bus, in a seat with another woman beside me, smaller, younger, but smelling like the previous one. She was wrestling with three parcels, a shopping bag, and a baby behind a large yellow dummy. I took the baby whilst she sorted herself out. It fixed me with a beady eye, grinned fiendishly, and wet down my left leg. Then promptly started to howl, blaming me for the accident. The child was snatched back, I got a glare from the mother which became a nervous smile of apology when she saw the stain on my lap. I shrugged it aside, gave my attention to the same drab outlook all the way to Douai.

Another police check, but in the milling swarm of human ants I slipped clear, made for a bus labelled Aniche. Much too crowded, I settled for following its direction on foot. A

129

walk that went on forever, it seemed, but it could have been the lift that was back in my shoe. After three mis-directions, an urchin picking his nose removed his finger long enough to point out the street. The way to the door I wanted was blocked by small boys playing football with a bundle of rags tied with string. The doorway was one of the goals. It brought home another pearl of advice given by my peers . . . houses with children are more dangerous than sleeping with women . . .

Ah, well, in for a penny, in for a pound. I weaved a way through, knocked on the door. An angular creature in black stockings and a pinafore jumped out from behind it, shrilled the boys away with a shake of the fist and some high-velocity abuse. Finally, her eyes came to rest on me and my case.

'Whatever you are selling, I don't need any.' The lips set into a thin, straight line.

A promising start.

'I'm not a salesman.'

'Why knock on my door, then?'

'Max lives here?'

'You know him?'

'Would I be here if I didn't, madame?'

She liked the 'madame' bit. No one had used it on her in years. Possibly because she wore no wedding ring. Her hands scuttled out of sight under the pinafore. The jawline melted a fraction.

'I don't know . . . you wouldn't be the first.' Her eyes went up and down the street quickly, then the head jerked for me to enter.

I wiped feet, removed my beret. The jaw melted the more. Her eyes said, this is a gentleman. And gentlemen were strangers to Aniche. You'll have to watch it – my mind told me – learn to hawk and spit in gutters, scratch your crotch in public.

'Wait while I fetch him,' she said. 'What name did you say?'

'I didn't, madame. But it's Patrice.'

130

'Patrice?' A closer stare at that. 'Yes . . . you look a Patrice.'
She left me.

Was there something peculiar about a Patrice? I eyed myself in the hall-mirror. Sallow face, a bit drawn, in need of a
shave, nothing out of the ordinary . . .

A step behind me. The reflection gave me a man in shirt-
sleeves, collarless, eyes screwed up against smoke from the
cigarette in his mouth. Slight build, five-six or thereabouts,
thirtyish but hair thinning fast, dark-brown eyes when he
removed the cigarette and opened them. And, when I turned,
a club foot. Genuine. Not like mine.

'Max?'

No answer. He just stood there surveying me.

'Mules are fetching good prices,' I said, giving the password.

'I wear lace-up corsets myself.' The grin was sour. He
made a thumb over his shoulder.

I was in.

TWENTY-EIGHT

'You think you can do it?' The man called Max shrugged,
answered the question himself. 'You would not be here otherwise. Moulin-Bas is the complete professional.'

No comment.

He lit a fresh cigarette from the old. 'No need for modesty.
It is all around what you did in the Pas-de-Calais.' He waved
the butt at a stack of newspapers piled in the corner. 'Réseaux
news is my business.'

'I'd rather not be news,' I said.

'I can make no promises. Much will depend on the help
you require.'

'Two or three picked men. Men who work at the plant for
preference.'

'Men who won't give a shit about their livelihood going
up in flames?'

'You could put it that way.'

131

'Is there any other?' He scratched his chin. 'While they work at Paix there's less chance of being drafted across the Rhine. No man wants that.'

'Understood. But if we don't do it, the RAF will. And bombs don't discriminate.'

'You think we don't know?'

'I know you know. Why else am I counting on support?'

'Smells of blackmail,' he grimaced.

'Commonsense is a nicer word.'

'Some would agree with you,' he shrugged. 'Those who resent the place working for the Nazis. A few have even tried their hand at sabotage. Small stuff, to slow down production. Nothing on your scale.'

'They might be the very people.'

'Possibly. You'd like to meet them?'

'Soon as can be arranged.'

'Tonight. It's newspaper delivery.' He nodded towards a window that looked over the back of the house. 'We have a van. La Mouche drives it.'

'La Mouche?'

'We call her the Fly, the way she buzzes around. No better driver in the Nord.'

'I look forward to meeting her.'

'You have.'

I made a finger at the door. 'Not—?'

A nod. 'And she's taken a fancy. Patrice – a nice name for a nice-looking boy was how she described you. Wanted to know if you were staying.' He curled a lip at my wariness. 'I'll tell you for nothing she's a good cook and her bed is well-sprung, even if she may rattle a bit in top gear. You'll do worse, but I haven't committed you.'

'Somewhere more handy for Paix,' I said, diplomatically.

'I know the place, if you prefer to be a monk.'

'I'm here to work.'

'Spoken like a true Englishman, hein? What about extra accommodation? You will be inviting some friends to the party?'

'With the local *réseau's* permission.'

'Take it for granted. We run our cell on democratic lines, but the Action Committee make the decisions. Two of us.'

'You and you?' I asked.

The sarcasm was sand under a Bedouin's armpit.

'La Mouche and myself.'

'Which one is Trotsky?'

No smile. 'Come the Revolution, we'll find out, comrade. First we depose the Czar of Berlin.' He changed the subject, gave a half-shut eye to the case beside me. 'You'll need storage space, too, I suppose? You can't do it all from your little black bag?'

'Hardly. Ordinance are full of bright ideas. But they've yet to come up with an explodable jock-strap.'

'Pity. Castration might stop the next war.'

The supreme optimist.

Sam was a Pole. One of a half-million in the area. Like most he was fluent in the language of his country-of-exile and had taken French identity. He called himself Sam because it meant 'alone' in Polish. His wife, children, family – if they still existed – were in Sosnowiec, now absorbed into Greater Germany.

I had been instructed to avoid Poles. EU/P's in the area was known as *Monica*. But *Monica* was beset with difficulties, over-cautious since *Interallié*'s betrayal. Sam had lost heart and it was apparent from the first moment of meeting. A mood of reluctance, disbelief, even, that this 'boy' could be capable of planning such a venture. Envy, too, I suspected, that I had the means to do what had been denied him. Yet he had to be the key man in my operation. He was a foreman at the Paix plant. Could he get me inside for a thorough recce?

Reluctantly he supposed he could, if Max could arrange a forged pass. Could he point out to me the technical possibilities and strategic points where the most damage could be done? That depended on me, or rather, my knowledge of my craft and capabilities.

The ball was in my court. I began to talk of deflagration and detonation, of the chemical composition of gaseous mixtures and the velocity rates of Cyclonite compared with granular TNT, of the best uses of LOX and Cheddite 60/4. It was meant to impress and succeeded. His mood changed. There was a warming towards me. Back in Poland, in the far-off days, this had been his particular field. I could match him in text-book question and answer. He was more satisfied than I was that I knew my job. And when I mentioned that the time pencil activators we would use were of Polish design originally, he smiled, slapped my shoulder. He could do better than get me inside the place, he'd take me on as a trainee-worker, then he could really show me the ropes! Where was I staying? Never mind what Max had suggested, I must come *here*, in this house! The beds were clean, no bugs, and the kitchen wasn't bad. He had trained the 'woman' to make a fair *chlodnik* soup and tomorrow we would have *zakaski* made by his own hands. Without the vodka, alas, we'd have to put up with French *marc*. We must drink now to celebrate; two of his friends would be joining us – Jajo – so-called because he was as bald as an egg – and Níc, who who was so thin you could thread him through a needle. Both worked at Paix and would want to help, *O której zaczyna sie przedstawienie*, when does the performance begin?

Max and La Mouche came in as if on stage cue, their delivery round completed.

'There will be no performance.'

'Why the devil not?' I came back at him.

'Because you're in trouble. Bad trouble . . .'

'*La Geste* trouble,' added La Mouche. 'There's a price on your head.'

TWENTY-NINE

I lowered the drink that Sam had poured me.

'Since when?'

'Since someone informed on you at Aire.'

I stared in disbelief. Max thrust the French equivalent of the Police Gazette into my hands. 'We have a friend in the Commissariat. Every gendarme in the department has orders to arrest you on sight.'

Two words jumped out at me . . . *Patrice Morgat.* The description that followed fitted like a glove. Only the clothes differed. Felix had fitted me out with fresh ones at Epernay. I thought of the two checks that morning . . . but for the virago with her umbrella at Hénin Liétard and the bustle at Douai . . .

'Wanted for questioning in connection with sabotage and terrorist activities against the armies of the Occupying Power . . .' La Mouche was at my shoulder, pointing out the words with a bony finger. 'Two hundred thousand francs reward . . .'

I only half-heard her. My mind was racing towards Aire. Who had done the informing? Had Maurice and his group been rounded up? And Solange . . . had she walked into a waiting trap?

I lowered the paper, aware of three pairs of eyes watching me. I felt them transfer to my hand as I picked up the glass of *marc.* A liqueur glass, filled to the brim. Spill a drop, my sub-conscious said, and they'll notice it, have doubts, the 'boy' is not strong enough, too dangerous, better wash our hands of him, two hundred thousand francs was a thousand sterling, a temptation in any language . . .

I eyed the hand myself. Steady as a rock. A reaction learnt at pseudo-interrogation school. They had stopped at nothing short of physical torture, taught by a man who had spent four months in Dachau. The glass went to my lips, I drank half, put it down again. All three exchanged looks. I knew I was right. I felt La Mouche's hand press my shoulder. The gesture was acceptance. 'We'll see you through, Patrice,' she murmured.

'Hand me your documents.' Max was brisk. 'And get rid of the lift in your shoe.' I did not need to ask how he knew, a man with a genuine disability knows a fake. 'Peculiarities must be *néant* if you're going to be Edouard Bouchon.'

'Edouard Bouchon?'

'My nephew,' said La Mouche. 'Dead a year and buried in the Cornquaille. He won't object to being Lazarus for the cause.'

'You had this all thought out beforehand,' I said, looking up at her.

She moved round, sat down opposite me. 'When Max told me who you really were I thought it a wise move. You are like my Eddy – build, looks, accent. My sister married a sailor from Brest.'

'Aren't you putting them at risk?'

Her smile was thin. 'The Boches will have to dig them up to hang them.'

'What happened to Eddy?'

'He joined a local *réseau*. They tried to destroy a U-boat pen at St Nazaire . . . before the British had the same idea. He was hit by a bullet, several, but escaped. He wrote from Quimper, asking for help. When I got there he was dead, buried in a coffin along with an old man who was having a legal funeral. The only souvenirs I have are his papers.' Her eyes were bright but hard. They said don't let my nephew down.

'Thank you,' I said.

In twenty-four hours, Patrice Morgat was dead and Edouard Bouchon reborn. I was now two years younger, a native of Plougastel, an apprentice-engineer. A piece of information I seized upon, it made Sam's task of taking me on at Paix that much easier.

'You are going ahead with it?' said Max.

'Give me a reason why not. Moulin-Bas is out of the way, nobody need wet their drawers. What news from Aire?' I had pressed for more details of the betrayal.

'None. But see that as a good sign. Bad news travels fastest.'

136

'I'm concerned about my courier.'

'You never mentioned any courier,' he said, sharply.

'Didn't I?' I said, blandly. 'That had to be obvious. Where did you imagine the rest of my party were coming from?'

'I took it for granted they would travel with your stores.'

'Let's take nothing for granted, Max – including each other. We're neither of us infallible like Karl Marx or the Pope.'

'You could have told me more.'

'I didn't, because you didn't ask. And you didn't ask because you know well enough that the less you know the less can be squeezed from you if things go wrong.'

'This courier of yours knows the Aniche address?'

'Along with a dozen others, surely? The Carvin cell, the group executed a fortnight ago. Don't tell me you had no contact with them or they with you?'

'The Delvals – Roland and Julien, yes . . .'

'They didn't talk?'

'They were men? Your courier isn't.'

'Did I say so?'

'A guess. You Gaullist people use them a lot.'

'I'm not Gaullist people. Just someone doing a job. Anyway, how do you classify La Mouche?'

'I know her. I don't know your woman.'

'I do,' I said, tartly. 'She's scared out of her wits like each and every one of us. Not a bad thing. It means she'll be that much more careful. The only reason I gave her the job.'

'If she is caught . . .?' he persisted.

'She knows what to expect. Talking her head off won't save her.'

'It has done. That and opening the legs. The Cat was a good example.'

'A French trollop!' I spat. 'My girl is Jewish. If they want her body, they'll take it without asking. Take it, use it, then dispose of it. If she does squeal along the way, if she betrays anything or anybody she knows, there's a point she'll stop – *me!*'

'Like that, is it?' The hint of a sneer.

'Very much like that! And *me* includes your pissoir of an address! Now get off my back, your Gallic arse is safe!'

The sneer faded. 'I'm Jewish, too,' he said. He clumped out of the room.

Two days added years to my life. I was house-bound. Even with a new identity it wasn't wise to move outside. Sam returned each time, his face long with gloom. French and German police, everywhere, working in pairs, checking, re-checking papers. Around the station area and main bus-stops were plain-clothes SD and V-men, part of an auxiliary French Gestapo. Posters carried my name and description, the price was up to three hundred thousand. The consequences of harbouring me were imprisonment and deportation. His gloom was tinged with respect.

'It would seem they know you are expected here,' he said. 'Is that possible?'

'All is possible. But I don't think so. It's more likely the usual rash of Teutonic thoroughness – *gründlichkeit* – which passes for efficiency. The same thing could be on in a dozen towns.'

'It happens,' he nodded. 'We went through it two months ago. So many here you'd have thought they had evacuated Berlin. Forty-eight hours later, it was back to normal.'

'What is normal?' I asked, wrily. 'At Prix, in particular.'

His eyes lit up. 'It is still on?'

'It was never off. And not just the refinery and the mine. I want to hit when most Germans will be there.'

'That would be the morning after the sabotage,' he said, shrewdly. 'When the engineers and damage assessment experts arrive.'

'Plus security troops and Gestapo, top brass, the more high-ranking the better. That is where the eight-hour time-pencils come in. They finish off what we start the night before.'

He gave me a strange look. 'Bloodthirsty, aren't you?'

'No. Logical. Sabotage hampers the war machine. But to me it is only a minor target. My enemy is people. I shall never understand the attitude of those who sink a U-boat, for example, then pick up survivors. The menace is not the submarine, but the men who fire the torpedoes. The same goes for bombers, tanks, artillery, rifles. Left alone, they are inanimate objects that will gather rust. It's the finger at the trigger that needs to be chopped off, the mentality that created the monster eradicated.'

'You see all Germans as Nazis?'

'In those uniforms they have to be. Those who endeavour to differentiate between *Wehrmacht* and SS overlook one salient point – *both* are fighting to win, and the victory will be Hitler's, no one else's. The anti-Nazi German is a myth that will not become a reality until defeat. Then they will all come crawling out, making the SS their alibi.'

'You know them well, Patrice.'

'And I detest what I know,' I said. 'Draw me a sketch of Paix.'

He took out paper and pencil.

THIRTY

Max appeared before Curfew with the pass that would get me into Paix. An excellent forgery, down to stains and grease-marks that come from much handling. 'You'll be glad to know your courier is safe,' he said, casually. 'La Mouche went up there first thing this morning. She brought this back for you.'

He handed me a letter addressed to Edouard Bouchon and marked *privé*. The envelope had been slit open. 'La Mouche was within her right to check the contents,' he said, swiftly, anticipating my anger. 'She was carrying it. If there had been anything incriminating, well . . .'

'I trust you are happy, too,' I said, sarcastically. I unfolded the letter, read it.

Dear Edouard – it is a long time since we met, I wonder if you remember me? I was only a little girl then, but your

139

*auntie says you have grown into a handsome boy. I would
have liked to come to visit you, but that mean old guardian
of mine, Uncle Maurice, won't let me travel. He says it
isn't wise for young girls with all the soldiers around – so
silly, they can't be so that bad and, anyway, he is sending
me to Aunt Blanche in Paris where there are so many more!
Of course, those two bores, Phillippe and Bernard, will
be there to chaperon me. So ridiculous, I am nearly seventeen! Which reminds me, how old is Lena? Uncle insists
she must be eighteen or even nineteen. He says Grandmama should know, he heard her so say so quite definitely.
But the important thing is your birthday. I would have
baked a cake, but we are short of flour. But Aristide is
bringing some eggs and fruit in time for the celebration.
So when you have the party, spare a thought for me – your
ever affectionate Solange.* There was a postscript. *There
has been measles in the family, but they have not infected
me. There are no germs on the enclosed lock of hair!
Love, S.*

Written in French, in a schoolgirlish hand I recognized as
hers, the lock of hair was no sentimental touch. It added confirmation that the letter did come from Solange and was not
written under duress. The contents contained a number of
messages, based on an elimination process using a combination of numbers known only to both of us.

SINCE I HAVE COME MAURICE SAYS SENDING
PHILIPPE AND BERNARD TO LENA STOP
INSISTS EIGHTEEN OR NINETEEN GRANDMAMA
SHOULD KNOW STOP ARISTIDE BRINGING
EGGS AND FRUIT IN TIME FOR PARTY STOP

There were other points in the phrasing. The reference to
being *only a little girl* meant she was safe, whereas if she had
written *I am a big girl now* would have spelled danger.
Measles in the family implied the German variety – the
Abwehr or Gestapo. *Aunt Blanche in Paris,* however, suggested that Maurice was moving her away from Aire but
minus her transmitter, proof he was taking no risks. It was
included in the most important part of the letter that started

140

and finished with a crossed-out *so*. This also gave me fresh instructions from London – *Grandmama* – 18 or 19 meant dates when the job should take place.

A change that gave me extra breathing space. But why? I could only suspect something big was planned for that time and our job was no more than a diversion. Not a happy thought. Diversions, all too often, collected the most stick . . .

Max interrupted my thoughts. 'Satisfied?'

'I'd like to know more about the measles.'

'A youth named Albert. He was challenged at a road-block, tried to get away. He collected a bullet in the thigh for his pains, was captured. He got the usual boot and butt treatment, but it seems he only divulged your name and description.'

'Kind of him.'

'He didn't like you very much. You had called his family a bag of shit or something, threatened to shoot him. He was so sensitive about it, he would have left the cell if you hadn't moved on. When la Geste accused him of butchering three SS men, he said you had done the chopping. Is that so?'

'Guilty on all counts. How does Maurice know he said no more?'

'Figure it out for yourself, no one else was taken. Also, it seems, Albert took a turn for the worse. The bullet in the thigh slipped upwards and somehow lodged in his throat before he could say more.' Max clucked his tongue in mock sadness. 'Francs-Tireurs get edgy about faint-hearts, especially when they are caught. And it's amazing the accidents that can happen when one is not guarded too well. A police *boîte* in Aire is not quite Fresnes jail.'

'That sounds reasonable.'

'More than you do, if I may say so. Your tongue is sharp. It can make you enemies, Patrice.'

You can talk, I thought. 'Edouard,' I said, tapping the letter. 'Even my girl knows that.'

'Edouard,' he said. He picked up the letter and envelope. 'If you have finished with this, we'll file it our way.' He

141

rattled a box of matches. 'Or perhaps you would like to keep part of it?' He hooked the lock of hair with a finger.

I probably would have done, but saw the gesture as yet another test. 'No . . . it doesn't go with my own.'

'Suit yourself.' He burned the lot in a metal ash-tray. The paper flared, charred swiftly. The blonde curl was more defiant. It took a second match.

Sorry, *mon ange*, sorry . . .

THIRTY-ONE

Monday, the 10th of August. I couldn't afford to wait any longer. Police checks were a chance I must take. Sam and his friends were starting a spell of night work – the nine to six shift – ideal for our purpose. He found the necessary overalls and headgear and we set off in a thin drizzle of rain.

The Paix complex was guarded by a *Sonderkommando* – a force of *Feldgendarmerie* boosted by elements of the Standarte Deutschland, an SS regiment that had moved to the area in recent weeks. Security was strict. Twice in twenty yards of entering the main gate my pass was checked by men in black slicker capes and armed with the inevitable Schmeissers. To one side of the gate was a watch tower with a spotlight and a Spandau. In 1937, I had seen Dachau from the outside and the tower served as a grim reminder. A reminder reinforced as the road took us past the pit-head. The closed trucks that had preceded us in were unloading squads of forced labour. Shaven-headed wrecks of men dressed in thin denims, each marked with a large letter denoting their country of origin, some with the Star of David. Kicks and curses helped them on. I saw one hit the ground on all fours, his face thrust into loose shale from a vicious blow on the neck. His head rose in mute appeal, turned towards our straggle of 'free' labour. Then, to escape the boots, he began to crawl like an animal. The others shuffled past, unheeding, fearful of becoming involved. He tottered to his feet, took a punch in the kidneys that spun him round. He went backwards in a stagger, tripped, and fell again. More blows began to rain upon him ...

Sam jerked at my arm, whispered. 'Don't look.'

'But—'

'The bastards enjoy an audience. It shows they are the masters. It's a warning also, not to interfere.'

'When we do the job, one thing I know. I'm going to get those poor devils out.' I muttered.

'They won't thank you for it.'

I stared at him.

'I mean it,' he said. 'So you open the gates, tell them they are free to go . . . but where to? The town will never hide them. It isn't a question of changing clothes, obtaining a fresh identity, the way you have. They're branded, tattooed numbers or symbols seared into the flesh. Home to them is some filthy bunker in the camp they've come from, under the eye of a 'trusty', a German political prisoner. A Communist, as a rule, who makes life only a little less hell than the man wearing the swaztika. But *it is home.*'

'You know so much ... how come?' I asked.

'The letter *P* on some of them stands for Pole, right? Níc and I, we tried to help one who made a break for it. We hid him up in the refinery for sixty hours. He told us what it was like. Go sick and you either rose again on the third day or it was into a cattle-truck and shipped to another camp. A death camp. Only one way out of there. A gas chamber, an oven, or slow strangulation in a twist of piano wire. The lucky ones get a bullet in the neck. He knew it was so because a number of guards had boasted about it. With that kind of alternative, they've reached the stage where survival is measured by each breath they draw. Dying is not a merciful release. It's more brutality, more pain, more degradation. No escape.'

'Didn't your man?'

His smile was grim. 'They brought the dogs in. They found him soon enough, savaged him like a rat. Then the guards took over, dragged him across a slag-heap before fling-

143

ing him into a truck and taking him away. That is why I say you will be doing no favours by freeing them unless you can ship them to Britain or Switzerland. Nothing less will do. They will just sit down and cry and wait for fresh guards to round them up and hope to God they won't be beaten for something they didn't do!'

I shook my head . . . was he right? He could be. I still had a picture of the wretch on his hands and knees and no finger raised to help him. Create a degree of terror where self-preservation is the dominating, all-devouring factor and the thousand-year Reich was no longer a lunatic dream, a sneer in the press of the free world . . .

Beyond the slag-heaps and the rattling conveyor belts was the refinery. Another fence surrounded this, with warning signs slashed with a lightning fork to denote it was live. We passed through a gate and a third check. Along one side of the plant were railway sidings, where sentries patrolled in pairs between wagons at either end, mounted with Oerliken guns and searchlights. In the refinery itself, more guards patrolled the lanes between a jungle of pipes that hissed and juddered. The odd one, too, was on the catwalks high above. Lights came on with the night – red, green, blue, and white – little pre-tence at black-out. A siren doused them and then only if the bombers were overhead. According to Sam when the lights went, the guns spoke a message of steel so thick and continuous it was a miracle anything above survived. He had seen four bombers become flaming coffins in as many minutes in a previous raid, the net result of which had been three streets demolished a mile away and a cortege of civilian dead. The only German casualty had been a broken leg when part of a brothel collapsed.

We could hardly do less than that, I thought, as I moved around with Sam, a wrench in my hand to show I was not on a sight-seeing tour. One or two workers gave me a curious glance, but Sam covered it by direct introduction or snide reference to apprentice-engineers fresh out of college who

144

knew it all. My response was to grin sheepishly and hope I would be accepted with no questions asked. My eyes were everywhere, making mental notes of places where the charges could be set. Sam offered no suggestions. They would come later when I revealed my ignorance.

Midnight found us in the canteen. It offered lentil soup and a brew that passed for coffee. The main part of the meal we had brought with us – bread and some unappetising meat loaf I found impossible to eat. We were joined by Níc, who took it from me in exchange for a rubbery wedge of cheese.

During the meal, a Frenchman slid along the bench and whispered at Sam, throwing me a side-long look as he did so. A muttered discussion developed in which Sam threw up his hands and rolled his eyes. It ended with him slapping the man's shoulder and giving assurance. 'Leave it to me, it will be done right away.'

The Frenchman left. I looked at Sam. He grinned, shrugged. Níc chewed at the meat loaf, removed gristle from his teeth, said : 'Union card?'

'CTG. You have to join or they'll stop you working,' said Sam to me. 'That's the shop steward.'

'Do the Boches know?' I murmured.

'Hardly. But it makes no difference. For the sake of peace and quiet, I said you would apply immediately.'

'Thanks for nothing!' Of all the sweet irony . . . in order to blow up this bloody place, I must first have a union card! 'What about the poor sods we passed coming in? Do they pay their dues?'

'Our friend doesn't approve of them,' said Níc, still picking his teeth. 'They are blacklegs taking the bread from French miner's mouths.'

'You are not serious?' I looked hard at him.

'And you, evidently, are not a good trade unionist. It isn't enough to fight for liberty, it has to be for time-and-half as well.'

I looked at Sam. I saw no smile, merely a nod of the head.

'More than a few resent the presence of slave workers rather than pity their plight.'

145

'Christ Almighty!' was all I could say.

Níc answered that, looking me straight in the eye. 'Never in this world. Not *him*. Not now . . . nor anytime.' He rose, left the table.

'A man of decided opinion,' I said, quietly.

'He should know,' said Sam. 'He was once a priest.'

THIRTY-TWO

Come the morning, I had made a thorough recce of the refinery. Once only had I met a direct challenge from a guard, when I strayed too close to the laboratories. Sam had quickly straightened it out, apologizing in German. I was a new kid who didn't know his arse from his elbow; then he castigated me for not observing signs like *Eingang Verboten!* and *Avis! Defense de Entree!;* didn't they teach me to read at school, ignorance would get my head blown off. It had been followed by a sharp back-hander. I had dodged a second cuff, deliberately finding a patch of oil to slither on and fall, to come up black and greasy, which brought a hoot of laughter from the guard. As I slunk away, I heard him compliment Sam on his German and offer a cigarette. Both had lit up, despite the *No Smoking* notices in both languages. One couldn't get chummier than that. Without Sam, there wasn't a snowball-in-hell's chance of bringing off the operation. Jajo, too, was indispensable. He worked in the dynamo house, the source of the power that must be cut at a crucial moment in my plan.

Níc, too, made his position clear. He caught up with us on the way home, thrust a large envelope into the top of my overalls. Back at the lodgings, I unfolded the contents . . . a detailed scale plan of the whole site. My eyebrows must have registered surprise.

'Why not?' answered Sam, pulling off his boots. 'He works in the administrative block. All it required was a wax im-

146

pression of the keys. He did that on Saturday, the new set were made yesterday. You now have the result.'

'How much does he know?' I asked, quickly.

He wiggled his toes. 'Not a lot from me. But a mind that spent twelve years of its childhood under the Black Monks will not miss much that is devious.'

'Has he completely rejected the Church?'

'More a case of God having rejected the human race and Níc seeing it as a wise decision.' Sam eyed a large hole in one sock. 'He could be right. Out of this may come a new Garden of Eden with a different species.'

'Make it a tortoise and I'll be back.' I cracked my jaw in a yawn. Six months' hibernation would be bliss. I went to my own room, threw off my clothes, climbed into bed to sleep and sleep . . .

. . . for three hours. Max was shaking me, slapping my face.

'Visitors!' he whispered.

I was out of bed and across the room, behind the door, hands ready to chop and gouge the moment it opened. Then I caught his grin.

'Aristide and Maurice,' he said.

'Bastard,' I muttered. I brought my hands down, swung the door wide, hauled the pair of them in.

'*C'est du bon sport!*' enthused Aristide as I outlined the plan.

Maurice was cautious. 'Excellent, but not easy. How many of us will there be?'

'Four already inside. Sam, Níc, Jajo, and myself. Then Raoul, Le Claque. Philippe, Bernard, and you two. And Felix from Epernay. Eleven . . .' I hesitated, glanced at Max, seated, as usual, behind a halo of tobacco smoke.

A hint of sarcasm in his answer. 'If you are not superstitious, La Mouche and I will make thirteen.'

'Reserves?' asked Maurice.

'I can find three,' Max went on. 'Capable of handling guns and grenades. I'm not sure I'd trust them with explosives.

They've not had the opportunities of some.' A sour note, almost one of animosity. Jealousy at chairborne level was bad enough. It could be disaster here.

'That can be arranged,' I said, sharply. 'If they fail the level required, you'll be told in no uncertain terms.' I turned back to Maurice. 'Solange said you were bringing eggs and fruit...'

He nodded. 'A dozen eggs, phosphorus kind. Twenty kilos of fruit, almond flavour. Oh, and a present for you, Patrice.'

'Edouard,' said Max.

'Edouard,' said Maurice, with a frown. He fished inside his jacket, came out with a Luger. The frown went as he passed it to me. 'Those horse-dung mines, remember? They took out a staff car. What was left of the officer we found in a tree. The pistol was his. Afterwards, we all agreed it should be yours, a commandante's weapon. A small token, you understand...'

I understood perfectly. It was a way of getting around the Albert business without loss of honour to his group. A form of apology, a proof of faith. My acceptance meant subject closed, no call for a post-mortem. 'Thank you,' I said. 'I always wanted a Luger.'

Max had been watching with half-closed eyes, a curl of the lip. Everyone is happy but Albert, the sneer seemed to say.

'Diversions,' I asked him. 'Trial runs for your three men. Can you suggest targets? Small, not too much risk involved.'

'Several,' he said. 'But not German.' He outstared Maurice and Aristide. 'That's right, my friends ... *French*. Our enemies are not the Boches alone. You can't object to a *coup de main* against Doriot's Légion Tricolore? Or Déat's scum who work with the Gestapo? Or is all French blood sacrosanct except where the treason is personal?'

A direct taunt at Maurice. But the older man was not rising to the bait. He looked at me, raised an eyebrow. You're the commandante, it said, show your steel.

'Political vendettas are out,' I said. 'If the Légion want to die on the Russian Front that's their funeral. And knocking

148

off V-men is corner-boy stuff. The idea was to teach this bunch of yours to use explosives.'

Max changed his tune smoothly. 'A target I had in mind was the Darnand Mobiles. Their garage at Denain.'

'*D'accord*,' said Maurice, drooping an eyelid in my direction. 'Put them back on their flat feet and they'll lose effectiveness.'

'Fair enough,' I said. 'Give me two others.'

Max shrugged. 'If we can't hit the Légion itself, why not their recruitment office at Valenciennes? I'm told they keep a well-stocked armoury in the cellar. Another idea is a warehouse on the outskirts of Lille rented by Action Francaise. It's full of French editions of *Mein Kampf* and other gutter-press literature. It would make a nice bonfire.'

'Big deal,' I felt like saying . . . 'if that's the best you can come up with, go command a brigade in the Irish Republican Army!' On the other hand, French Nazi objectives would not be a bad smokescreen. It might suggest that the presence of the SS had made Boche targets secure and were forcing the Francs-Tireurs to vent their frustration elsewhere. It might even draw off a flying column to deal with a rumble of civil disturbance. And, in all fairness, I had asked for small targets . . .

I nodded acceptance. A gesture that threw Max completely. He, in his cantankerous way, had been spoiling for a fight. Now he had one, not quite in the manner expected.

'You want to discuss them in detail?' he said.

'No. Maurice, I am sure, will help out as required—'

'Of course!' said the man from Aire.

'—and all I want are the dates,' I continued. 'To co-ordinate with the job here.'

'You know about the eighteenth or nineteenth?' said Maurice.

'Yes. And I'm wondering why. Have you any ideas?'

'Is a Second Front possible?'

'We've been over that ground before—'

'—I know. But I can only report the signs. The Schloks have been on the move through Merck St Liévin. A whole division back from Russia, according to Claude. He could be exaggerating, but I don't think so. He is becoming a very good Intelligence officer. Artillery units, too, 15-centimetre guns. The rumours are around, talk of British-American landings any day.'

'Places?' I asked. With the whole of the north-east coast-line a forbidden zone, one might wonder how such information was known. But it was, and not always flights of imagination.

'Hardelot, some say. A party of Commandos landed there in April, looked around and left. God help them if it's true, the dunes are one big mine-field now. But the talk is more of Berck and Mahon, Le Crotoy and St Válery-sur-Somme. I've heard about St Válery from another source, a cousin from Abbeville. People are already shifting out, he says, they had enough in 1940.'

'If the locals know, the Germans must know more,' I pondered. 'Does London know they know, I wonder?'

'It might be a deliberate leak?' said Max.

'There's always some cunning bugger who plays it clever-clever, intent on outwitting the *Abwehr*. What makes a nice twist in a book or a film, doesn't necessarily work out in practice. Canaris's crew are not bloody fools. They're more likely to pinpoint places *not* mentioned.'

'Is there anything we can do about it?' asked Maurice.

'Not with Solange in Paris and without her transmitter.'

'If you could get a message to her, she might find a way to pass it on.'

Via one of the *Confrérie* network, that was true. And she would rather be doing something than twiddling thumbs in a safe house, fretting what we were up to. Nothing worse than time to think. She had said that on more than one occasion.

'La Mouche will deliver the message,' said Max. 'She has met the girl before, so there's no problem of a stranger. A short note from you is all that's required. Any details you want sent to London, she can memorize. A photographic mind, that one. She could quote word-perfect the letter you received,' he added, with a sly grin.

He had to spoil it with that kind of remark. But he was right, of course. La Mouche was the logical one for the job. 'Tomorrow then,' I said. 'No later.'

THIRTY-THREE

Three days and nights passed uneventfully. I did odd jobs at the refinery under Sam's supervision, studied the various sections of the plant in detail, made notes on the scale drawing afterwards. We brought Níc and Jajo into our discussions and both offered valid improvements to the original plan. A problem unsolved was the one of the slave labour. I was not prepared to ignore them as Sam had suggested. We reached a measure of agreement. It would have to be a last-minute decision as in the case of the local workers. There was no question of bringing others into our confidence. A solitary hint on the grapevine and someone would see us out, if only to protect his job. The most dangerous of them was probably the shop steward. He had accepted my union dues but had made a pompous demand that Brother Bouchon be ready to attend an interview by the works committee on Friday, the 21st, when my application for membership would be formally considered. By then – with luck – there would be no works for the committee to adjudicate upon.

Maurice, meanwhile, made a recce of the minor targets with Max. He reported that only the garage presented problems and Max had grudgingly accepted it was not work for beginners. The new men would go along as observers on this, the first of the three tasks.

La Mouche left for Paris with a short note for Solange. I had sealed it in front of her, saying the contents were personal, that the only incriminating information was that which she carried in her head – the result of a briefing session with Maurice. I didn't defy her to open the note. Rather I played on her womanly instincts. Solange was a sensitive person, there was scant privacy in wartime, anything between us was between *us* and no-one else.

It worked. Her face softened as it had done the first time I had addressed her as 'madame'. She departed, a female Cupid, in buckle shoes and a flapper-style cloche hat.

A strange lady . . . not a bit my idea of the nympho Max had hinted she was. But, then, I had only met one in my life – a WAAF at Ringway – and had seen her for a lesbian at the beginning, the way she walked, talked, and shook hands. It was after several days and rather more gin-and-limes and an erudite dialogue on the merits of Aristophanes that she had suddenly bussed me voraciously and unbuttoned her blouse. She was sorry she wasn't a virgin for me but her father had raped her at thirteen, and she had had a guilty conscience ever since for having enjoyed it. The only way she could purge her guilt was to do it again with someone as understanding and sympathetic as me, here today, gone tomorrow, no emotional come-backs, she gave her word . . . I was to learn later from another trainee-parachutist, that she had been deflowered by her uncle at the age of eleven with the same consequences. We had both reached the conclusion that the lady in blue with the singular double-maidenhead, was part of a sadistic conspiracy to sap our strength before we were launched on the first unnerving balloon jump. On second thoughts, we'd agreed she had performed a very loyal service in taking our minds off the next morning's worry. How many thousands would pass through Ringway before the conflict was over one had no idea, but one woman's 'war effort' deserved recognition! If not by a medal, at least by a plaque in that corner of the field behind Number Two hangar, made from a chunk of the runway and inscribed simply *We Salute You, Nickers* – an apt corruption of her real name.

Saturday, the 15th, saw the arrival of the Epernay party with the materials. Felix had got them on to a long-distance heavy lorry, crated as railway workshop spare parts. The driver himself was a member of an FTP group in Lille and had been only too pleased to oblige. The goods were placed in a safe store at Corbehem, handy for the plant. All that remained was to smuggle them in and put them where they would do most good.

We drank to that in champagne they had brought with them, Sam rustled up some of his *zakaski*, and a party began to develop. It augured well that the two groups were making friends, and even Max wore a smile less sour than usual.

La Mouche returned in the middle of it. After two glasses, she caught my eye, manoeuvred me into a corner with her back to Max. She slipped me a letter slily.

'How did it go?' I asked.

'Very well. Solange is hoping to see someone this evening.'

'You have no idea who the contact is?'

'No. She was very discreet about that. Nor did I have to tell her there was to be no connection between the information and our operation. She said as much herself. Not only is she pretty but wise. You are a lucky man. But, then, she is a lucky girl.'

I rewarded her with a peck on the cheek.

She blushed, pecked me back. 'I promised to pass on *that*, too.' She moved away to join the others. I went to my own room to read the letter. As I had expected, it was unopened.

Partice chérie, so wonderful to hear from you! Your letter could not have come at a more needed moment. Aunt Blanche is kindness itself, but I do miss the comforts only you can give. I am sorry to hear about your rash, it sounds nasty, but nothing serious, I hope. I may have a probable cure. The prescription is an old one of Auntie's. I have tried two pharmacies she suggested but one is closed down and the other out of stock of the necessary ingredients. However, there is an old so hag in the village who might make it up. Auntie says it is diet deficiency. Plenty of fresh vegetables and fish is the answer, so so silly, as if we didn't know! I can't wait to see a mussel on a plate, let alone a lobster! But for real choice, I'd rather have you. If I'm good and patient I'll get both, yes? Your fondest, most loving Solange. And, again, a postscript. *No lock of hair this time, I'll finish up bald and that would mean a nunnery! S.*

Clever girl, apart from the opening slip, calling me Patrice. But the rest was neatly worded—

RASH SOUNDS SERIOUS STOP I HAVE PRESCRIP-TION STOP TRIED TWO SUGGESTED BUT ONE CLOSED DOWN THE OTHER OUT STOP HAG FISH THE ANSWER STOP CAN'T WAIT TO SEE MUSSEL YOU BOTH STOP.

The important words were *Hag Fish.* The code name meant he or she was Section RF of SOE. 'In the village' was Paris and almost surely 'I' personnel equipped to handle the information we were passing on. I wasn't overjoyed at the thought of an unknown contact, but ditching her transmitter at Aire was a safety measure I had approved of under the circumstances. The second fish reference – *Mussel* – concerned our escape line when the job was finished. I echoed her sentiments on that score. A pity about the lock of hair, I might have kept it this time . . .

I turned the letter to ashes, rejoined the party.

THIRTY-FOUR

That same night saw the destruction of the garage at Denain. Raoul accompanied Maurice, Aristide, and Max's three trainees. He went in like a cat, across a roof and through a skylight over the workshop. He christened Poulainette on the duty officer and spannered a mechanic into silence, let the others in by a side door. Four cars, a Black Maria, and eight motor-cycles got the plastic treatment, as well as a gasoline storage tank and pumps, a spare parts and tyre store, and drums of lubricating fluid. Ten minutes after they departed the place was burning nicely.

Sunday was the Légion's turn. Maurice again, with Bernard and the same three newcomers. The Légionnaires were holding a recruitment rally in another part of the town. A solitary corporal clerk had been left in charge. He died at his desk, to become one of Doriot's martyrs. But Max had been misinformed about the armoury. The basement was only a pistol range, no guns, no ammunition. Charges were set, the group withdrew, only to find they were four, not five. One of the trainees had gone back inside, not sure he had activated his detonator correctly. He was never to find out. The charges blew prematurely, the front of the office erupted into the street and with it, the man's body. Bernard got there first, took a quick look. Stumps for hands, the face sheered away, there was no point in removing the corpse. Identification was an impossibility, there was no trace back to Douai. On these operations, I had laid down a rule – no papers carried on the person. And it was for Max to see that was carried out.

The death itself posed a new problem. The other two got the jitters, wanted to pull out. There was nothing heroic about death in a gutter, but their excuse was the unreliability of the explosives. It was pointless telling nervous men that their comrade had died because he was a bloody fool. So far as the Paix job was concerned, they were both written off. And though they knew nothing about it, the fact remained they could put the finger on Maurice and three of his group. On Max, too, but that was his affair. I made it plain that either he made certain their tongues didn't wag or we would do it for him.

A chastened Max offered no argument. He persuaded both men to accept the principle of 'voluntary house arrest' for a limited period of time. It was a kind of Inverlair that ensured their silence. The alternative was explicitly final and I would have had no compunction about carrying it out. There was too much at stake to allow for further Alberts.

Monday night was the warehouse. Max elected to take the place of one of them; Felix took the other. Philippe and Le Claque made up the team, the latter partly to try out an incendiary device he had been working on at Epernay. La Mouche drove them up, delivering them almost to the door.

155

A surprised night-watchman let them in, allowed himself to be bound, gagged, and deposited in an outside dustbin where no harm would come to him if he kept his head down. They were well on the way home before the first rumble came and the clouds reflected red with flame. Even so, it was La Mouche's skill at the wheel that eluded a road-block ten kilometres out and yet a second cordon further on.

For my part, I was glad it was the last of such *estrapades*. They had not achieved their intent – from my point of view, at least – of supplying extra trained men for the main operation. The only significant success had been the removal of a section of *Feldgendarmerie* from patrolling the sidings at Corbehem to other duties. Two men at the most, at any given time, but they might prove a vital factor in the preliminary assault. Against that, there was always the danger of increased vigilance on the part of those left to cover this deficiency. If we came out of this unscathed, I felt, it would be little thanks to Max.

I went to bed on Tuesday morning in a restless, uneasy mood. Yet commonsense told me there was nothing more to be done beyond putting our plan into practice. Success or failure, there would be little opportunity for sleep afterwards except in the ultimate one. Something, in all truth, I gave little thought to and even less discussion. Fear of death is pointless, it's the one thing in life that is inevitable. The most one can hope for is no accompaniment of misery and pain, that one might go peacefully, unaware, with dignity. Sam was probably right about those poor wretches of slave-workers. All they really wanted now was death in sleep . . .

I yawned, eyelids heavy. Death and sleep . . . someone once wrote about it . . . Shelley, of course . . . how did it go? *Death and his brother Sleep, one pale as yonder wan and horned moon . . .*

There would be a moon tomorrow . . . *tonight* . . . pale, I hoped . . . very pale and horned . . .

I was gone.

THIRTY-FIVE

Tuesday, August 18th . . . pale moon rising in a summer evening sky, to set around two-thirty the next morning. Spread your skirts in a veil of cloud, Mother Goddess, and I shall cherish you until eternity. The BBC French Service gave out its first stream of messages . . . *Yolande's cat has had four kittens . . . the Tinker can expect new pots to mend . . . Monica is busy milking the cows . . . the lower windmill will turn tonight . . .*

I grimaced at the *will* in the last message, visualized a fat arse comfortable in a chair, pink gin at elbow, face smiling and nodding . . . 'One off *your* messages, dear?' from the little woman, clicking needles over a balaclava, her bit for the war effort. 'All this secret work is so exciting, I wonder what the man is like who's listening over there?' . . . he's a dumb bunny, darling, shit-scared, with no appetite for what might well be his last supper.

I switched off the radio, eyed the soup-stew of stringy mutton, onions, and butter-beans, found a wan smile for Sam's derogatory observation . . . 'if the explosive don't work, we can always fart the place down.'

I took a last-minute look at the scale plan over the meal, then burnt it, stirring the ashes into the remnants of the casserole. Back in my room, I dressed for work. Ordinary clothes under the overalls, knife in its shoulder sheath, Luger taped to the thigh, pocket slit for quick access. I had practised walking around like this for several nights, using a spanner instead of the pistol, and had found it the most comfortable and best concealed method. Sam and Níc had done the same, but they would be taking in wire-cutters. A glance in the mirror, no suspicious bulge; a scrutiny of the room, nothing left but the imprint of my head on the pillow; all else in the small suitcase to be collected by La Mouche within the hour. No matter how the Lower Windmill turned tonight, it was goodbye to this place. I went out, shut the door gently.

Entering the gate at Paix, I noticed a difference. Two guards instead of the usual four checking passes. Six instead of the usual dozen hustling the slave-labour. Up at the refinery, the quota had been reduced. Maybe I had been too hasty in my assessment of the diversions. I muttered as much to Sam. He had been opposed to them from the outset.

His look was dour. 'The credit isn't ours.'

'You've heard something I haven't?'

'You weren't listening. Monica is busy milking the cows. The message before ours. Max may think what he likes, but those road-blocks last night were not for his benefit. The railway was blown in three places between Lille and Arras.'

Monica was EU/P. It tied in with the overall strategem, something big was in the wind. 'Nice to know we're not alone. And tonight?'

'I can only guess. The loco sheds at Fives are fat udders for squeezing.'

'And you think the Boches have made the same guess?'

His shrug was answer enough. It explained the sudden withdrawal of men from here. Good for Monica, more power to her fingers. Only the cynic in me found it hard to credit such co-ordination at top level. But let it be so for one night, a few hours, even; long enough for us to convert this complex into a scrap-yard.

Our plan was in three stages. Stage One dealt with the refinery, its retorts, storage tanks, and key machinery. Stage Two was the mine, the pithead, winding-gear, and conveyors. With this would go the powerhouse and dynamo. Stage Three was the delayed one, dependent on the efficiency of the extra-long fuses, aimed at the laboratories and administration block when technicians and Gestapo were there to assess the damage.

H-hour was midnight plus fifteen. The hour when the top dog of the powerhouse took his meal break. The hour when

158

Jajo must blow a set of fuses, plunge a section in darkness and remove the current from the high-voltage fence.

As luck would have it, this was not an uncommon occurrence. Much of the equipment in this section was not geared to work at the peak the Germans demanded, with no shut down for maintenance. Consequently, blown fuses were more a cause for annoyance rather than suspicion, and a scheme was in hand to rectify the trouble. The top dog – Weiss – was not happy delegating authority. It would take him sixteen-and-a-half minutes to stumble back in the dark from the canteen, find and remedy the fault. Jajo had worked the trick for a trial run the previous Friday and we had timed it. Sixteen-and-a-half minutes for Sam and Níc to make the required gap in the fence for the outside party to come in.

The point of entry was well-marked. Three oil wagons bearing the *Imperator, Willems* sign had been in the siding for a week. A shape easy to define in the dark and their size gave reasonable shadow in low moonlight. Raoul and Aristide would be scouting ahead, dressed as railway workers, wheel-tapping or whatever such folk are supposed to do. The remaining five would tag them, each carrying ten kilos of explosive, as well as grenades and the two Chicago-type 'choppers'.

The other fifty kilos were already inside. The three Poles and myself had smuggled it in five kilos at a time, the final ten by Níc and Jajo this night. Placed in seven storage points, handy for various targets, and safe, we hoped, from prying eyes or fingers. If by mischance any one of the seven was discovered, the finder would become its permanent keeper . . . they were bobby-trapped.

This last precaution had been Sam's idea. He had argued that no innocent could stumble upon the stuff by accident. It would have to be one of several 'noses' who curried favour with their German masters. Níc had gone further, pointed them out – the men who must not be warned, even at the last minute. If they expected me to demur at killing civilians, they were wrong. I had no interest in lackeys and their subsequent fate. They must take the same chance as the rest of us. But I was determined – and here Maurice and the others had agreed with me – to try to save the poor sods facing entombment in the mine.

At eleven-thirty, Sam and I defused the booby-traps. A simple enough process for those who set them. They were marked with an empty cigarette packet, a thin strip of metal in the base of each. Soldered to the metal and running out through the bottom of the packet were three wires. The trick was to remove it just enough to reveal the wires and snip them in a given order.

Five done, two to go. We were at the solvent wax extraction unit. Our store was deep under a network of pipes and the drill was for one to work while the other kept watch. Sam was taking a long time over this sixth one. He came out muttering, glancing at his watch. I gestured with the pliers I was holding. Abandon the drill, move on to the seventh, I'd complete this one by myself.

I ducked in, wriggled forward to the cache. The difficulty was soon apparent. The niche had become oil-slimy and the concrete beneath was a skating rink of dripped wax. I eased the booby-trap out of the way, pocketed the pliers. I decided there and then to move the explosive to a drier, more accessible spot. I was restowing the last kilo when a hand dropped on my shoulder.

'What d'you think you're doing?' said a voice in French.

The shop-steward. This was his area of employment, one of the reasons why we had chosen an extra-safe hide. A flashlight flicked on, played over the sticks of HE. The voice went smug. 'I suspected you all along.' He spun me around.

A foolish thing to say and do. A stiff right hand took him across the throat, snapped the hyoid. A second chop as he crumpled broke the neck. The knees hit the ground, the head was that of a rag doll. His suspicions would go with him to his grave, a sump feet deep with congealing wax. I picked up his flashlight, played it over the pit. One heel was visible. I jabbed that down and it was as if he had never existed. As I turned away to rejoin Sam, he no longer did for me.

THIRTY-SIX

Twelve-twelve. Sam, Níc, and I, six feet from the wire and sweating. Beyond it, the curved shells of the *Imperator* wagons; beyond those, others, clunking and clinking under the pull and push of a fusspot shunter hissing steam and smoke. But no sign of Aristide or Raoul. What was keeping them? Not Germans – or a klaxon would have sounded, the arcs would be sweeping the fence and sidings. That self-important locomotive, possibly, but they had been warned to allow for such a contingency. Christ, come on, come on . . .

Twelve-thirteen. The lights flickered and went. Two minutes early. Sam raised a hand, a six-inch nail in the palm, to be lobbed at the fence as a safety check. Before he could do so, one of the arcs on the guard trucks spluttered into life. We shrivelled back into shadow as it swung and bathed the fence in blue-white light. Not part of our plan . . . Jajo, damfool, was supposed to ensure that the junction cables were disconnected. One obviously wasn't.

I hurried away to the open culvert where the cables lay. The path took me between storage tanks. Coming round one, I saw the reason why. A guard, on patrol, had spotted the break. He had reconnected one, was bending over the other. Four feet from him, in the shadow of a gantry, the knife left my hand. It welted into his kidneys. He pitched forward, made a different connection in a blue flash. Then he hurtled backwards in my direction, flung by the shock.

A shout and clatter on the catwalk above. A second guard swung out and slithered the steel ladder. The nearest weapon to hand was a two-foot length of iron pipe, jagged at one end. I swung it as he touched ground and turned. Meant for his face, he was an extra-tall bastard, and he took it in the chest. He gasped as the rib-cage stove in, went down, mouth wide open in silent alarm. I swung again as he began to cough

161

blood and vomit. A more accurate second swing, and definitive. It ripped open the throat.

I turned to the first guard. Unconscious, but still breathing. I hooked out the knife, sliced the jugular, came up on a new sound. But it was Jajo this time, looking bewildered. I gestured at the cable junction.

He snapped the connection. The arc died. Darkness along the fence once more. He helped me slide one body out of sight, hesitated over the second.

'Weiss,' he muttered. 'He'll be back any minute.'

The guard's Schmeisser lay near his feet, but I wasn't sure Jajo knew single shots from a burst. Now wasn't the time to teach him. I dug deep down my trouser leg, ripped the tape, came out with the Luger; flicked off the safety catch, passed it to him. 'Point at his belly and squeeze. And on anyone else who doesn't jump when you say so.'

He grinned, nodded. I tapped my watch. 'Give us a few extra minutes for the time lost.' I caught the second guard by the jackboots, dragged him away, lowered him behind a lubrication drum. I paused, listened. No alarm, no panic. I collected up the two machine-pistols, headed back to Sam and Níc.

They entered the Ark two by two . . . Maurice and Felix; Philippe and Bernard; Le Claque and Raoul. Aristide came solo with a rucksack containing the two tommy-guns. Sam and Níc rolled the wire back into place, hooked it together, closing the gap. 'Only if you have to,' I whispered, handing the machine-pistols to Felix and Níc. 'That goes for you, too.' The second warning to Aristide and Raoul, now armed like Mafia henchmen.

'Yours, I think,' murmured Maurice. He handed me a haversack.

I nodded. 'Stick to the plan and we're out in one piece. Or should be. *Merde,* anyway,' I added, using the word in terms of good luck.

'*Merde,*' came back from nine throats.

162

We slid our different ways into the night.

Maurice, Philippe, and Felix were to deal with the storage tanks and water hydrants. Sam, Le Claque, and Aristide were handling the more complex polymerization and alkylation units. Níc and Bernard would set the long-delay charges in the admin block and laboratories, the latter reduced to a skeleton staff at night and, at this hour, at their meal break. Then they were to move on, help Jajo wreck the power-house. For Raoul and myself it was the wax extraction and cleaosol sections. With all charges prepared beforehand it was a simple matter of application, setting and activating to a correct sequence, and beating an orderly retreat. Two-fifteen was the deadline for moving out of the refinery and on to Stage Two. Anything undone must be left undone, for at two-ten Raoul and I were to create instant chaos and draw off the guards.

Twelve-forty-four. The lights were back, but emergency power only, a sharp reduction all round. Jajo had taken over the powerhouse – whether at pistol-point or not was unimportant – and he had restored light to the arcs to allay suspicion. A key measure. So long as the enemy had light, the better our chance of keeping them in the dark.

Raoul and I finished our first tasks with a minute to spare. I counted on the fingers of one hand the times we had to freeze deep in shadow – two guards going off duty, two coming on. With Raoul scattering gravel for boots to crunch we had ample warning. The other occasions the clack of French tongues reached us long before their owners.

I jerked my head and we moved towards the fence. Parked inside the wire, on a length of track, were three railway coaches. They comprised the SS canteen and sleeping quarters – two Wagon-Lits couchettes and a restaurant car with its own galley. All Mod Cons for the Master Race. We wriggled underneath, slapped plastic 808 at intervals on each coach and five-minute pencils. It was feeding time for the pigs and the sty above us sounded full. Loud laughter, a group singing *Bräuslieder* filtered down to us. Grunts and snores from the sleepers. The last charge fixed, Raoul gestured upwards with the tommy-gun. I shook my head. A burst up through the floor might turn the choir into sopranos but most, with luck, would be a heavenly chorus very soon, so why waste ammunition? I gestured to him to leave.

He made a fresh sign. At the path, this time, that ran beside the coaches. Two pairs of jackboots – one arriving, one leaving. They stopped close, a match flared for cigarettes, a scrap of conversation in German . . .

'Leaving us tomorrow, *nicht, nicht whar?*'

'Ja, a leadership course at Junkerschule.'

'Then to the Lebensborn, I suppose? Playing stallion for the state, you lucky bastard!'

'Not *me* the bastard! Only the five or six I plan to make!'

A hoot of laughter at that, but no indication of the two parting. The five minutes were down to three, we could wait no longer. I slid my knife free. Raoul followed suit with Poulainette. I came upright between coaches, brushed the concertina link. Two short steps, no need to throw, my man had one foot on the mount, a broad back for the taking. He was telling some joke about a whore on his last leave. His companion was lapping it up with dirty giggles. Giggles that died in a sudden gasp as Raoul slid out and struck upwards. I plunged mine. And both fell in a heap, one across the other. No time to bundle them out of sight. We moved fast, putting obstacles between us and the coming blast.

We found cover with only seconds to spare. Then all around was bathed in yellow and red. Seven thumps in rapid succession and an eighth that was two merging together. Rain that was metal, wood, glass, china, leather, and flesh pattered in large spots. With it came screams, shouts, followed by whistles shrilling alarm and a pounding of feet. Three guards went past us, coming from the refinery gate-house. A fourth showed, hesitant at leaving his post. I tapped Raoul's gun, pointed at this fourth man. Get him. He was jinking for new cover before I could lower my hand.

164

When I did it was to the haversack Maurice had given me, to open the flap. I turned and wormed back towards the coaches. Two had been lifted sideways, one straddling the fence. All three were burning.

There were survivors, some staggering about in a daze, beating out flames. Others were being helped from the last Wagon-Lits by guards appearing from all directions.

The grenades in the haversack were phosphorus. The first caught two men making a 'chair' for an injured third, a guard with stumps for legs. All three blossomed into fire. Grenade Two took a window where faces were shrieking for help. Grenade Three found the lap of a survivor seated on the ground. He became a torch. Grenade Four flared a guard 'piggy-backing' another. He began to run in circles, his companion clinging tenaciously, fear dominating comprehension. They collided with others huddled together in shock. All went down like nine-pins, flames spilling over them.

I viewed the scene with utter dispassion. Each and every one was as much the target as the complex of pipes and machinery that made the refinery. The more the terror, the fire and confusion, here, the better the distraction, the less hindrance to our own getaway. Calculated mayhem, them or us . . . as simple, as logical as that. As I watched, a fire-tender appeared, a *hauptscharführer* clinging to it and yelling for clearance. Close behind came an ambulance. They parked only feet from my cover. Grenade Five hit the tender, flared the *hauptscharführer* from the crotch upwards. He fell away in a screaming, writhing ball. Grenade Six dropped neatly into the ambulance as men scrabbled for stretchers.

The heat grew too much for me.

I left.

THIRTY-SEVEN

No guards at the refinery gate. Only a milling throng of French workers, shouting and arguing, some with faces turned upwards at the cluster of searchlights frantically roaming the sky. I caught snatches of words as I threaded past them . . .

'an air-raid—'

'how can it be, no planes, listen—'

'sneak-raiders, low flying—'

'Americans, they've developed a silent engine—'

'bombed rail-yards at Rouen—'

'broad daylight, yesterday—'

'out of the blue, no warning—'

'idiot talk, trying to scare the wits out of us—'

'they did Abbeville on Friday, I tell you—'

'old wives' tales, nonsense—'

'you'll see, they'll come skimming over the slap heaps—'

'stay around if you want, don't expect me at the funeral—'

At such a time, trust Frenchmen to hold a meeting and argue the toss. My watch read two-twenty-five. Any second now there would be a mad panic and a rush . . .

No time to finish the thought. One almighty flash and the first storage tank was attempting to outclimb the searchlights. The others followed swiftly, then the furthermost sections of the refinery. A klaxon sounded off somewhere, the two guard trucks in the sidings switched their arcs upwards. One gun started pumping tracer into the sky, convinced, too, that it was a sneak-raider. The other followed as the solvent wax unit rose in the air and started to pelt flaming great gobs of wax and jagged slivers of metal.

I was well away by then, skirting the first of the slag-heaps. Behind me the last waverers were high-tailing it for safety, seeking cover. Above me, a conveyor-belt rattled on, still tipping shale to the bitter end.

The first person I saw as I approached the pit-head was Raoul, face wreathed in a broad grin as he flapped a hand in the direction of the refinery.

'Forget it,' I mouthed. 'What about the mine?'

'Charges fixed and ready to blow.'

'The workers?' I said, pressing on.

'Maurice has it in hand. The shaft-winder at the end of

a pistol, eager to please. One lot up already. Christ, have you seen—'

'Opposition?' I cut in.

'Six rounded up and disarmed, you'll see—'

I saw. Lined up against a wall, part of an outbuilding at the rear of the pit-head. Hands high, legs apart, backs showing, guarded by Aristide and Felix. I went close, barked a command.

'Umdrehen sich!'

They turned about and I took a good look. Their insignia and collar patches told me all I needed to know. Of all the stinking brew that was the Third Reich, the scum that floated on the surface was the *Totenkopf* – the Death's Head SS – the concentration camp bully-boys. I stopped in front of one of them. He wore the rank of *scharführer* – sergeant. Six feet tall, about my age, his face was pale, the mouth working, hate overcoming discretion. He spat at me. *'Crapule,'* he sneered. *'Crapule, crapule.'*

'An interesting command of French,' I answered, in German.*'Mazltov. Tsurfridn aykh tsu kenen.* That's Yiddish for "congratulations, glad to meet you".'

The eyes dilated, the mouth worked for a second spit. Then stopped as I relieved Raoul of his tommy-gun. 'My very first *Totenkopf,'* I went on. 'Let's have a Heil Hitler as only you can. Schnell!'

His heels came together, he flung out his right arm. I flung out mine, ram-rodding the gun, smashing him hard in the balls. He went down clutching himself, sobbing with pain. I wiped the spittle from my face, looked along the line. 'Any more heroes?'

Not a spit. Nor a sneer. Five very nervous, very frightened men.

Philippe appeared at my elbow. 'The last batch up . . . *mon Dieu,* like men from the grave!' The pistol in his hand was trembling, his face tight with rage.

'I know what's in your mind, Philippe. But there's a more fitting solution.' I gestured at the others, handed Raoul his

167

gun. 'Bring them around but *this* one crawls on hands and knees!'

I kicked the *scharführer* in the mouth.

They came to the waiting cage, sullen, scared, unbelieving. In the dim light from a single bulb the faces were greyish-yellow. Like their sergeant, they were all in their early twenties, von Shirach's protegés who had graduated to higher things. This wasn't the way the Führer had told them they would die for Germany. Lower lips quivered, piss-stains appeared, shorn of tunics and helmets all military posture was gone.

'Christ, but you can't,' muttered Felix, as the truth dawned on him.

'Christ, but I can and will!'

I snatched his machine-pistol, herded them into the cage, sprawled the crawling *scharführer* amongst them with a second kick. The gate clanged shut. I pressed the bell to send them downwards. I flung aside the machine-pistol, dipped into the haversack.

'Roast in fucking hell!'

Two grenades went down the shaft after them.

THIRTY-EIGHT

2.55 am. In twenty minutes, the pit-head and its workings would blow, all that remained was to get away. Not as simple as it sounds. Two hundred metres away, at the main gate, were the *Feldgendarmerie* reinforced, it seemed, to at least a score of men, plus the tower with its mounted Spandau. It was also apparent that the order prevailing was *Ausgang Verboten* . . . No Exit. The French workers who had streamed to the gate had been turned back by a volley over their heads. It remained to be seen if the rule applied to the Totenkopf slave-trucks.

Sam was raising the tail-board of one of these. Beyond it,

168

I got a glimpse of gaunt, oil-smeared faces, packed cheek by jowl, eyes glazed with bewilderment and fear.

He glanced at me, creased his mouth in a thin, bitter smile. 'A few sharp words in German and they scrambled like sheep.'

'Who drives?' I asked.

'I do,' said a voice. La Mouche appeared out of the shadows. She wore one of the tunics taken from the six Totenkopt. Underneath a pair of man's overalls. A steel helmet was in her hand.

'And I the other,' Max, this time, dressed in similar gear. He grinned at my surprise. 'You didn't expect us to wait outside nibbling our fingernails?'

It was no time to ask how they had got there. One could presume he had forged passes similar to mine. I acknowledged the *fait accompli* with a nod, waved them back to the driving-cabs. I now checked our team. All present except Níc and Jajo. Bernard gave the answer. 'They stayed behind, unfinished business.'

'Me, too,' said Sam.

'But—'

'You fight your war, we Poles fight ours.' He took the sting from the remark by gripping my arm, squeezing the muscle, then patting me on the cheek. '*Bardzo Panu dziekuje*, Patrice. Tonight you give us hope and honour again. For that we salute you.' He stepped back, brought up his hand. Then turned away towards the inferno beyond the slag-heaps.

What further he hoped to achieve at Paix I had no idea. But I knew better than argue with a Pole who had made up his mind. '*Uwaga!*' I called after him, an expression he had used often at me. Take care. A singularly inane remark under the circumstances.

3 am. Maurice looked strange in SS tunic and helmet. He was to ride shot-gun next to Max in the second truck. Philippe and Bernard were dressed the same, complete with machine-pistols, acting as 'guards' at the rear of the first,

169

along with the workers. Part of the bluff we hoped to pull, to get through the main gate without a fight. I had been relying on Sam's fluency in German to help in case of verbal argument. Now it would have to be mine alone. I shrugged on the sixth tunic – the *Scharführer's* – with distaste, and climbed in beside La Mouche.

'Roll,' I muttered, donning the helmet, 'Slow and steady. Foot down hard only if and when I say.'

She eased the truck away from the cluster of buildings that screened us from the gate. The wheels began to grit on loose shale. I checked my machine-pistol. Catch off, set to fire a burst. A final phosphorus grenade lay on the seat beside me. We bounced off the rough ground on to the road. I surveyed ahead.

One hundred and fifty metres to the gate. An arc of light sprayed down from the platform tower illuminating the area immediately before it, revealing the *Feldgendarmerie*. Two files, strung in line, shoulder to shoulder, uniform stance, like toy soldiers in a box. Charge them suddenly, fast, and they would scatter, we would be through. But the danger was that Spandau in the tower. The light would blind La Mouche, the gun would stitch both trucks from stem to stern. I saw little sign of civilian workers. Discretion had become the better part of valour, they had probably gone to cover in the air-raid bunkers provided.

One hundred metres to go. Bells clanging strident beyond the gate. A gap opened up in the two files as tenders raced through. A quick gesture at La Mouche. She pulled over to let them pass. *Feuerwehrmacht,* the elite of Nazis fire-troops. Nothing but the best for our bonfire. I eyed the wing-mirror as they sped past. They had to pass close to the pit-head. A quick glance at my watch. Still a pair of minutes left. Cross fingers and hope . . .

An ominous rumble. Our stationery truck slid sideways as if on shifting sand. The rumble began a roar, then the pit-head exploded. The second of the fire-tenders danced high and out of the mirror, a clockwork model thrown away by a petulant child. The first was swallowed in a heave of slag as the mine-workings caved in.

My eyes went back to the gate. The powerhouse should have gone at the same time. And with it, the arc light on the tower. But, no, that still blazed down.

La Mouche looked at me. I nodded. We would have to take the chance. The longer the delay, the greater the possibility of a mobile column arriving. And even the dim-witted *Feldgendarmerie* would get suspicious.

The hundred metres became seventy-five, then fifty, and still the light held. Forty, thirty, and there was a silhouette running towards us, arms waving. A *feldwebel*, he came around to my side, shouting. Over the thump of minor explosions, I got the gist of his words . . . orders of the *Sonderführer*, no one permitted to leave the area, not even German personnel . . .

At that moment, the arc died.

'*Now!*' I snarled at La Mouche. Her foot jabbed down, we lurched forward, gathering speed. The *feldwebel* jumped for the step, took a purchase on the door handle, came up beside me. His face was inches away, mouth open as he bellowed a halt.

There was nothing else for it. I thrust the machine-pistol into it, fed him a short burst. He dropped away, headless, six bullets exploding his skull.

The file in front of us broke formation. The one behind it began to scatter. We clipped a pair of them, flung one aside like an old sack. The other rose high, sprawled across the bonnet like a stranded starfish. I snatched up the grenade, leaned out and lobbed it high, aiming for the Spandau. It spewed flame on the platform, but not enough to stop the gun chattering. Maurice and the others in the second truck must do that now, for we were through the gate and out on the cobbled road beyond, swerving wildly from side to side. So much so, I thought for a moment that La Mouche was hit and we were out of control. She was hunched low, hands on the wheel, shouting something, nodding her head at the windscreen.

171

The stranded guard was still with us, on the bonnet, alive, and clinging desperately. She had been trying to shake him off.

'Hold it straight!' I yelled. And brought up the butt of the machine-pistol, knocked out a section of glass.

The man half-raised his head, showed an imploring eye. He was pleading in a thin screech as the gun jumped under my finger. The eye became a red mess. He slithered away to the road.

Back to the mirror. The second truck had made it and was tight on our tail. Beyond it I got a glimpse of the burning tower beginning to tilt crazily. Some sporadic firing from the road, but the Spandau was silent. Then La Mouche was swinging the wheel again, throwing us around a corner.

A long, dark road ahead. But no enemy. I knocked away the rest of the windscreen. A clear field of fire, just to be on the safe side.

She changed direction several times. Buildings gave way to trees. I threw her a glance. She responded with a quick smile.

'Clear now.'

'You reckon?'

'Certain as can be . . . cigarette?'

'Haven't any . . . sorry.' Situation normal with me.

'In my pocket. Lighter, too.' She lowered her chin at her right breast, kept her hands on the wheel.

I fumbled gently, found both. Lit two, gave her one. 'Thanks,' I said. 'For a lot of things. You were a bloody marvel.'

'You were not so sure before we left,' she murmured.

'Peeved a little at the trick being pulled behind my back. Am I so difficult I couldn't be told?'

'Max and I suspected the Poles wouldn't leave. It was never on once you decided on Stage Three. They were determined that the follow-up should not be a failure.'

I could understand that. Sam, I knew, had been dubious about the efficacy of the long-delay fuses. I had had doubts myself. But one had to gamble somewhere along the line.

If he, Níc, and Jajo were that insistent on being in at the kill, it could include themselves. A tenacity that bordered on lunacy. 'Their skins!' I muttered. 'But I had been relying on them to get these camp workers away.'

'Did they say they would?'

'No . . . not a promise, if that's what you mean. Sam, in fact, saw it as a waste of effort. On the other hand, come the crunch, I did not see him refusing to help fellow-countrymen.'

'*These* are not,' she said. 'Nearly all are wearing "T"'s.'

'Czechs?'

An abrupt nod from La Mouche, a grimace. 'No great love between *them*, I'm afraid.'

'Aw, Jesus Christ . . .' I flicked the cigarette out of the window, pushed back the helmet. Another case of a common enemy not being enough, they had to go on fighting a private war. I had a sudden thought for the poor wretches crammed like cattle behind us. 'How soon can we halt, and where?'

'Another kilometre. A place checked out yesterday. Max suggested it.'

My face must have revealed my thoughts. Another little smile from her, rueful. 'You don't like Max . . . a pity. He thinks very highly of you.'

And elephants wear button-boots, I thought. 'What is this place?' I asked.

'A coal mine.'

I stared at her.

'A worked-out one. Flooded a long time, since before the war. Even the Boches know better than try to use it.'

'I'll take your word for it,' I sighed. 'Beggars can't be choosers. One of the drawbacks of our kind of army. When the battle is over there's no QM detail to bring up rations.' I was talking more to myself than to her. The danger past, I was suddenly both hungry and thirsty. The others must be the same. 'I have a lot to learn,' I said.

'Maybe.'

'I *know!*'

'Do you? You gave Max one hundred thousand francs ten days ago.'

'So . . .'

'Patience,' she said. And pointed a finger.

Ahead, and to the right, was the gaunt skeleton of a pit. We left the road, began to jolt along a rutted track. A gate hung askew off hinges at the end of it. A nudge from the fender pushed it wide. We went past rubble that once had been buildings into the shadow of a winding-gear house, came to a halt.

I pushed open the door, jumped down. One glance at the back of the truck and my heart sank.

The canopy had been stitched by the Spandau. The moans confirmed my fears. We had been driving a bloody abbatoir.

THIRTY-NINE

4.45 am. Wednesday, August 19, The dark hour before the dawn. And for me it had become very dark. Philippe and Bernard were dead. Le Claque, Felix, and Aristide were wounded, as well as seven of the slave workers. Another sixteen of them had merely exchanged death in one pit for burial in another. That was the sorry story of our escape. And the fault was mine. If only I had given as much thought to dealing with that bloody Spandau as I had to the rest . . . *if only*. Wise words after an event.

It could have been worse, of course. The failure could have been a complete disaster. That it wasn't was no thanks to me. Max – whose part in the operation I had dismissed with summary contempt – might yet save the day. He had looked beyond the destruction of Paix, to our immediate needs once we got away. Here, at the old mine, had been a first-aid station, a doctor, and a nurse; mattresses and blankets, bandages and sulpha powder, a means for sterilizing instruments, an acetylene lamp to operate under. The two men whom I had condemned as useless and put under 'house arrest' had prepared a hot meal for our arrival. There was fresh clothing, from berets to boots, for the survivors. A plan, too, for ferrying them north to Lille, Roubiax, Tourcoing – towns where the FTP were strong in numbers and more able to absorb and hide them from their masters. All this was salutory proof that there was more to being a partisan leader than skill in the art of killing and destruction. I was beginning to learn but, the hard way, as usual, at the expense of others . . .

The main slag-tip had bonded since the pit closure and much of the ugly, black scar was covered with coarse grass and weeds. I had climbed to the top the better to see, but mostly to be alone. Now, as I watched, the first grey fingers of light clawed up over the trees to the east. But it was to the west and north-west that the sky was most brilliant. Clusters of searchlights weaving blue-white patterns, yellow-red flares and flashes that were guns or bombs or both. Beyond them lay the coast, the Channel, possibly alive with ships and men making for the beaches. For some of them only minutes left of living. Not for them, again, the further shore, the comparative safety and freedom that was Britain. The comparative safety and freedom to be a miner in Kent, for example, and go on bloody strike in this year of grace, 1942. What was the excuse, hardship manning the pits? Drop in here, brothers, or anywhere in Europe that knows slave-labour, then you can squeal hardship, brothers . . . but until then, pardon me while I spit!

A crunch of feet brought Maurice beside me. He looked to the south, the view behind my back.

'Still burning,' he said. A reference to Paix.

I made no comment.

'Are you not interested?' He turned, looked down at me.

'That was yesterday.' I plucked at a strand of grass. 'If I remember it tomorrow it will be because of Philippe and Bernard and sixteen others who might have lived if I hadn't played God.'

He came down in a crouch, pressed my shoulder.

'If you had not played God, as you put it, a great many more Boches would still be alive, both here and in the Pas-de-Calais.'

175

'So . . .?'

'So stop feeling sorry for yourself, my Patrice. Go on the way you've begun. That way your own dead will have not died in vain.'

'Tell that to their families,' I muttered.

'I shall have to, non? Two of them, anyway.'

I had no answer to that.

'Give me a cigarette,' I said.

He did so, lit it. Then rose to his feet. I did the same. We walked down the slope to rejoin the others.

FORTY

We travelled westwards, seven of us. Max at the wheel, myself at his side. Maurice, Raoul, and the three wounded partisans in the rear. Our aim was Arras, a distance of forty kilometres, by six am. One hour of bluff we had considered worth the risk. Unless we were much mistaken, the enemy would have more urgent problems than a hue and cry for a missing SS truck.

A fact that was, ironically, our very undoing . . .

The route took us across the main Lille-Amiens road. But access, we soon discovered, was blocked. A scout car parked squarely in our path, a red torch being wagged in our direction. Beyond it, streaming south-west, was a convoy of half-tracks, guns, and motorized infantry.

'Back up,' I muttered to Max. 'Find another way.'

The only way was south. Max tried two more approaches with the same result. The convoy held the crown of the main road, the only traffic in the reverse lane were outriders and controllers. Our distance was beginning to stretch and the fuel gauge was hovering low. 'The reserve tank?' he queried.

Max pulled a face. 'We're on it!'

'So much for Boche efficiency.'

'So much for their supplies. If you must go around destroying their resources, make sure we fill up first.'

'It has to be the next crossing, shit or bust.'

The fourth approach was narrow with a scum-green dike on the right-hand side. At the end of it a solo motor-cycle, engine running. The man in the saddle turned his head, looked at us, then brought the machine round, rode towards us. Max swung the truck to the left, keeping tight to the grass verge. The motor-cycle had to swerve, come up to my side.

'Halt!'

Max braked, slid the gear into neutral, let the engine idle. We were sixty metres from the main road, with a screen of trees along the far bank of the dike. The mirror told me it was just us and the motor-cycle in the approach.

A *feldgendarme*, rank of corporal, he remained astride his machine, feet planted on the ground. Authority was stamped in his upward glare. 'No way through!' he bellowed, in German. 'Can't you see the convoy?'

'*Ja ... Wehrmacht, nicht wahr?*'

'What else, blockhead!'

I leaned close to the door. He could now see the SS insignia and rank. 'Repeat that!'

A quick change of tune. 'Sorry, sergeant. But I have my orders. The main road must be kept clear.'

'*My* orders are to cross it! Your manoeuvres can wait!'

'No manoeuvres, sergeant. There has been a landing!'

'So ... where?'

'Dieppe!'

'Dieppe, hein?' I made a sign with the left hand at Max. Then brought it higher for the corporal's benefit. 'And you need all those to throw them back into the sea? Work for two SS men and a dog!'

We were moving on the last words. The corporal brought the bike around hurriedly. Max swung over again to the right. The bike tried to squeeze between us and the dike. Almost, but not quite. The truck clipped his rear wheel, spun him sideways. He let the machine go, jumped clear, moving backwards, hand going for his pistol.

Silly sod. The knife thumped into his chest. His movement

177

became a stagger, a splash as he hit the water, the green tinged red. We crunched over the front wheel of the bike, headed for the main road.

Max took the truck out, horn blasting, determined to force a gap. A question of nerve, who gave way first . . . us or a half-track. The half-track braked, slewing sideways in a screech of sparks, tangling with one of a pair of outriders who had opened their throttles at the sight of us.

We had our gap and we were across into the lane opposite. A glance in the mirror showed the second outrider swinging in behind us. Yet another silly sod, keen to die for Hitler.

Maurice or Raoul granted him his wish. A Mills grenade lobbed out and bike and man disappeared in a sudden spread of black smoke and metal fragments. A moment later we were curving a corner, rocking as we went.

'Dieppe,' muttered Max. 'So that's where it is.' He sounded disconsolate.

'It can stay there . . . Arras,' I reminded him. 'How far?' The fuel gauge had dropped to zero.

'All of twenty.' He, too, looked down at the gauge, shook his head.

'I doubt if others will break convoy to chase us. But ditch at the first likely cover. If we can hide the truck, so much the better.'

I scanned ahead. The road was straightening out, running north. To the right of us, flat, open fields, all the way to the main road we had just crossed. To the left, more fields, then the rise of a railway embankment, converging gradually to keep line with us. In the far distance, a slow-moving goods-train heading in our direction. But no cover worthy of the name anywhere.

The engine coughed, cut, coughed again, then soared into life once more. Max grinned his relief. 'Life in her yet.'

A grin I didn't share. A premonition hit me. It had to do with the goods-train and the half-track we had stopped at the crossroads. A gun. A 20 mm Oerliken, the kind that had

178

fired tracer skywards from the sidings at Paix, suspecting a sneak low-level raider . . .

'Kill it!' I screamed. 'Out! Fast!'

I thumped the back of the cab three times, a signal to the others.

Max looked at me. 'But you said—'

'Don't argue, for Christ's sake—'

Even as I spoke, the whine came, increasing in tempo and sound. The train was closer, the gun in the foremost wagon swinging, holding, beginning to fire. Not at us. At something behind and above. Something that spat cannon-shells back and went past with a roar and a rush of wind . . . a Spitfire.

Max slammed his brakes, held the truck in a controlled slide. I kicked open my door, jumped. I hit the road, feet, knees, hands high to protect the face rolling clear. The rear of the truck slid past wheels locked, a glimpse of Maurice and Raoul hanging on to the tailboard. I came up, moved to them as they let it fall. One each to a wounded man, we got them out and into the ditch, treading ooze and water, putting distance between us and the truck, as the Spitfire rose, banked, turned, and swooped down for a second run.

Wagons became matchwood, began to burn. The engine rose up on its nose, turned turtle, spilled down the embankment in a shriek of escaping steam. The plane climbed once more in a flash of wings, came in for a third attack. With a menacing shift of direction.

We all flopped low in the ooze, scrunching tight to the bank of the ditch. Cannon-shells hammered the road above us, lifted it, threw it aside, rained debris upon us. Then it punched our truck into a great surge of flame . . .

. . . the Spitfire was gone. Seven heads rose warily, seven bodies turned and floundered up the far bank, away from the heat, the acrid stench of burning rubber. Max gazed back at it, bewildered.

'How could it go like that . . . without gasoline?'

'*Without?*' said Maurice. 'There were six full jerrycans in the back . . .'

My jaw dropped. 'Oh, *no* . . .' I began to giggle.

179

Max turned to me. 'And the attack . . . you knew before . . . how did you . . .?'

My laughter died. I shook my head slowly, shrugged. How does one explain away a cold finger on the spine, a silent whisper in the mind? When it happens, one should obey and be grateful.

I removed the SS steel helmet, tossed it into the ditch. 'We have a bonfire,' I said. 'Let's be rid of our fancy clothes before someone else gets the wrong idea.' I began to unbutton the tunic.

FORTY-ONE

The Dieppe raid has been referred to as a classic operation of war – a polite term for an utter balls-up. At best, it could be called a gallant failure; at worst, a bloody disaster, involving as it did two brigades of infantry and a tank battalion largely comprised of untried Canadians, but spearheaded by three of the best British Commandos, a detachement of US Rangers, and assault units of the Royal Navy. What purpose it served only Christ knew and the planners might learn from hindsight. That it was political, there can be no shadow of doubt. It was, in effect, a blood sacrifice to the Little Father, Iosif Dzhugashvili – better know as Stalin – who had been muttering in his moustache about action in the west. If Whitehall and Washington fondly hoped it might inspire the comrades, then tough titty, Moscow was most reticent to give the raid a mention. Then, as forever before and after, it was the Red Army alone who fought whilst the capitalist-imperialists sat on their fat arses like Nero doing his Sunday thing at the Colosseum. A point one can imagine, that all those who died on and around the beaches that Wednesday morning would have appreciated.

For myself – who could only hazard a vague guess as to what was happening at the time – Dieppe was to play a crucial part in my eventual destiny. A tarot card dealt in the game of chance that is living or dying.

We reached Arras during the afternoon, keeping to the fields for most of the way, moving as fast as the slowest amongst us – Le Claque. All three of our injured were able to walk, but the frantic exodus from the SS truck had re-opened the wound in Le Claque's side and he had lost more blood. We eventually parted company on the outskirts of the town, Maurice and his FTP members to return to Aire.

A separation not without emotion. That we would meet again was a remote possibility and both parties knew it. I embraced Aristide, Raoul, Le Claque, in turn. I knew that wherever the war might take me I would count myself a fortunate man if I found others of their calibre. As for Maurice, it was a bear hug, a rough kiss, and a simple 'Bonne chance, mon Patrice.' Then a husky chuckle, a finger laid along the nose to hide a glisten of tears. 'Or should I say *"buona fortuna, pis-pis"?'*

'In Poland we say *pánskie zdrowie,*' I answered. Another expression of Sam's which I suspected meant much the same thing.

The reply threw Maurice for a moment. Then the chuckle became a belly laugh, the hug a slap on the shoulder. 'You'll do!' And we were back full circle, our first meeting in the Renault by the canal. How long was it . . . less than eight weeks? It did not seen possible . . .

'*De toi á moi,*' I whispered. And turned away quickly, to follow after Felix and Max.

Arras was a constant rumble of *Wehrmacht* vehicles over the cobbles, moving through towards the coast. As I entered the Rue St Auber I had a feeling in my bones. What I was here for wasn't on. There could be no Lysander pick-up this full moon, not *here*, with the enemy all around in such strength. Whatever London may have decided, DF *Mussel* – my escape route – wouldn't want to know. And I, for one, wouldn't blame them.

Yet I had to go through the motions. Motions, on the face of it, utterly ludicrous for a sweaty, unshaven male. I could think of more self-effacing procedures than entering a corset shop and buying a female 'all-in-one'. Then I remembered it should have been Solange doing this instead of me . . .

The counter assistant who came to me was in her thirties, cool, poised, expressionless under her pencilled eyebrows. My mumbled request might have been for a bag of nails for all the reaction it received.

'What size, m'sieu?'

'Size?'

'Yes, m'sieu. You must know madame's size, non?'

I didn't know madame's size, non. I vaguely remembered Solange saying something, but she had been in her own underwear at the time and I hadn't been paying much attention to her words. She had joked about it being a garment for a very large lady . . . what the hell was *OS* in French?

'Enorme,' I muttered.

That brought the pencilled eyebrows into half-moons. 'Enorme is a matter of opinion, m'sieu. Not measurement.' The words were tart with it, conscious, maybe, of her own rather ample endowments.

'I – er – let's start with the biggest you've got and work down,' I said, playing for time. Playing with fire, too. The eyebrows came into a straight line, she had found a *double entendre* where one wasn't intended. I was plainly a *voyeur*, I would be inviting her into the fitting room next to try it on and not merely the corset . . .

She sidled away to another assistant. An older woman and severe of face. This one eyed me with a frown, dismissed the younger one. She picked a book from the shelf beside her, came over.

'The garment is for someone in particular, m'sieu?'

Icy polite, but much better. It was the question I should have been asked in the first place.

'*Mais, oui* . . . Madame Anguille,' I said, quietly.

She opened the book. 'Madame Henrietta Anguille?'

Catch question. I shook my head. 'Marie Anguille . . . d'Hénin.'

'D'Hénin Liétard?' Still studying the book.

'D'Hénin-sur-Cojeul.'

'When did she order it?'

'At the end of July. The thirty-first, I believe.'

The book snapped shut.

'*C'est ça. Cent-vingt-cinq, n'est-ce-pas?*'

One hundred and twenty-five? What was this mythical Marie Anguille – a barrage balloon? Stupid of me, of course, she was talking in centimetres, not inches. It still made her a barrage balloon.

'Exactly,' I said. 'Enorme.'

'Comfortable is the word, m'sieu.' The severity relaxed a fraction. 'But I very sorry to disappoint Madame. But we are out of stock for the time being.'

'I understand. Too many Germans in the market. A popular size for their women, I'm sure.'

A ghost of a smile. 'M'sieu – and Madame – might do better to try Paris. They have a wider range.'

'You can suggest somewhere in particular?'

'Maïson Blanche, perhaps. I'm sure Madame Anguille knows of them. If you have no luck, you could try here again in, say, a month's time. Things might be different then . . .' The smile was there, now, sympathetic. 'Bonne chance, m'sieu.'

'*J'y suis de moitié avec vous,*' I said, and left the shop.

Felix and Max both were in the station cafe. Felix's wound was upper left arm, but not serious. It had stiffened up during the day and he wore it Napoleon-style. A tough old bird, he was fit enough to travel the long trip to Epernay. But I sensed he was glad of my promised company as far as Paris. He rose and went to the counter to get me a coffee.

I glanced at Max, wondering where to begin.

He did it for me. 'I'll travel with you both . . . if you don't object,' he added.

183

'Why should I?'

He grinned. Friendly, not his usual sour curl of the lip. 'Well, we haven't exactly been two tits in a vest, have we?'

'I don't know. We bounced one another enough.'

'You know what I mean.'

'I know I owe you an apology,' I said. 'I under-rated you badly.'

'And I thought you – or your reputation – had been over-rated. Before Paix, that is.'

'So we both know differently.' I offered him my hand. We shook. 'What about Douai?' I asked.

He shrugged. 'It'll get along without me. I would have left before but for you coming. A job in Paris, working on an underground newspaper. The chance I've been waiting for. The pen rather than the sword. I know my limitations.' He stretched out his club foot instinctively. 'And having see you work has made me that much more aware of them. No sour grapes, you understand?'

I understood. I could also have argued with him about his potential with the FTP. I chose not to. I accepted his reasoning along with one of his cigarettes.

'What about La Mouche?' I asked, lighting up.

'Don't worry about her. By the time she has finished mothering all those Czechs . . .' He left it at that, with a sly chuckle. Then, very quiet: 'This girl of yours . . . is she really Jewish?'

'She says. Not a thing one shouts about these days.'

'Get her out of it, Patrice. Get her out and keep her out . . . for the baby's sake.'

The cigarette fell from my lip to the floor. I stared at him.

'Oh, Christ,' he said. 'You didn't know?' He buried his face in his hands, mumbled on. 'I thought you must . . . I mean, I knew she sent you a second letter, privé, I thought that must be it.'

I took a deep, deep breath 'How . . . do . . . *you* . . . know . . .?' I said very slowly.

He lowered his hands. The eyes held a look of infinite misery.

My teeth grated in a snarl. 'How do you *bloody* know?'
The answer, a whisper. 'La Mouche . . . how else?'
'And *she?*'
'In Paris.'
'*How* . . . not where.'
'She's not just a woman, she's a trained midwife. She saw the signs.'
'What signs?'
'The . . . usual. You know. Morning sickness.'
'That's proof?'
'I don't know.' He shook his head. 'But it confirmed what your girl already believed. She begged La Mouche not to tell you, intimated she was doing so herself . . . in the letter . . .'
My mind had already reached back for that. No hint. Nothing. And there wouldn't have been, not then before Paix, not now whilst we remained in France, not even afterwards, possibly. But they were not to know that.
'Jesus Christ, my shitting big mouth . . .' tumbled from Max, then tailed into silence.
Felix was back at the table with the coffee and a *marc*. I felt his eyes on me as he pushed the glass forward. 'You look as if you need that,' he said. 'Is something wrong?'
Something wrong? I picked up the *marc*, hand unsure, spilling some over my fingers. Something wrong? The spirit caught my breath, almost made me retch. Something wrong?
Solange, Solange, *mon ange*, what have we done?

FORTY-TWO

The Paris train was interminably slow. One glance out of the window and the reason was manifest. For mile upon mile it was a procession of burnt-out wagons, shattered engines, torn-up sections of track. At Amiens, the yards were still smouldering, a ruin of rubble, a tangle of metal; a world of mooncraters and gangs of men harvesting with crowbar and shovel, the sterile thanksgiving of a bomber raid. Such destruction to

185

a man trained to destroy should have given much satisfaction. In truth, it didn't. I found it all too impersonal. One day, I could imagine, they would dispense entirely with the human element and fly the machines push-button, robots from the sky, the ultimate in civilized savagery. Its very indiscrimination made it so for me. War has a certain morality, a code of justice, so long as it is kept on a personal level. And whatever I may have said to the contrary to Maurice on Bastille Day, this affair was very personal. It had started for me the night I had killed Willi Eigenbrodt in Heidelberg. It could only finish in one of two ways – with my own death or the final retribution on all the Eigenbrodts of this world.

A naive dream, perhaps, but without it there was no driving force that could have impelled me to fight. I was not in it for king or country or the advancement of generals. In that respect I would never make a soldier, even less a good officer. I wouldn't have lasted five minutes with any regiment of the line where blind obedience is demanded, regardless of whether the orders are stupid and suicidal. I was still too much of an individual, too cocky, too intolerant of seniors who held rank merely by length of service. Once, already, I had avoided a courts-martial by the skin of my teeth. At Omagh, on receipt of a particularly outrageous order, I had told a certain Major Bint to 'get stuffed.' He had coloured to a puce of apoplexy, repeated it twice more in front of a mess full of officers. I had repeated my answer. And the drink in my hand would have gone into his face, glass and all, but for the restraining influence of Jack Allen. The next day, Jack had managed to soft-talk Bint into dropping the charge. How he succeeded I never knew because I was posted away that same week. With Jack Allens in short supply in the British Army, it was as well for me that there were such organisations as SIS and SOE. A great many of us were, I am certain, square pegs unable to adjust to round holes. And – with some arrogance – none the worse for being so.

The train clattered on, a snail-crawl into the dusk. Shapes beyond the window blurred into a merciful smudge. I was bug-eyed with need for sleep, yet could only doze fitfully. I had been trying hard to put out of my mind what Max had said at Arras, but to no use, it kept coming back . . . clacking with the train . . . could it be true? Could it be true? It had not been said for the sake of the saying, it was a possibility I had to face, cling as I might to Solange's words that first night in the barn. When the ecstasy was over, the body supine, a worm of conscience had surfaced. 'Don't fret, chéri, I wanted you as much as you wanted me. And *please* don't worry about the other thing, this Keziah is another Hannah whose womb was shut by the Lord. I couldn't have a child if I asked you for one . . .'

Words said to ease my mind, to overcome my doubts . . . or out of bitterness of belief because she had failed to perpetuate her lost husband? Either way, it was a question never raised again. I had accepted it because I wanted to, I suppose, and our love-making had been idyllic and without tension, the perfect antidote to the work we were engaged upon. Only now, much too late, I remembered that the Lord of Israel had relented towards the other Hannah and she had become pregnant. And the ego within me felt I had the right to know, to be party to any decision about the future. I was too confused to be sure whether I was pleased or sorry, whether it would be a disappointment or a relief if it wasn't true. So much depended on Solange's own attitude. How she thought dominated my thoughts, I wouldn't rest until I knew . . . oh, come on, train, come on, how much longer, for Chrissake . . .

We emerged from the Gare du Nord with less than a half-hour to curfew. My goodbye to Felix was brief, bordering upon rudeness. How much he knew or guessed I had no idea, but he smiled understanding, wished me well, there was a bed at Epernay anytime I needed it, not to forget. Then he was gone in a *vélo*-taxi.

Max and I made for the Metro, breaking all the rules in doing so, it was a leprosy of SD agents and V-men. Logically, the safest place to pass the night was in a *maison de passe,*

one of those near-to-brothel hotels where registration was not
demanded. So numerous were they, so frequent the comings
and goings, not even the Gestapo got around to more than a
desultory checking.

But there was no logic in my mood. It was Maison Blanche
or nowhere. With five minutes to spare we found the house,
rang the bell.

A shuffle in the passage, the grating of bolts, the slide of
a chain, and the door opened a fraction. I got a part-view of
a heavy woman in a dressing-gown, curlers under a hair-net,
a handkerchief held at her nose. She appeared to be suffering
from a cold. Her French was hoarse and thick.

'What do you want?'

'*Tante* Blanche?'

A long moment of hesitation. Then: 'Oui. And you are—?'

'Edouard and Max.'

'Should I know you? I don't think so –' She made to shut
the door.

I got a foot in the gap, held it. 'Friends of Marie Anguille.
The corset queen. We left a plate of mussels just to come
here.'

'You should have telephoned first –'

'I know, madame. But it is close to curfew. There wasn't
time.'

She thought about it, then sniffed. 'Very well, then . . .'

I withdrew my foot. She withdrew the chain. The door
opened a few centimetres wider. We were in, and the first
thing I noticed was the gun in her free hand. An Italian
Beretta.

I pushed it aside gently. 'Thank you, madame, but you
won't need that, we're not armed.' And watched it disappear
into the dressing-gown pocket. 'M'slle Perrin?'

'Solange Perrin?'

I nodded. She waved the handkerchief at the stairs. 'Second
flight, the left door on the landing –'

I was climbing before she finished. I found the room,
paused at the door, trembling. I gave it a little tap.

'*Entrez.*' The voice was quiet, muffled.

The door opened at my touch. She was there, across the room, at the wash-basin, stripped to the waist, her blonde hair up in a turban of a towel. A sight for any man's eyes . . .

Except mine.

She wasn't Solange.

Neither were the two men with Lugers who kicked the door shut behind my back.

FORTY-THREE

Hands caught my arms, wrenched them high up my back, forcing the head forward and down. The girl turned with a laugh, came towards me, breasts flaunting. She cupped one with her left hand, thrust it in my face. 'Suck that,' she said, in German. 'Richer milk than you'll ever get from your Jewish whore!'

If I was living dangerously, so was she, the bitch. Another inch and my teeth would have torn the nipple away. As it was, I spat on it.

The sneer died, the breast fell, the fingers were coming, at my eyes. I got my head sideways in time and the nails raked bloody tramlines from cheek to jaw. Then the punching began, swinging in from either side – mouth, chest, belly, groin. I hit the floor, twisting in pain, got a bug's eye-view of the door swinging open, the landing outside. Then I was out there, the boots taking over from the fists, going backwards down the stairs. A kick in the mouth snapped a tooth, I gagged as it lodged in the back of the throat. I got up a hand, but it was knocked away and stamped upon. Alien hands prised the jaws wide, alien fingers jabbed inside, to make me vomit. With it came the broken tooth – not the poison pill they had suspected. A boot in the kidneys showed their indignation. Another in the ear had me looping the second flight all the way to the hall below. Now the hair was caught, jerked at the roots, face turned upwards. The woman in the dressing-gown, no *Tante* Blanche with a cold, her voice thick with the accent of Alsace. 'Filthy, stinking swine!' She spat in my face, went on repeating *'Crappule, schmutzig, crappule, schmutzig!'* over and over again, saliva dribbling down her chin, eyes hard marbles of hate.

Then it was the men once more, trampling, kicking, yanking me upright, slamming me from wall to wall, along the passage, out into the street, impaling me on the sharp edge of a Citroën door, before bundling me in the back, clambering in around me, and driving away. But no respite, the fists kept coming incessantly, senselessly. Senselessly from their stand-point for after the first impact of pain back at the house, the nerves were dulling to a numbness. I was a punch-drunk boxer now, rising at the bell, going on without knowing why . . .

Then we were there . . . wherever *there* was . . . out of the Citroën in a fresh flurry of blows, half-carried, half-dragged, across a hallway and into a lift. Narrow, more confined even than the car, but it still went on, kicking, kneeing, thumping. One, two, three floors, was it? I couldn't be sure, but too high, I thought, to make a jump for it if I got near a window. No percentage in breaking your neck just to stop these buggers' fun. And beating, beating in the back of my brain, one thing, one thing only. They had my girl, they had the child within her; if any harm had come to either of them then, by Christ, I *mustn't* die, I had too much to live for. The very personal war to date would become a private vengeance. And the *if* didn't come into it, they will have hurt her, they know she's Jewish, the cow with the tits said so, so what are you waiting for, you may not get another chance.

My hands had been forced up to stop me shielding my crotch. One covered my face. Through spread fingers I saw the eyes of one of my escorts. China-blue and cold, the acme of Germanic perfection. Concentrate, *concentrate*, remember the STS training, the speciality of the house, a score of eight out of ten on the dummy, can you do it for real?

As the lift juddered to a halt, China-Blue-Eyes brought up his knee for the umpteenth time, searching for the groin. I swayed back, letting out the moan he was after, but riding it instinctively to take in its turn the other one's knee in the base of the spine. Then I lurched forward, turning my hand from my face, thumb hooking, the fingers flicking. And the right china-blue splashed to a crimson, the eyeball was out on his cheek, a pulpy mess, he was screaming high and thin, trying to fumble it back into place, but he needn't bother, he wouldn't be using it again, not with the pupil ripped, the retina, choroid, and cornea caught on my clawed fingers.

I smeared them across the lift-gate as I was propelled out, spun away to a door, and booted into a room by the second man. He was in screaming hysterics like the one in the lift. 'This dirty bastard has just injured Kurt! Do for him! Do for him!'

How many did for me I cannot say. My own eyes were puffing into slits, all I saw was a fuzz-whirl of faces, of hands swinging leather belts with buckles as they bounced me from one to the other in their concept of a merry-go-round. When they tired of that, they stripped and handcuffed me, starting all over again, but systematically now, from head to foot and with special attention to the genitals. I don't know how long it went on, I was way past the point of caring, it would have to stop sometime I knew, even the Master Race took time out if only to shit. With no resistance offered, no more sound coming from me – nothing to do with stiff-upper-lip, just cracked ribs and difficulty in breathing – I was fast becoming a blue-black-and-bloody sack without meaning. The kicks and thumps lost much of their vigour, the tempo flagged in a stink of sweaty endeavour. Only the yelling went on, the insistent flow of parrot imprecation, the *schweinhunds, schmutzigs, feiglinger verbrechers, jüdisches abfalls,* and the rest of the Neanderthal noises that pass for the German language . . . and, of course, the spittle, forcing my mouth open to deliver that.

Then came a new voice, one with command in it. It brought a sharp, heel-clicking silence from the ape-man. Hands lifted me, threw me into a chair. Ice-cold water splashed down from a bucket, stinging the bruises and cuts, trickling over the lips. It tasted salt, but that could have been the blood in my mouth, one wouldn't want to do them an injustice, they had behaved quite normally up until now.

'Open your eyes,' said the voice, in English.

That was a joke. I pass.

I smelled the sweat, the heavy breathing behind me, sensed the hand raised to slap, waited for it to fall. But the new voice said *'Nein,'* and went on to repeat the question in French.

I opened one eye as best I could. I saw a tall man with sharpish features. But it was the mouth that held me. It was almost feminine in its mould, with moist lips. As he bent forward I got a hint of perfume. Then he was poking at my penis with a cane, lifting it, looking at it, letting it fall. 'Not a Jew,' he said, straightening up. 'Not like the other one.'

What other one? Max, of course. I had forgotten about him. I hadn't seen him since we had entered *Tante* Blanche's. Deep down, I supposed, I had hoped he had got away, but with the big cow there with her gun and others like my two waiting in a room downstairs . . .

'Je le regrette,' I managed to say. *'Pas Juif.'*

He sat down on the edge of a desk, swung a varnished jackboot. He put aside his cane, took out a pair of nail-clippers, eyed his left hand. 'You are sorry you are not a Jew? It can be arranged if you wish.' He repeated the words in German for the benefit of the apes. I thought they would kill themselves with laughter, but the gods were not on my side. Their *Oberst* was a wit, the nail clippers gave it point. It was psychology the way he snipped a nail, an old one from the book. Warned about it during interrogation training, I knew it for what it meant. But sitting there naked, it made me squirm inside just the same.

'Your name,' he said, without looking at me.

English again. I passed a second time.

'Votre nom.' He snipped a second nail.

'Bouchon.'

He glanced away, behind me. Another officer appeared. A Hauptsturmführer, this one. Squat, fleshy, pebble-glasses bridging a bulbous nose. He handed the *Oberst* my wallet.

192

'*Danke*, Karl.' The wallet was flicked open, the contents removed by the nail-clippers, then spread on the desk at his thigh. The nude picture never even got a glance. He picked out my identity cards, read it.

'Edouard Bouchon.' A look for confirmation.

'*Oui.*'

'Native of Brittany.'

'*Oui.*'

'Born 16th of May, 1922.'

'*Oui.*'

'Apprentice engineer.'

'*Oui.*'

'Eyes blue-gray.'

'*Oui.*'

'Height one metre seventy-five.'

'*Oui.*' Any moment now, the catch one.

'Distinguishing marks—'

'*Néant.*' If my dear mother could see me now . . .

'Patrice Morgat was a Breton.'

'There are a lot of us around.'

I saw the mouth go prissy-thin. 'Yes, that is so.' He motioned at the one named Karl. 'Our friend is sweating. Cool him down.'

Karl nodded, picked up an electric fan from the desk, switched it on. He paid out the flex, came to me. He kicked my legs apart, placed the fan between my thighs. Cold air hit my belly. And cold sweat beaded my brow.

'Patrice Morgat was a Breton,' repeated the *Oberst*.

'If you say so . . . *oui.*'

'He *is* a Breton.'

'*Oui.*'

'He is also known as Moulin-Bas.'

I made to shrug, but more to slide back from the fan. But hands caught my shoulder, pressing me forward. Karl thrust the fan further along the seat of the chair.

'*Oui or non?*'

'*Oui.*'

'A terrorist parachuted in by the British. *Oui or non?*'

'*Oui.*'

'He committed acts of murder and sabotage in the Pas-de-Calais – *oui or non?*'

'*Oui.*'

'He moved to the Department du Nord, three weeks ago, to Douai – *oui or non?*'

'*Oui.*'

A fractional hesitation on that one had brought the fan yet closer.

'He was responsible for a series of terrorist attacks culminating in sabotage to the mine and oil refinery at Corbehem – *oui or non?*'

'*Oui.*'

'You worked with him on all these crimes – *oui or non?*'

'*Oui.*'

The pressure on my shoulders was growing. The sweat coursing down the back was curving the buttocks, making them slippery. Only will-power kept me from sliding into the blurring blades.

'You *are* Patrice Morgat . . . alias Moulin-Bas . . .'

Karl's eyes glinted behind the pebbles, his lips were thick, moist, slightly parted with excitement. He couldn't wait for me to give the wrong answer, so that he could have the pleasure of turning the fan sideways and thrusting it home for a bloody emasculation job.

'. . . *oui or non?*'

Heads you win, tails I lose. I shut my eyes, let out a little sigh.

'*Oui . . .*'

The first sharp sting of the fan-blade slicing . . . but it was lower in the thigh. Karl had to have his little joke as he pulled the fan back, switched it off. He was returning it to the desk as I opened my eyes. The pressure was off my shoulders, I slithered forward as far as my arms would allow, being handcuffed behind the chair. I brought my legs together and hoped he hadn't cut the artery.

The *Oberst* was smiling, gesturing with the nail-clippers. 'Up and get dressed.'

Someone dumped my clothes beside the chair. Another unlocked the cuffs, gave me a push. I found the shirt, ripped a sleeve to bind the cut. It was filthy, but it was all I had.

The *Oberst* tut-tutted at that. 'You French, so primitive in matters of hygiene. You want blood-poisoning?'

I want your fucking head on a platter, mate, à la Salome and John the bleeding Baptist, only let me do the chopping myself, eh?

I ignored his snapping fingers until I was pushed back into the chair again. 'Do it for him, Fritz,' was the order.

Fritz was middle-aged with liquid brown eyes and tapering fingers. He came at me with a first-aid box, simpered as he trickled iodine into the cut. I arched momentarily in agony. He pushed me down and stroked my testicles with his free hand. 'Want me to kiss it better, darling?' he murmured in German, pursing his mouth. Then he wadded some cotton wool and fixed it with strips of plaster. 'There now, thank Fritz, you sweet little Frenchie bastard . . .' He balled a sly fist and punched where he had stroked before. 'Sorry, darling, my hand slipped, all the blood and piss on the chair . . .'

I got into my clothes except for the tie, belt, and shoelaces they had been careful to remove. I mustn't have the opportunity to hang myself, it was early days yet. Just because I had confessed didn't mean it was over, this had been the preliminary softening-up, it would be the other names next and the addresses. I tried to assemble my mind. Gestapo or SD, I had landed in a queer's convention, unless Fritz had been camping it up. Not likely in front of the *Oberst*. He was a genuine queen, if ever I saw one. What – or rather, who – did that make him . . . Major Y's Boemelburg? If so, this was the Avenue Foch, west of the Arc de Triomphe. Ironical names now in the story that was Occupied France.

I buttoned what buttons remained to the shirt, looked across at the bastard. He had put away the nail-clippers and had taken out a hip-flask. Poor devil, he had worked hard, he needed that drink. He caught my eye, picked up a cigarette packet, offered me one.

I made no move. He creased his mouth in a smile.

'Go on, take it. It won't bite you.'

I took it. It was English, Virginian. One of Solange's was my immediate thought, oh Christ, I wanted to ask but dare not. Any concern shown would make it the worse for her. Karl stepped forward with a lighter. For a change he was acting abnormal.

'That's right,' said Boemelburg. 'Enemies we may be, but we can be civilized, *non?*'

Indeed, what's a threat of castration between chums? *'Danke schön,'* I said, with heavy politeness.

'Ah, *sprichst Du Deutsch?'*

'Danke . . . bitte . . . ja, nein . . . pas plus,'

'A pity,' he said, lapsing back into French 'Show me your hands.'

I showed them. He touched them with his cane, turned them over. That's wise, don't come too close, have you been told what they did to one of your fancy boys? But then you wouldn't see his face, he's usually backside up, yes?

'Good hands,' was the verdict. 'The look of an educated man. Lad, perhaps, I should say . . . a second language for sure. Perhaps some schoolboy English, hein?'

'Un peu.'

Rather more than a little for Moulin-Bas I imagine.' He switched to English. Possibly to impress the apes, but I wasn't certain, it might be a trap of some kind. ' "He did not wear his scarlet coat for blood and wine are red . . . and blood and wine were on his hands when they found him with the dead." Do you know that? And the writer?'

Aren't we clever . . . Oscar Wilde, another one like himself. I had my answer but I thought it wiser to remove the cigarette from my mouth first.

'Adolf Hitler?' I said.

His free hand came up to give me a backhander. Then it dropped. He smiled. 'You are either very brave or very foolish, Edouard Bouchon,' he said. 'We'll talk again tomorrow. And then—' He poked me in the crutch with the cane. '—you will tell me who is the real Moulin-Bas.'

FORTY-FOUR

Handcuffed again, I was removed to a cell. A room with a boarded-up window, a trap of foetid air, a fierce light in the wall above the door, a peephole in the door itself but that wasn't enough. The handcuffs had to be hooked to a chain-and pulley, hoisting me ceilingwards until only my toes brushed the floor. A fleeting thought as the first agony wrenched at the shoulders . . . not for nothing are they known as the Black Jesuits; we were back to the Inquisition. 'Hail, shitting Hitler, full of fucking Grace, Blessed Art Thou amongst bastards, Blessed is the Fruit of Thy mental masturbations the ninety-eight point seven per cent of all Germans who voted *Ja* at the last ballot, a nation of syphilitics solid behind Thee, I've seen them having their orgasms in Nuremberg and Vienna, in Cologne and Munich, men and women young and old in uniform and out, Seig Heil, their Christ cometh in a brown shirt and a Charlie Chaplin moustache, Seig Heil, Shitler, Seig Heil . . .' I shrieked on my version of the Litany in their own language partly because it took my mind off the pain partly to bring them to me, nothing they could do was worse than this . . .

They came back, outraged at such blasphemy, lowered me to the floor. And it was boots, boots, boots, until I had them worried, they thought I was dead I was so still and that mustn't be, something must be left for the morning shift, their brother National Socialists, their good comrades of the Workers' Party. They crept out, left me on the floor, crumpled, soaked in sweat, a mound of misery and aches . . . sleep, sleep, while you can tomorrow is another day.

Tomorrow was a bucket of water thrown from the cell door. Tomorrow was a bath before breakfast with the clothes pulled off me. Tomorrow was exercise in the nude, see how you run. A dozen or more willing helpers in the corridor outside, lining the route, belt buckles, straps, and ox-gut whips at the ready. Half of them female white blouses and BDM ties, the typing pool looking for entertainment in the morning break, pointing, giggling, they had never seen a naked man before, these whores of a thousand and one SS nights. Five times I ran the gauntlet. Once each for Hitler, Goering, Goebbels, Himmler, with a special one for Karl Albrecht Oberg, SS *Oberführer* and top Gestapo thug in Paris. No phantasy on my part, each run was named and chanted. The sudden appearance of SS *Standartenführer* Doktor Helmut Knochen, chief of the SD, warranted a sixth, but he declined the honour with a modest smile, a shake of the head. He and his retinue passed by, one of them scooping me aside with a jackboot like some dog turd fouling the path.

'Piss first,' they said, in the bathroom. 'We are not having you do it in the bath, the usual filthy French habit.'

It was slow coming and painful passing and when it did it was as much blood as urine. And those who had crowded in to watch gave a cheer and the girls clapped their hands; they hadn't enjoyed such sport since they last played basketball with a Jewish baby. If the idea was to cause embarrassment, humiliation, being forced to perform under the gaze of women, the exercise was a failure. The bitches meant nothing to me.

The bath-water was icy cold and the object was to bring the victim as near as dammit to drowning then to revive him by a crude method of artificial respiration that entailed vomiting. It was all utterly pointless, for it was not done to make me talk, to answer questions, to reveal names and contacts within the Resistance. Nor was it punishment for my mutilation of comrade Kurt in the lift and other crimes against the Reich. These apes were as vociferous as those of the night before, the same, meaningless chanting. It was being done quite clearly for the simple pleasure of the doing, a vicarious thrill, a sense of Godalmighty power over another, a desire to demonstrate superiority.

To call it animal behaviour is to be unfair to animals. To term it savage is an insult to primitives. To attribute it – as those who seek an alibi have since done – to the system, to the brain-washed training of the SS, is to suggest that body possessed supernatural powers. Less than 300 in strength in 1929, only 30,000 when Hitler came to office, they were never in a position to subjugate, to terrorize a population of eighty million into ways of barbarism. The seed had to be there in the nation as was the anti-semitism, the swastika, the love of uniforms, the Hitler salute, part of a *Freikorps* inheritance that existed before the brown-shirted worm crawled out of the arsehole that is Austria. A master of rhetoric, that one hadn't an original idea in his head. He merely capitalised on the situation, giving them in full measure the ideology they had long accepted as their birthright.

They were a race apart. And being such, the Germans were, by their very nature, the logical argument for the code of conduct they pursued – mass genocide. This small, overcrowded planet would be well rid of them. And to those who shriek the crap about a people who fathered Beethoven and Goethe, I would say that one Persephone is no justification for incest, go fiddle the Eroica over the ploughed-in corpses of Belsen, recite *Mein Ruh' ist hin, mein Herz ist schwer* to the ashes of Auschwitz, you can do both without fear of competition, the cries of the children are stilled, the last whispered *Eli, Eli, lama sabachthami* has faded away . . .

The guardians of Kultur brought me back from the 'dead' for the fourth, fifth, or sixth time. As with the beating of the previous night, I had long passed the stage of no-response, and it was becoming a bore to spectators and participants alike. I was caught up by the feet and dragged, face downwards, back to my cell. I was bundled inside, sodden wet, ordered to get dressed into sodden clothes. So what am I, Houdini, still wearing handcuffs?

No more than a gesture, a mute explanation of my difficulty, yet it was enough to earn a vicious stamp on the fingers, to show yet again who was boss. The ignorant sod of a Siegfried couldn't prove it any other way, he was that unsure of himself. Even as it brought a groan from bruised lips, tears from swollen eyes, a darkening of blood under crushed nails, I knew, in some strange way, that I was the eventual victor; he, the defeated. All I wanted was to be there to see it, to mete out the justice. And never mind governments, politicians, peace treaties. I would be my own judge, jury, and executioner. Necessity knows no law.

FORTY-FIVE

Boemelberg again. Back from a heavy lunch by the way he belched. An equally loaded drinking session, too, judging from the brandy-waves and slur of the voice. I was ordered to strip, to occupy the same chair as before. There is some psychology crap behind this interrogation in the buff business – the removal of one's dignity, the sense of defenceless, bare the body the easier to bare the soul. It probably works on the uninitiated, but SIS training had included it, several hours at varying temperatures, straddled on wall bars in a gymnasium, a target for insult and jibe. A form of innoculation, an antibody build up of resentment and strength of will our good Colonel Rabagliatti had called it – a nice turn of phrase from a top British Intelligence agent with an Italian name. And, on this occasion, I was glad to be out of damp clothing that chafed the many bruises.

'Exercised and bathed?' said the *Oberst*, in French.

'*Oui.*'

'Watered and fed?'

'*Non.*'

'Never mind. There are millions in Asia dying of famine every year. You have a long way to go, hein?' He prodded me with his cane, gave me a cigarette.

Karl of the pebble-glasses was there to light it, but there was only one other present – a *hauptscharführer* by rank. A pretty youth, fair-haired and willowy, with notebook and pencil at the ready.

'You lied to me, Edouard Bouchon,' said the *Oberst*. 'That

200

was very wrong of you. I give you a chance to retract or face the consequences.' He paused, allowing the words to dwell. I expected the nail-clippers to appear, but they didn't. Maybe he had used them so often, he was down to the quick. Then he added: 'You are not the one they call Moulin-Bas.'

'I'm not the one they call Moulin-Bas,' I said.

'Better . . . but you know him, don't you?'

'I knew him . . .'

'Know him, *knew* him – there is a difference?'

'There is when he's dead.'

'Ah! So he is dead now, is he? When did he die? And where?'

I drew on the cigarette before answering. He knew about Douai, about the mine and the refinery, the work in the Pas-de-Calais. Some of it likely guesswork, but some of it was due to talk . . . Max? Solange? 'At Corbehem,' I muttered. 'If you know about that, you'll also know that some were killed during the getaway.'

'In stolen German vehicles, aiding the escape of political prisoners, yes? Further crimes to those of terrorism and murder and sabotage. And the worse crime of all . . . the wearing of German uniform!'

'I agree,' I murmured. 'Nothing could be more criminal.'

He was in too much of a lather to get the studied insult. Karl was too thick. Pretty Boy's blue eyes flashed signals, but Boemelberg ignored them, pressed on. 'This Moulin-Bas, Patrice Morgat, was one of those dressed as a *Totenkopf*. *Oui or non?*'

'*Toten* . . .?' I said, warily.

'. . . *kopf*. SS. Oh, yes, I forgot, you do not speak German. A few words only. Not enough for you to have impersonated a member of the Reich forces!' The last sentence said in his own language.

I made no answer, sensing a trap. My eyes slid to Karl, standing behind him. A slight tic in the face as he peeled away a glove to reveal a heavy signet ring. He made knuckles for my benefit.

'Not enough, I repeat,' Boemelberg went on, in German.

201

'Only enough to indulge in a foul obscenity of blasphemy in your cell after you left here! But, then, perhaps, you are a quick learner, ja? We shall see, ja, we shall see!' He jabbed the desk bell hard and long then rose, beckoned to Pretty Boy. 'We will leave you awhile to think on it. With tutors. For the record we will call it an examination, a lesson in behaviour.' He glanced at Karl, smiled. 'If our young friend needs a cigarette to help him concentrate, see that he gets it, hein?'

'*Jawohl, Herr Oberst!*' A glint behind the pebbles.

Alone with Karl, I watched his left hand. But he was in no hurry to start, preferring to wait for the summoned reinforcements. He took out a Luger, lay it on the desk as a warning not to try anything. Then found a cigarette, lit it, barely inhaling, then laid it down carefully in an ashtray beside the gun. Nothing untoward in the gesture, yet I found it ominous. I stubbed out my own on the underside of the chair, tried not to think where he intended to stub his . . .

. . . not long to find out. I'm not the strongest man in the world, but it took four of them to hold me across the table as he went to work, starting at the soles of the feet and moving upwards. I was shrieking so loud by the time he reached the genitals I doubt if he knew whether he was inflicting first-degree burns or more. As I felt it seeking the anus, nature made its own protest. A twisting knot in the gut and what I would have performed with pleasure in the giggling mouths of those bitches in the bathroom now took place on the table. A violent, total, semi-liquid bowel movement, a diarrhoetic evacuation that must have spattered Karl and the two at my legs, because they went back yelling curses and I was writhing, rolling free, off the table, hitting the floor with my heels, only to be caught by those at my arms and twisted over as someone screamed 'Rub his face in it!' and they did and they did and they did . . . and somewhere, along the frenzied pounding and the din of hate and hysteria, I passed out . . .

. . . conscious again, I was given a bucket of water, a single

square of toilet paper, and a toothbrush. I was told to clean
the table and myself, in that order. The toothbrush was for
the table, it had to be scrubbed spotless. The water was salt,
the better to make the burns and cuts sting. And the toilet
paper had been spat on first . . . these boys didn't forget a
thing. But don't think I am complaining, I was lucky to have
what I had. If such a thing had happened in a camp, I would
have been made to use my tongue and nothing else like the
mangy cur I was. I know. They told me so as they kicked me
around afterwards, thrust me under a scalding shower then
under an icy one, hot, cold, back and forth, mop it up after
you, you bastard, you dirty, filthy, French *crappule*, now get
dressed, *schnell, schnell, raus*, and run on blistered agony-
feet before them, into another room, another office . . .

'You are Moulin-Bas' said Boemelberg. '*Oui or non?*'
   The three of us. All cosy. He, on a settee. Pretty Boy, round
little arse in a swivel-chair. Me, standing room only, serve
my blisters right. And if my troubles weren't enough, the
broken tooth had got back into the act, adding its share of
misery.
   '*Oui,*' dribbled out..
   'You said "*oui*" the first time. "*Non*" the second. Now it
is "*oui*" again. Are you or aren't Patrice Morgat?'
   'I'm whoever you want me to be.'
   'That is no answer.'
   I peered at him through the one eye which had anything
approaching vision. Sitting there, sprawled out, legs apart,
belt off, an oldish man with a mottled complexion, he re-
minded me of someone . . . Major bloody Bint, back in
Omagh. Not only was this Boemelberg a queer and a lush,
he was close to being useless as an interrogator, so obsessed
was he with his cat-and-mouse game.
   'I repeat,' he said. 'That is no answer.'
   '*Alors, un autre* . . . get stuffed.'
   He frowned, not understanding. '*Que dites-vous?*'
   I could have suggested he asked Pretty Boy. Instead, I

203

said: '*Rien*', and pointed to my mouth. 'No drink, no talk. And if you don't like it, call in more of your apes and I'll shit on them, too!' The words came in a croak that was bravado, contempt, but mostly from a feeling that they couldn't hurt me anymore . . . not with effect, not this day.

Pretty Boy snatched up a metal ruler, swung in his chair. But the *Oberst* waved him down, gestured at the door. 'Coffee . . . for three.' he said, with a thin smile.

Pretty Boy dropped the ruler, left the room. Boemelberg took out his flask, poured a drink into the thimble cap. He eyed me rather like a headmaster dealing with a recalcitrant schoolboy.

'I have been patient with you, young man,' he said. 'Very patient, indeed. Last night I said you were either brave or foolish, but more than either, I think, misled. Misled into believing you could fool me.' He gulped back his drink, screwed on the flask-cap, put it away, dabbed at his lips with a handkerchief. 'I know you are not Moulin-Bas for a number of reasons. Firstly, the man is an officer. French or English, it matters little. Not French, because you have not the accent. I was here, in Paris, before the war, with the deplomatique. I know the style of the Saint Cyr, they would never have accepted you as a cadet. As for being an English officer . . . again, you have not the manners nor the breeding. Your behaviour pattern, your speech is of the gutter, not of a gentleman. Physical similarity to the man we want is not enough, you see.'

He rose, came to the desk, picked up a folder, flapped it at me. 'We have a dossier, statement, even a letter . . .' He paused, pushed forward Pretty Boy's memo-pad and pencil. 'You will write for me "Solange cherie," and sign it "Patrice".'

I took the pencil, wrote the words with the left hand. He turned the pad, looked at it, then opened the file. He produced a letter, the second one I had written to Solange. I thought she had slipped when answering it, calling me Patrice. Now I saw why . . .

'Compare,' he said.

No need to. The letter was written in the right hand, the natural one. Use of the left was a defence mechanism; an extra finesse of SIS training. Write the first chapter of Genesis, as much as you can in twelve minutes, wherever you finish write the remainder one hundred times until fluent . . . a third time winner, clever boy, ambidextrous, fly him for a quid and he'll write it upside down and backwards, too . . . but he signed a bloody letter *Patrice* and she had kept it and it was as if I had signed her death warrant . . .

Boemelberg took my slump of dejection as further proof of his thesis. So sure he couldn't be bothered with a finger-print check. Mine must be all over that letter, but he merely returned it to the folder.

'Your going to the woman Perrin's room immediately upon your arrival was another mistake,' he crowed. 'Too elementary for someone who had organised a terrorist network, an operation such as Moray Eel. You see, we even know the code-name, its link with the invasion attempt at Dieppe!' He peered at me closely. 'Did you know that? I think not! Such matters would hardly be privy to an ignorant Breton peasant named Eduoard Bouchon who mouths filth and blasphemy learned from some wretched Marxist Jew!'

He jabbed at me suddenly, sharply, using the metal ruler. It took me in the groin, ripping the blisters, sent me to my knees in the sheer agony of it. Tears welled and rolled down my face. I could only sob my rage, hatred, determination to see him in the same position, no matter how long it took.

Yet the bastard was so thick, so stupid, he saw the tears and the posture as signs of contrition. 'You have left it late to be sorry! There is nothing so degrading as a man crying. It is not how Moulin-Bas would behave. Nor would he expect it from his decoy – for that is what you are, yes?'

You're so fucking clever, *Obersturmbannführer* Karl Boemelberg and all the other Karls and apes and queens of the *Sicherheitsdienst*, you know all the answers, I'm my own decoy, yes. I nodded my head slowly.

'Now on your feet! I am not finished with you yet! At once, do you hear? I'm not a man who indulges in violence,

205

but you have tried my patience sorely. There is a limit beyond which I cannot go.'

I bet there is, I thought, groping my way to my feet. What did you do in the war, daddy? Old enough to have fought in the last one, but not even a piddling Iron Cross, third class, like Corporal Hitler . . . not much from an army that hands out medals as so much pork and sauerkraut, that time, this time, anytime, a goose-stepping gutless shower . . .

Pretty Boy came in with the coffee. Three cups, cream, sugar, on a tray, with a plate of *petit fours*. Such a nice mover, no need to ask how he earned his first promotion. At Jugend camp, under Baldur von Shirach? He simpered his pleasure at the tears still wet on my face, at the ruler in Boemelberg's hand.

'Does he still get coffee, *Herr Oberst*?'

'Yes. He has learned his lesson – haven't you, lad?'

I nodded again. I had learned my lesson very well. All I wanted was the chance to apply it. If Maurice and Felix had thought my attitude towards the enemy inhuman, they hadn't seen half . . .

FORTY-SIX

A new cell, with all the amenities. Four walls and a bucket. And a visitor. Dressed like a priest, he walked like a priest, he reeked that moth-ball odoured sanctity of a priest.

And spoke like one. 'Can I be of help, my son?'

'Yes, father.'

'Tell me . . .' He pressed a gilt crucifix in my hand. God strike you dead if you lie, it said. I had no intention of so doing.

'Get me out of here.'

'I wish I could, my son. But, how?'

'Strip your soutane and beads. I'd make a lovely priest.'

'My son, my son . . .'

'Why not? I've got the stigmata, father. On my balls. Pope

Boemelberg's boys gave it me. You take my place, you could be so lucky.'

'My son, my son ...'

'Give over the Absalom crap.'

'I am here to offer you the sacraments.'

'If there's cheese with the bread I'll take it.'

'Don't mock Our Lord Our Saviour, my son ...'

'Your Lord Your Saviour should come down off his shitting cloud. His crucifixion was patty-cake compared with what goes on in the camps.'

'If you continue to talk that way, I will have to leave—'

'You've got the message at last! Take your Christ-badge with you before I stuff it up your arse!'

He took it and went.

Was he a genuine priest – or a plant? I don't know. I certainly didn't care. If I needed a crutch at that moment, it wasn't the ginger man from Nazareth. One made of teak, solid, preferably with a metal ferrule on the end ... all the better to kill the next bastard who showed his face in the cell. A pox on my soul, Satan could have it with pleasure, just get my body out of here, breathing, able to carry on the fight, forever and ever amen ...

An hour passed. Or three. No way of telling, they had taken Maurice's watch, along with my other few possessions. I lay on the floor, half-naked, shivering, but it was better than the irritation of clothes against the burns. I tried shutting Solange out of my mind. Max, too. What was happening to them was a torture I could do nothing about. I knew that neither had betrayed my true identity. Obtuse idiot that Boemelberg was, one or the other or both had given him reasons to believe what he believed. Subsequent questioning had revealed more to me than to him ...

—Moulin-Bas, Patrice Morgat, or whatever the real name – he is British, *oui?*'

—*Oui.*'

—A member of British Intelligence, *oui?*'

—*Oui.*'

—He is not dead, *non*?'

—*Oui, Non.* I don't know.'

—Why don't you know?'

—I am not God. Nor am I a fortune teller.'

—Don't try to be clever.' The metal ruler stroked my cheek.

—I am trying to be honest, *Herr Oberst.* I do not know.'

—Where did you last see him? And when?'

—Yesterday morning? Whatever morning it was when I was last free.'

—Wednesday. The morning of Dieppe. Where?'

Only one man could make me a liar. Max. It depended on what he had said.

—I'm waiting . . .'

—And I'm trying to think, *Herr Oberst.* It was early, we were in a truck, travelling south-west, I believe . . .'

—Does it help your memory if I say it was Abbeville?'

A catch. Max would not have said that. But he had said something to me in Arras, when I had told him that was off. He had felt all along it was a waste of time, if London really wanted me out why not somewhere closer to the landing area, in line with any advance, such as . . .

—Not Abbeville. Amiens.'

—Why Amiens?'

—Because . . . I don't know.'

—Because he was deserting you, planning to get to Dieppe alone, to escape back to England with the British Navy, *non*?'

My silence had brought that thin smug smile of triumph. 'He deserted you as the British always do, as they did at Dunkerque. Why can't you French learn who your real enemies are, have always been? Your Joan of Arc knew, so did your Napoleon . . .' He had gone into a lecture on French history, he loved the sound of his own voice, sycophantic to every syllable, it would have been a joy to vomit in his mouth . . .

—And you came from Amiens to Paris?'

—Eh?'

—From Amiens to Paris, you and the Jew?'

—If you say he is a Jew – *oui.*'
—Are you saying he isn't?'
—I'm saying I never asked him.'
—But you knew the woman Perrin was.'
—Did I?'
—Why did you go directly to her?'
—The one who offered me a tit to suck, you mean?'
He had blushed at that. Such talk was indecent, I might
have been speaking of his own mother, this prick of a creature
who had been farted out under a haystack, this consequence
of copulation with a goat.
—You know who I mean!'
—By name, yes. But no more. I was only the messenger
boy.'
—And the message?'
I had been waiting for that question. Such a long, cumber-
some build-up to it, the answer had to be something that
would not put further pressure on Solange. Someone had
betrayed her and I could only suspect the source – the con-
tact she had made in Paris to pass on my information about
troop movements to London.
—The message?'
—It made no sense to me. Such rubbish.'
—I will be the judge of that!'
—Mind what you eat. Hag Fish is poisonous.'
—That was the message?' His mouth had gone tight.
'Nothing more?'
—Nothing more.'
—You had better be very certain about that. You are not
made for playing the hero, Eduoard Bouchon—' The ruler
stroked my cheek again.
—I am sorry, *Herr Oberst*, there was something else—'
—Ah!'
—Best wishes, Patrice.'
End of interrogation. A brusque dismissal, through lips
gone thin with inward rage. Not with me, rather my 'message'.
On the button as I had hoped it would be. *Hag Fish*, I had
surmised, was either a Sipo plant or a captured RF agent

209

turned round . . . another *Capri*. Well, he wouldn't be the first nor the last, but if the Gestapo and the SD were sold on my inference that London knew of the substitution or defection, they wouldn't use him again. Something gained . . .

New visitors. One, obviously, the guard commander, with his keys. The other, youngish, slim, an *obersturmführer* lieutenant – in rank. The latter stood and looked down at me, grimaced. Then he stooped and examined the soles of my feet, gently. There was a visible wince as he straightened up.

'*Unangenehm,*' I heard him murmur to himself. '*Und unnötig.*'

Unpleasant and unnecessary. That goes for the company, I thought. What was this bloody place – Victoria Station?

His eyes flickered around the cell, his head shook slowly, then came back to me.

'I am the duty officer,' he said, in halting French. '*Comprenez-vous?*'

'*Ich verstehe,*' I answered. 'Have I any complaints, *nicht wahr?*'

'You speak Geramn, *ja?*'

'A little, *Herr Kapitan!*'

A little smile at that. '*Lieutenant,*' he said, careful to avoid the SS ranking. 'Have you complaints?'

'Not about the food, Herr Lieutenant. I haven't had any.'

He frowned, turned to the guard commander, muttered something I couldn't hear. The guard commander began to hedge in a Rhenish accent. I gathered he had received no orders to feed me or to provide me with any form of bedding. The duty officer's voice raised, sharp, waspish – had he been ordered *not* to feed me, not to bed me? No-o, nothing specific to that effect, but it was rather late to do anything about it now. Was it, indeed! – from the duty officer – it was never too late, no such word in the German army, this man has to be fed and found another cell at once, *schnell.*'

I got to my feet slowly, trying not to smile as the guard commander clicked heels and clattered away. A pretty charade for my benefit, the more so because I understood the language. I had been wondering when I would get the sweet treatment,

210

the soft approach. In fact, I thought I had slipped up over the 'priest' on that score, if I had been more amenable I might have got something out of it. But I had played it according to the book. The more intractable one's manner towards any attempt at kindness, the more they will lay it on if it suits their ploy.

The duty officer turned back to me. 'You need any help?' he asked.

'I can manage, *Herr Lieutenant*.' I held my pants in my hand. 'I won't dress, if you don't mind. The blisters are more bearable uncovered.'

He averted his eyes from my penis. 'As you wish. Take your time.' He motioned to a pair of guards outside. Between them, they hoisted me off my feet and carried me along the corridor, up a flight of stairs.

The new cell was the Ritz. Bed let down by chains from the wall, a straw palliasse, a bolster, two blankets. A tap and the usual bucket for offices. Where was Jeeves and the morning tea?

'*Danke schön, Herr Lieutenant,*' I said. '*J'emmerde,*' I thought, 'on you and all yours!'

'It is nothing,' he said. 'No more than the humanities demand. I believe they should be maintained even in time of war.' He took out a cigarette case, offered me one, lit it for me. 'I must compliment you on your German. I have been trying to place your accent.'

I bet you have. I expelled smoke slowly. I had thought I would never touch another cigarette after Karl Pebble-Glasses' performance, but it was different taken from the other end.

'Bayern, *ja?*' he prompted, gently, checking the tap to make sure it worked.

'She might have been,' I said.

'She?' Eyebrows high.

'A girl. She was studying French, but found it difficult. She was too pretty to be clever, especially after dark.'

'Bed is the best place to learn languages, they say, *ja?*'

He winked, and laughed. And was itching to kick my teeth in, the idea of this *infecte crappule* laying some pure Aryan

211

maiden. I got the warning sign as fingers savaged the tap shut.

'*They* may say, Herr Lieutenant, but *I* did not.' An answer that was diplomatic. I still hadn't had the meal he had ordered. 'Inger was not that type, she was Bund Deutscher Mädel.' BDM. Hitler's Own. The sweet, unsullied flowers of young German womanhood – if you cared to believe the legend. On their backs with their legs apart before you could unfrock a french letter was much nearer the truth. BDM also stood for Bang a Dozen for a Mark, they're even cheaper wholesale.

But if the *Herr Lieutenant* was aware of the fact rather than the fiction, he didn't show it. 'A pity this Inger did not teach you also about Germany. You would not be in this trouble now,' was all he said.

'Perhaps. But if France had conquered Germany instead of the other way round, don't you think you would have been in my position?'

'But France could never conquer Germany!'

'With respect to your views, *Herr Lieutenant,* but the *Herr Oberts* Boemelberg spoke to me today of the glories that were Napoleon and how he conquered Europe—'

'But that was before the Führer, before Bismarck, before we were united . . . and, anyway, we Germans defeated him at Waterloo!'

'The *Herr Oberst* didn't mention that. He blamed it all on the English. He said they were the traditional enemies of France.'

'Yes, well, but—' The *Herr Lieutenant* was a bit lost for words.

'I find it all very confusing, *Herr Lieutenant.* Both you and *Herr Oberst* had had more education in these matters. It could be that I have been led astray, though what I have done or tried to do is only what I would imagine any German would do in those circumstances. But having lost I must take my punishment like a man . . .' Christ, how much longer do I have to rabbit on like this, a mixture of German and French, before the food comes? I knew I had this silly

212

young sod slightly mesmerized, not sure whether to bark or
bite or wag his tail with satisfaction at having got me to talk
so freely. *Too* freely, was his dilemma, how to channel it in
the right direction without making me suspicious and clam
up again . . .

The sudden appearance of the food saved both of us. Hot
soup and cold sausage, a crust of greyish bread. The *Herr
Lieutenant* smiled his relief. *'Bon appetit,'* he said. 'I may
look in later when I have finished my rounds. I would like to
continue our little chat, M'sieu—?'

'Bouchon. Eduoard Bouchon.' I stubbed out the cigarette,
raised my hands. 'One other favour, *Herr Lieutenant* – would
it be possible—?'

'The handcuffs. Yes, of course. Looser, anyway, while you
eat.'

Big deal. But it was better than nothing. If they went on
being so kind and generous, they would have me believing
in fairies again, the variety that don't wear *Chanel Numero
Cinq* on their jock straps

FORTY-SEVEN

The duty officer never came back that night, nor yet the next
day. For some reason best known to themselves I was left
alone, except for the guards. One brought me a bucket of
water laced with carbolic and a brush to wash down the cell.
When it had met with approval, I was given breakfast –
another stale crust and a brown, muddy mess that passed for
coffee. Lukewarm, it softened the bread sufficiently to get it
down. Then I was paraded to the lavatory, watched over while
I performed. But only a perfunctory interest, to ensure I didn't
attempt to steal the chain.

The day passed in total darkness, except for a blaze of
sudden light whenever the guard was changed and a new eye
appeared at the peep-hole. A long, unwinking stare was all I
got for lunch. After the sixth time, I reckoned twelve hours

had passed, and now the door opened and I was brought supper. Supper was the same as breakfast, except that the brown, muddy mess sported a tired dumpling and a float of cabbage and was called soup. The guard was the same one who had given me room service the previous evening. A thickset man in his thirties, thick of neck, thick of hands, with two fingers missing on the left one.

'War wound?' I asked, in German. For all I cared they had been torn off by a Montmartre tart, but interest might earn me a cigarette.

'*Ja, ja,*' he nodded, held them up for a closer look.

I eyed the medal ribbon on his tunic. 'Russian front?'

'*Ja, ja. Taganrog, ja,* near Odessa. Panzer trooper, me, *ja?* Kill many, many Russians.' He opened and closed his hands three times. 'This medal I am given for that many, *ja?*'

More likely for sniffing Hitler's bum, I thought. I said: 'You are Swabian, *ja?*'

'Ho, *ja,* Swabian, me. Augsburg, *ja?* You know Augsburg, *ja?*'

'*Ja.*' I knew Augsburg. 'A town built by the Fuckers, *ja?*' Puzzlement. 'Fuckers?'

'The Princes Fuckers, *ja?*'

'Ah, *ja,* you mean Fuggers, *ja?*'

'*Ja.* Fuckers'.

'Very old, Augsburg. Very beautiful, *ja?*'

'Very big *Rathaus, ja?*' Rat House was an apt name for a German town hall.

'You like *Rathaus, ja?* You like Augsburg food, *ja?*'

'*Ja, ja.*' Just like the swill I was eating. Only more dumplings.

'And Augsburgh girls you like, *ja?*'

I was watching his hands. But they were not fisted. They were making curves like dumplings.

'*Ja, ja,*' I said. 'Girls, big, like the *Rathaus.*'

'Ho, big, *ja,* plenty to get hold of. Big like the *Rathaus,* ho ho, that is good, *ja?* Very good.'

The joke had earned me a cigarette, I reckoned. I broached the idea whilst he was still laughing.

'Cigarette, *ja?*'

'*Ja, bitte.*'

'*Nein.* I don't smoke, *ja?* Big like the *Rathaus*, very good, very good, I like that, *ja!*'

The Fugger from Swabia left me.

By the time the duty officer came back, two days later, I'd had time to think, time to plan. The Fugger from Swabia had helped without knowing it. I refused to be beaten by such turds, refused to acknowledge that such crap could dominate me, let alone the world. I'd had a belly-full of the *Herrenvolk*, and the Fugger from Swabia reduced them to the appropriate level, something to be flushed away.

The Lieutenant came in behind the Swabian, who was carrying a tray on which was real coffee, real meat stew with dumplings, and a couple of slices of good *schwarzbrot*. I watched the Swabian eye it lustfully when he set it down; at his rank he'd still be eating *ersatz*. The was even a chunk of *mettwurst* and a sweet-sour pickle.

'Here it comes,' I thought, but now I was ready for it. Now the training had taken over. Pain is in the mind, okay. Nobody ever died of pain, okay? That's what the pimply medic in Andover, Hants had said. Pain is a message the nerve ends send to the power house, telling it to blow the master fuse that plunges you into the darkness of unconsciousness, the peace of oblivion. Okay? Then he tightened the vice in which he'd strapped my wrist. Now I had the real thing, the pain of all the blows they'd given me, the blisters of the cigarette burns, the cuts and what my pimply friend in Andover would have called abrasions and contusions. And, fuck 'em, not one could affect me any more. Mind over matter? Right! And the matter was this creep of a Lieutenant, thinking he could buy me with a hunk of *mettwurst* I wouldn't even bother to shove up his arsehole.

'You've made them very angry with you,' he said. Masterpiece of understatement – I knew damn well they were furious. 'First you say you're Patrice Morgat, and then you say you're

215

Moulin-Bas, but the next time they talk with you, you deny it. You've confused them, and they don't like that.'

Head down, contrite. Eat the *mettwurst*, quick. It contains energy. And the bread. They might take it away again. 'Sorry,' mumbled among the crumbs. 'I didn't mean to confuse them, but they asked me so many questions. And then, the beatings. My mind's in a whirl . . .' Yes, a whirling dervish dance of death, his death, not mine, the Swabian's death, not mine. *Obersturmbannführer* Karl Boemelberg's death. But not mine.

'I understand,' the Lieutenant said. 'It must have been very confusing.' He leaned forward to pat my arm, then overbalanced slightly, or so it appeared, and the cuff of his jacket caught the bowl of dumpling stew and sent it crashing from the tray. Instinctive reaction; I flinched, waiting for the blow and the screamed abuse that would call me a clumsy crapoule. But it never came.

'What a clumsy person I am,' he said, then turned to the Swabian. 'Take this mess away, and bring another tray.'

The Swabian's eyes were wide open in astonishment.

'But, Lieutenant . . .' he started to say, but the Lieutenant's voice snapped out at him like a flicked razor blade. '*Schnell, dummkopf!*' he said, his voice lancing the air of the cell.

The Swabian took the tray, wiped the table top clean with his hairy paw, and went out without a backward look.

But he closed and locked the cell door behind him.

As soon as he heard the lock click, the Lieutenant leaned closer to me and, when he spoke, his voice was a whisper. 'I have a message for you,' he said.

Page twenty-seven of the manual they hadn't even had time to set in print, but had reproduced in purple on one of those gelatine pads. The print on my copy had faded across one corner, and the man who'd had it before me had inked it in with a fountain pen. Instant recall; the whole page photographed, drawn from the appropriate file in my mind, read again. I could even smell that purple ink.

'A message? From whom?' Play it straight and simple.

'The woman you went to see.'

'Big tits . . .?'

His face wrinkled at the coarseness. 'No, not her. The one you thought you were going to see. The one who's having the baby . . .'

Red in front of my eyes and an almost irresistible urge to smash the thin solemn owl-eyed face of this bloody foolish boy who was playing a man's game without realising it.

'What's the message?'

'She wants to see you!'

'Where?'

'Here. She's in this building.' Despite my certain knowledge that all this was fiction, all this was the method of page twenty-seven, a part inside me came to life, the part that had died when I saw the figure bending over that washbasin and realised it wasn't Solange. Romantic hope? Love's young dream? Hearts and Flowers?

'Here, in this building . . .?'

'We haven't much time,' he said, earnestly. He was good, no doubt about that. He had the technique, and the face that went with it. He was desperately, earnestly, believable. 'Look, I can arrange it, if you'll co-operate. At the moment you're guarded by the specials. All prisoners are guarded by them until they've confessed. After that, well, the specials move on and you're left in my care, awaiting transfer. I can relax a bit, take things more easy. I could even fix a meeting with your girl.'

Sounds easy, doesn't it? Spill your guts and you can see your loved one again. No guarantees, no promises. 'I *could* even fix that.' Yes, and I *could* fly to the moon on a broomstick.

'You see already how I can fix better food for you, a better cell . . .?'

What about the River Suite at the Savoy, roast beef with all the trimmings . . .?

'Why? One simple answer. Why?'

I didn't give a damn why, but one of the sub-sections of page twenty-seven had said 'It's important to sound sceptical when the first approach is made. Don't forget that you must

217

put them into the position in which *they* have to convince *you*.'

He licked his lips. A right Donald Wolfit, this one.

'I'm not a Nazi. Never have been. I hate them all for what they've done to Germany.'

I almost laughed. That stock answer was even printed on page twenty-seven. 'They'll probably say something like 'I'm not a Nazi. I hate what they've done to the Germany of Mozart, Beethoven, Bach, Goethe . . .'

'Beethoven, Bach, Mozart, Goethe, Schiller? *Kennst du das Land . . .? Alle Menschen werden Brueder . . .?*'

Only now the bully boys were re-writing the lyric, weren't they, to say that all people should be *German*. Or, at least, German ruled, *German* dominated.

'Germany was once a proud and beautiful country,' he said, 'a man could be proud to belong to it. Now . . .'

'Now you want to help me meet my girl again . . .?'

'It seems such a small thing, but I'd like to do it.'

'And she's in this building?'

He beckoned up towards the ceiling. I wished he'd pointed downwards. Nearer the front door. Okay, so I'd go along with him, see how far he would lead me.

'I don't mind telling them what I know,' I said, suitably humble. 'You understand I don't know very much. The people I was with always worked on what we call, 'the Need to know.' Only tell people what they *need* to know to complete the assignment. But if they'll just interview me quietly, without all these beatings, if they'll just give me time to gather my thoughts together, I have no objection to telling them whatever they want to know. After all, my share in things is over, isn't it? Everything I know is in the past, isn't it? I can't see any harm in telling them that. But without the beatings.'

Page twenty-seven, again. 'You must appear to be striking some sort of bargain . . .'

'I think that can be arranged,' he said. 'After all, what you can tell them, as you say, can't be all that important to them. And then, afterwards, I'll arrange that meeting for you.'

218

Back in front of Boemelberg again, stripped naked of course, because whatever he may say, he liked to look at my balls, to see my injuries, to assure himself he was a superior being, a man with the right to hide his privacies. Whereas I had no such right, not even the right to urinate alone. No nail clippers; they belonged to the past, when spirits had to be broken. It's so easy for these fools to be convinced of their own superiority, to be made to believe that theirs is the only might, the only strength. It's their biggest failing, their most vulnerable weakness, and they get it from history, from the whole disgusting story of rule by force, subjugation by might, not right.

'I hear you're going to tell us everything you know,' he said, 'to sing like a bird!'

A young man was sitting behind the desk, squirming on his chair. He'd set four pencils along the top of his writing pad. Neat orderly precision. Teutonic thoroughness.

'Ludwig takes shorthand in French, or German, or English,' Boemelberg said, smiling indulgently at his protegé.

I watched Ludwig blush with pleasure, realised I'd need to clean up my language if I wasn't to make him blush again. A delicate flower, this one. Look at any manure pile and you'd find his likeness growing tall, white, willowy.

'How are we going to do it?' I asked, keeping my voice humble. 'Are you going to ask me questions?'

'I think not. I want to know all about you. Where you came from. Who sent you. Who were your contacts. What were your codes. Who do you report to. We'll strike a bargain. You tell me what I want to know, and I will turn you over to the Lieutenant for safe keeping. Then we'll transfer you out of here. Somewhere more pleasant, in the country, where you'll have companions.'

Somewhere in the country. Where the air smells of gas and rotting bodies. Where the companions call a private roll each dawn to see who's died in the night, or gone to the 'final solution'. It wasn't going to happen to me that way. And page twenty-seven told me how. I gave them the whole story, chapter and verse. Names, dates, places. Code words, call

219

signs, transpositions. It was all accurate, all true, but all dead. They could verify all of it, but it all belonged to the past and not a word of it would tell them anything that would be the slightest use to them in the future. Except, for good measure, I threw in a few words to let them know for certain their contact with the Paris cell was blown, their Hag Fish had truly become poisonous to them, since I implied he had doubled back to us. For most of it, the face of the *Obersturmbannführer* was impassive, a granite mask behind which he hid any feelings he might possess. But when I said the words that would put the knife into Hag Fish, he took his little gold pencil out of his pocket, made an entry in his diary, and I knew Hag Fish had been sentenced to death. One less to bother with, one more traitor silenced.

My 'confession' took two hours, and cost Boemelberg the contents of an entire flask, sip by sip. I could smell the odour of flowers that wafted across at me every time he uncorked it – some exotic liquer that suited his personality. The trilingual shorthand writer Ludwig never stopped once, though necessarily I had to use French words, English, and German. The *Hauptsturmführer* with the pebble glasses looked in once was disappointed by not seeing fresh blood flowing from me, and left. The *Hauptscharführer* came in with his pencil and note book; his look at Ludwig was pure bitchy venom. Hell hath no fury like a pansy scorned. He pouted, tossed his curly locks, and minced away. Someday I'd get him to bend over for me, but it'd be a bayonet I'd use on him.

'That's all,' I said finally. 'I've tried to make it as complete as possible, to miss nothing out.' I was exhausted by all the talk, by the feat of memory. He asked half a dozen questions, but they were mostly expansions of what I'd said. One or two of them were tricky. 'The leader of the cell at Corbehems?' he said, without referring to the notes. 'You called him Mosquite?'

'That's right. I only met him once.'

'But we have information that the leader of the cell was called Max . . .'

So, they had got the poor bastard and he had talked to

them. I didn't blame him. But he'd managed to keep Maurice's secret.

'Max *thought* he was the leader, but Mosquite was the original contact. Mosquite was very clever. He worked just like any other member of the group. Nobody knew he was the contact with London, and with the other groups.'

Lively interest now, and the impassive look wiped from his face. Ludwig still scribbling. 'What were Mosquite's aliases; what other names did he use?'

That one was simple. 'I can give you his real name,' I said, 'I saw it once on a letter . . .'

One of Max's three trainees, the one who'd blown himself up in the office of the Legionnaires. Max had confiscated a letter when he searched him prior to the job. 'Jacques Etienne Duval, 5 Rue de Tourennes, Epernay.' Pencil out again, address jotted down. They'd check, find Duval mysteriously missing. When the body had been blown out of the Legionnaire's office it had been unidentifiable. They'd spend time looking for Duval, alias Mosquite. He'd told me that was the name the kids had given him in school. Someone would remember; it would tie in long enough for the brains of the *Sicherheitsdienst* to waste time on it. It would have just the right air of mystery, the right mixture of comfirmability and doubt that their rigid minds would appreciate. He put away his pencil. Took a last sip at his flask and found it empty. Eyed me speculatively. Time suspended because there were no more obvious things he could do to me, or about me. I knew that, so far as he was concerned I was already dead. The only problem that remained was the disposal of my remains. But the decision had to be reviewed, hadn't it? A fear-commanded society breeds its own lubricating fear; he wouldn't let me go until he knew for certain he'd extracted the last drop of juice from me. Page twenty-seven. Be humble, but strike bargains.

'Now that I've told you it all,' I said, 'I hope you'll realise my situation. My life wouldn't be worth a sou if you were to reveal the source of your information. I hope you'll keep my name out of it . . .?'

'Yes, you may rest assured,' he said. I could see his face brighten. Now he'd made his decision. 'So far as we are concerned,' he said, 'you just don't exist.'

Dead ironical. Hearty laughter, or the nearest thing to it that Ludwig could permit himself, as a smile flicked across his pallid, effete, face.

Then I made my mistake. I got up from the chair. Too energetically, too confidently. It was a small mistake, but it cost me. I didn't see what button Boemelberg pressed, but it brought two of them in, each the size of a gorilla. I hadn't seen them before. 'It wouldn't do to send you out of here in too good a shape,' Boemelberg said. 'Anyone seeing you might think you'd talked too easily. It might damage your reputation. After all, we want to make it seem as if you've been a hero, that any words you've spoken have been dragged from you by force. I'm certain you understand?'

I did understand. It wouldn't help his reputation any if word got about that I'd been an easy one. Ludwig's face was green. 'I'll go and translate my notes, Herr *Obersturmbannführer*,' he murmured, all he could say through clenched teeth.

Some prisoners used to masturbate endlessly, to reduce their strength to ensure they passed out quickly under torture. I didn't fancy the quick jerk-off method. I charged at the two gorillas, head down, arms chopping sideways. They were so astonished, I managed to split a lip with a side chop, and had my finger in the nostril of the other, prepared to pull and rip. They recovered quickly; one slammed a flattened fist into my kidneys and drove me down; I saw the knee of the other coming up. 'Not my throat,' I said to myself in that fraction of time before contact. It was the blow that can lift your head off your spine, a killer. I bent my head forward to meet it, and felt my nose splatter across my face, a roar of blood in my ears, and then quick merciful unconsciousness.

FORTY-EIGHT

When I awoke, I had forgotten where I was, what day, month, or year it was, what my name was. I was a suspended hunk of flesh criss-crossed and pierced by stabbing pain. Memory came back slowly, painfully, as I set myself to compile an inventory of what had happened to me. The physical side was easy. I'd been kicked all over my body. My hands had been stamped on. My face had been smashed, my upper lip torn. My chin was covered with a mixture of dribble and hardened blood. And then the other side came back, my names, my identities, a confused whirl of Moulin Bas, Patrice Morgat, Edouard Bouchon. Beneath those names was another one which wouldn't come to me; I felt the first sweat of true panic because somehow I felt that the other name, the one that wouldn't come, was the significant one, the key to my real identity. I had a terrible, frightening, vision of going through the rest of my life without that name, without the knowledge that name would bring of what kind of a man I was, what were my true loves and hatreds, my real pleasures and pains.

It took me an age to lever my body up until I was sitting on the side of my bed, hanging from its two chains. The chains themselves brought back a cold chilling memory of page twenty-seven and its awesome warning. *'It should be pointed out that the attempts we outline here to suppress aspects of one's own personality can, and sometimes have been observed to, result in permanent or semi-permanent loss of memory and/or identity.* And every one of us taking the course had said, 'Fuck you, Jack, that's not going to happen to me'.

The chains? Why did they mean something? What did they mean? Chains. What was page twenty-seven? Memories, half formed, half realised ebbed and flowed in my mind like

223

recurrent waves of nausea. Who am I? *Wer bin Ich? Oui est-ce que je suis?*

The room was approximately ten feet by eight feet by nine feet high. Hanging bed, on chains. Barred window. Barred door. It wasn't a room; it was a cell. It wasn't a hospital, my first thought, and I hadn't been run down by a herd of charging taxis coming out of a brothel in Lancaster Gate. I was in a cell, *ipso facto,* I was a prisoner. Blood, piss, all over me, ergo I had been beaten. Then the memory of that part of it came rushing back like bats into a black cave at dawn. The two gorillas, Ludwig turning green, Boemelberg beginning to smile with pleasure, the gold pencil fluttering over the pages of his book, and my run forward. Was it a boast that I remembered charging them? The chains. Page twenty-seven. *'No room can ever be completely emptied of possible weapons of offence'.*

The chains were my possible weapon of offence.

Set into a ring in the wall. Set into another ring, bolted through the iron framework of the bed. Black malleable iron nearly three sixteenths of an inch thick. Chain links forged into one piece. Okay, give me an oxy-acetylene torch and I'll be through the links in seconds. No oxy-acetylene. Tut-tut! Badly equipped, this cell! A bolt cutter? No? Right, I'll settle for a hacksaw, Sheffield steel. I'll gnaw them apart, or rather, I would gnaw them if I still had my teeth, or if the stumps they'd left me hadn't all been cracked ripping my tongue every time it made an incautious voyage round the bloodied mess that was my mouth. I got off the bed. Lifted off the stinking rag they called a blanket. Springs of flat steel welded to the iron frame. Lift the bed, slam it down. The couplings don't even tremble. Archimedes, where are you now with your principles? *Give me a lever long enough, and I will move the world.* Lift the bed. Let the chain hang down against the frame. Take one link round the frame, bring it back, and insert the link end through another link. The chain snags on itself. The bed's half lifted. Climb onto the frame. Now stand, one foot against the jammed link, the other on the outside edge of the frame. Stand upright. Pain in my left leg leads the march of a phalanx of smaller pains through my body. Okay, Archimedes, here we go. I leaped as high as I could, bent my knees, came down on my arse with the full force of my weight and gravity against the edge of that bed frame. Lucky aim. Just right. My arse on the edge of the frame. All my force behind it. Twice my force, plus the pull of gravity on the link I'd jammed back into the chain. It hadn't been designed for that, and sheared. The bed slammed down again, the other chain held, and I was tipped off onto the stone floor. But the link had sheared. Quick. Jam another link. Up again, jump, snap. Now I have a fifteen-inch length of chain in my hand. Other side of the bed, jam again, jump, snap. I was about to jump a fourth time when I heard foot-steps coming along the stone corridor. Slam the bed up against the wall, hold it with the snap catch. No time for subtlety. Drop the chain into my trousers pocket. Trouser's pocket? They'd dressed me, then, after the last time they'd beaten me. That means I'm on my way.

The Lieutenant came into the cell, found me standing upright against the wall, leaning against the folded bed.

'I felt sick,' I said, 'lying down. After the beating!'

Quick look around, from habit. 'It won't happen again,' he said. He held out his clipboard. On it was my transfer sheet. 'Now you're one of mine,' he said, 'until they complete their checks. Then you'll be sent to the country for a rest.'

'Do I get Horlicks, and Cod liver oil – and Malt?'

'I beg your pardon?'

'Forgive me. A joke.'

'I like jokes,' he said, his face showing how little he would understand them.

'That meeting you were talking about?' I said, 'was that a joke?'

He looked shocked. 'Of course not. It will take a little time, that's all.'

'And, while we wait, we play chess, or *muelle?*'

'I thought you might like to think over what you'd told the others. We could go through it again, if you want, just to

225

make certain you haven't made any mistakes, forgotten or omitted anything.'

The soft sell. Give me a chance to fill any gaps.

'After all, if they discover you've been inaccurate, or you've missed out anything, they might get angry and take you back to the other side.' He beckoned while he was talking and two guards came in. They bore no relationship to the gorillas, were ordinary *Wehrmacht*, chosen no doubt for their neatness, their 'ordinariness'. 'This is Petersen and Friedl,' he said. 'They will be looking after you. Anything at all you want, just ask them.' Friedl led the way, I followed, with Petersen behind me after he had closed and locked the door. We walked down the long corridor of cells, each with an eye. At the far end, we turned right into a cross corridor. About half way along this corridor, Friedl used a key to open a door and went inside. I followed him. The room was twenty feet long, ten wide, with barred windows down one side. Along one wall was a book-case, with a hundred or so books in it. A chess game laid out with military precision at the centre of a table, five or six easy chairs covered in leather cloth in a mottled institution brown. A gas ring in the corner, a sink, a kettle, a cupboard. In England it would have contained tea, sugar, milk. *In England.* So I was British. I realised with a shock I'd been thinking in German until that moment.

'You will spend your time here,' he said. 'Much better than the cell. Of course, you understand that any abuse of this privilege will immediately result in your being confined again. But here, I hope you can relax, while I make the necessary arrangements to honour our agreement.'

Honour. A dirty word, coming from one of them. Brutus was an *honourable* man.

More important, however, than any thoughts about the Lieutenant and his *honour*, was the sudden release of my mind, the return of knowledge of who I was, why, from where, when, and how. And with it, the memory of Max last seen in that downstairs hallway, and the sudden warm well of feeling for Solange. *Mon ange.* Mother of my child, guardian of my seed. When the time comes, you say to your-

226

self, I'll be brave. I'll accept what is inevitable. I'll go to my death contented by the knowledge of how many of them I'm taking with me, how much I've thwarted their efforts to conquer and rule the world according to their own bestiality. But it's not so easy when the death of another person is involved, the torture of someone you've held in your arms against the world outside. You can invoke all the formulae; she was a volunteer, old enough to know what she was doing. But suddenly I felt the remembered feeling of a child when he breaks a borrowed bicycle, and knows he must face its owner again. Only now we were concerned with human life, not toys.

Friedl sat down at the chess table. 'Do you play?' he asked me.

'Yes, but can I walk about a bit, first, to stretch my legs?'

'Why not wash your face at the sink. That will freshen you up.'

I did as he suggested. The cuts stung horribly but I was in that limbo where pain no longer has meaning. I had an objective, a target for that chain in my pocket, and the rest was just make-believe. Anybody who got in my way this time would either kill me, or be dead. When I'd finished washing and had dried myself on the clean khaki towel provided, I wandered aimlessly along the side of the room, glancing out of the windows, expecting at any moment to feel a hand on my shoulder. They knew I wasn't going anywhere. The bars had been cemented into the brickwork by experts.

Outside the windows was a courtyard. We appeared to be on the first floor of the building, five floors high. Another wing on the opposite side of the 'U', with a door into it. As I watched, a tall woman came out wearing a white medical coat. A slim young girl shambled in front of her, walking like a zombie, wearing a plain green sack dress and green plimsolls. Her hair was a tangled mess. One human, female, master races for the use of! With the one in the white coat to test for anti-social diseases.

I looked at the bookshelves, but could see Friedl was becoming impatient. 'De we play or not?' he said.

I expected no surprises from the books, so I sat down. He tried me with Ruy Lopez. I gave him the Bishop. Why not? With luck, I'd be taking everything he had later, including his manhood. He beat me in thirty moves. He could have had me in twenty but his closing game was atrocious. *Blitzkrieg, ja.* And then fizzle out. Another German trait, for which, if I could have been bothered, I would have despised him. But I was saving my emotions for my one big effort, nursing my hatred for the time when I'd be swinging that chain. I'd realised how much of my strength had been wasted in hatred, how much of my purpose diluted by the bitter bile of my contempt. Now the only thing that interested me was survival. And that meant, escape.

I had an anxious moment when they took me back to the cell, and Petersen went to the wall to let down my bed. No doubt they'd been instructed by the Lieutenant to offer me the creature comforts and hotel service. 'I'll do that,' I said, 'I'm not ready to lie down yet.'

As soon as they had gone, I let the bed down, clipped the length of chain back in position. It would hold and didn't look too apparent though the first real inspection would reveal it. Then I stood with by back against the wall and started my exercises, forcing my screaming muscles and limbs through the ritual that would strengthen them for the moment I would need them. It was two hours of sheer unadulerated bloody hell.

The Lieutenant came back. At three o'clock in the morning.

'Come quick,' he said.

I had no time to do anything about the chain, followed him out of the cell in a hurry. Twelve hours previously I might have permitted myself the luxury of hoping, but now, like Pavlov's dog, I was conditioned against hope of any kind, against despair, against hatred, against any emotion that would drain me. Friedl was waiting outside the cell, a Schmeisser in his hands, which surprised me.

I hurried with them along the corridor, turned left at the

228

end, walked down a flight of stairs to the floor below, back along the corridor to a room I estimated to be beneath my own cell. Every inch of the way my mind was photographing the corridor, the doors, the types of barriers I might have to pass on my way to freedom. The room into which they took me was square, with a low ceiling. It stank of fear, sweat, urine, and involuntary shit. And something too terrible to comprehend immediately.

Boemelberg was sitting on a leather covered typing chair, his arms draped over the back. His eyes held that partly glazed look I'd seen as he finished his flask. Two men against the walls, men I'd not seen before but whose type I knew perfectly well. Hold back your hatred, be dispassionate I willed myself. Ludwig at a table, looking greener than ever. One fierce electric light providing the only illumination. On a table, by the wall, a brass lamp with a black wooden handle. You fill them with paraffin, and pump a handle. Pour a little methylated spirits into a cup and light it. The burning meths warms a coil through which the liquid paraffin must pass; in that coil, the liquid is vapourised and emits from the end of the nozzle in a six inch long roaring flame. Human beings use them for stripping paint off wood, or in plumbing for melting lead pipe and wiping joints. The Germans had been using it to roast the skin of Max's chest. His eyes were slits, his face covered in a slime of snot and blood. His nose was wrinkled against the smell of his own burning flesh. I took a half step forward, involuntarily, and learned the reason for Friedl's Schmeisser when he poked it into my kidneys.

Boemelberg had seen me come in though he had not looked in my direction. 'The name of the leader of the operations at Corbehem, again?' he said. One of the men against the wall picked up the paraffin blow torch. The sound that came out of Max's mouth would have been a scream if they'd left him any teeth to form it with.

'Maurice,' he said. Was it my imagination that the slits of his eyes swivelled in my direction, that they seemed to say 'forgive me!'

'Who was "Mosquite"?'

'I don't know. I swear I don't know. I *swear* it . . .' Max's voice was a faint whisper but the silence in the room, apart from the sound of that burning blow-torch, was so absolute that we could hear every word.

Boemelberg beckoned the man forward with the blow-torch, and then swivelled his chair so that he was looking directly at me. 'This man, Max, is your friend,' he said, 'your comrade-in-arms.' Slowly he moved his hand and the man with the blow-torch drew closer to Max. I looked past Boemelberg, saw that Max was strapped to the chair by leather thongs and couldn't move away. He arched his back to the limit of the thongs, away from that serpent flame nearing his throat.

'Who did you say was the leader of the cell at Corbehem?' Boemelberg asked me, his voice quiet but nonetheless piercing, slicing like a razor-edged knife that you never feel until the artery has been severed.

I looked across the room at Max. He looked back at me as he bent his body backwards, every msucle straining away from that roaring flame. He was already in that madness that comes before death, that crazy optimism that tells you perhaps, after all, you're going to get away. But Max, you're done for, you haven't a snowflake's hope in hell. Go the easy way, Max, go quickly. It's an illusion to think I can end that pain for you, can save your life. These men are in the darkness beyond reason. But I'm alive, and still working. Maurice, so far as I know, is alive and still working, with a quiver full of the darts of vengeance. 'Max never knew who the leader of the cell really was,' I said. 'You know, because I told you that's the way these cells are organised. One man acts as the leader; he's the one the others hear giving the orders, the one they respect. But the true leader is one of the men in the cell, working quietly, seeming to take orders, not give them. He's the one who has contacts higher up the ladder, who receives the instructions and passes them on. The *apparent* leader knows nothing and no-one, other than that, one day, he gets a message or an instruction that tells him and his cell what to do. Maurice was such a man.'

I thought for a brief optimistic moment that perhaps we'd

got away with it, and we would have, too, except I'd forgotten the nature of the beast of unrestricted violence. The man with the blow-torch had smelled death; it was on his face, in his eyes, in the way his brutal nostrils flared, a man without reason, without compunction.

'Mosquite's the name of the man you want,' I said, loud as I could without actually shouting, but it was no use. The blow-torch completed its journey and above everything, above the roar of the force-fed flames, the bestial grunts of the torch-bearer for the new truth, the disciplinary shout of Boemelberg, I heard the bellowing screams, the last sounds Max was ever able to make.

'It was Mosquite you wanted,' I said, 'not Maurice, not Max.' But, by then Max had died a wanton death.

I was taken back to my cell; but not for long. I was standing against the wall, looking out of the barred window, remembering. 'A police *boîte* in Aîre is not quite Fresnes jail,' Max had said, when he reported to me that the Francs-Tireurs had disposed of Albert. And then, as we came to Paris – 'The pen is mightier than the sword!' Dreamer! The pen comes after the sword; the pen makes the apologies for all the obscenities the sword has committed. Dawn was breaking somewhere up there and the cold outlines of the building were softened by the first gleams of it. This had to be the day of my escape, somehow. Or the day of my death. One way or the other, I was past caring.

The door opened again and the Lieutenant came in.

'No sleep for the wicked, eh?' I said. He didn't understand, said, 'Pardon me?' in a puzzled Teutonic way.

'Grim sense of humour at this time of morning.'

'I shall never understand the British . . .'

He beckoned again for me to precede him from the cell. This time I had the chain in my pocket.

They stood me in the yard, in the dawn light. Freidl was beside me, at first. Then Boemelberg came out, with a *Scharführer* and a new flask. I'd seen the wall behind me,

231

the pock marks the bullets had made, on other dawns. The men came from a small building at the end of the yard, a greenhouse without glass. Eight of them. I counted. They were carrying Schmeissers. Did some of them have blank cartridges – that was the gentleman's way, wasn't it, so that any man could claim exemption from responsibility. They stood in one long line in the centre of the courtyard, facing me twelve paces away, the Schmeissers held at their waists, ready to lift and fire.

Boemelberg walked across to me, stood only two paces away. 'The name of the leader of the cell at Corbehem?' he said, without preliminary.

'It's still Mosquite.'

He waved his hand, and they brought out Solange. Grey green dress, plimsolls. Her hair, the locks of hair I'd held in my hand, were tangled and matted. But her face was clean and bore no marks. She looked across at me and I could see she recognised me, she knew me, knew every single minute aspect of me, as people will when they have spent a life together. And both of us knew our life together was now behind us.

They took her and stood her against the far wall, then walked away and left her there, a tiny defenceless figure, slim, upright, holding herself erect with pride despite all they had done to her. The firing squad remained looking at me, their Schmeissers held loosely but pointing at me. One member of the firing squad blocked my sight of her and, when I moved a pace to the right to maintain my view of her, the *Scharführer* shouted a crisp command and the left hand section of the file stamped further left to make a gap through which we could both see each other, Solange and I. We needed no words; the look in our eyes was a clear precise communion of minds more eloquent than any words. We had loved each other, given that part of ourselves to each other that is forever. Now we knew it was all over, our separation would be final and complete. She smiled. It was an act of bravery, derision and reassurance.

Boemelberg looked over his shoulder at Solange. Her figure

232

stiffened even more upright than before. 'It's still Mosquite,' I said, to forestall his question. Solange nodded, realising she was listening to the word goodbye, seeming to accept its inevitability.

They'd kill me now, but I was past caring. They'd kill me because they could make no more use of me. They'd keep her alive because she had a body they could use, but they'd kill me. And it wouldn't matter any more, to Solange or to me. Our life together had been brief but ultimately sweet; together we had known those moments that come so rarely to any man's life, moments that reveal with a heart stopping clarity the way life is intended to be.

The Schmeissers came up to waist height. I hadn't even heard the word of command. Boemelberg spread his hands in a gesture I would have loved to tell him was Jewish, but I said, 'It's still Mosquite.' He turned and walked back into the building. The scene etched itself on my mind. The firing squad before me, the *Scharführer* beside it, Friedl standing by the door, Solange against the wall, slender, upright, erect in an indomitable pride.

'Aim!' the *Scharführer* commanded.

Now the Schmeissers came higher and each one pointed at me. Friedl twitched as he stood against the door, his face turning away from me. Solange smiled again, tender, compassionate. I made the word, goodbye, with my lips.

'Fire!'

But it was Friedl's Schmeisser that chattered one long burst, not those of the firing squad, and it was Solange's body, not mine, that was slammed against the wall, blood spouting from the belly where my baby was forming. And in Solange's eyes was the look that said, 'Didn't you know? Hadn't you realised?' And I knew I hadn't understood this little scene, hadn't realised I was a bit player, not the principal actor. My fingernails bit into the palms of my hands; my teeth bit into my top lip but I said nothing, I didn't even cry out, as she fell sack-like to the stones at the foot of the wall and her blood, and the blood of our child, seeped from her.

FORTY-NINE

Stand still. Absolutely still. Wait. Command from the *Scharführer*. Schmeissers lowered. Right turn. March.

They went back into the greenhouse, one by one.

Beyond the greenhouse, the main gate. Large. Small door set in it. No doubt a guard outside, waiting for the meatwagon that would come for the day's consignment of bodies. Boemelberg's gone. The Lieutenant turned and went back inside the building. Friedl, walking across the courtyard towards me, the Schmeisser in his hands, though he hasn't changed the magazine.

He hasn't changed the magazine.

Quick, swallow air. Pump it down. Pump. Hand up to my mouth, belch out some of the swallowed air, turn round against the wall, belch it out again, finger down my throat now Friedl can't see my face, and vomit, chuck it up, retch the bile from my throat and the remains of last night's mettwurst. But my other hand, the one on the side away from Friedl, goes into my pocket and I don't wait to find the end of the chain, then whirl round in one swift movement because I can feel Friedl's hand on my shoulder and perhaps he's going to say he's sorry but there's no time for that, no time for words, only the start of a scream as he sees that chain with its hooked ends flaying out at him and catching him across the face and the throat, and my hand follows in with the fingers bent into hard knuckles, straight into his throat and knock his Adam's apple sideways as he goes back and down. That's a killer blow, and he's dead.

The big gate started to open. Bend down quickly, pull him to his feet beside me, slam him back against the wall, my left hand behind him, holding his back straight. His head lolls down but there's nothing I can do about that. Stick the Schmeisser under his arm and hold it there with the pressure of body. Now the gate's wide open and the truck backs in, and I can see the driver leaning out of the cab and he's too busy driving straight to worry about Friedl. The wagon came back across the courtyard, a big Benz with a soft top and an openable back.

One man out of the passenger side. Quick flick in the corner of my eye tells me the outside guard has pulled the big door closed again, but I've seen the street beyond the gate.

The driver jumped from the cab, came round to the back of the truck. He gave us only a cursory glance, then opened the back door of the truck. The two of them picked up Solange, one by the hands, one by the feet, and tossed her into the back of the truck. I dropped Friedl and went in swinging the chain. The driver took it behind his ear and dropped. I continued the swing and smashed across the other's face, but he was quick and used the door to stop it. Then he made the mistake of fumbling for his pistol but by the time he had opened the strap, his balls were somewhere up around his throat and I was smashing, left and right, at the points at each side of his neck. I swung around; no sign from any of the windows that I had been watched, but I wasn't going to hang around for applause. I leaped into the cab of the truck, started the motor, and drove slowly forward.

The guard outside had been listening for the sound of the engine, and, in a repeat of the morning routine that had firmly established itself in his mind, he swung the gate open. I didn't even have to stop the truck. By the time the front wheels were level with the gate, it was fully open, and I could drive through.

I had turned left and was half way down the street before the shooting began, round the corner and hiding in an alley when the motor-cyclists arrived at the abandoned truck.

The road ran straight through the centre of the wood, and narrow. There was a bend just inside the wood, a half-kilometre straight stretch, then another bend. I lay in the bushes at the side of the road, waiting and watching. In the three hours I'd been there, three motor-cycles had come through the wood, and two cars. It was late afternoon; I didn't have much time. Above all, I didn't want headlights. At the far end of the wood, telegraph poles straddled the countryside. At least, I thought they were telegraph poles, but I'd soon find out. I climbed the pole nearest the wood. The wire hung from porcelain insulators, but they were small. Take a chance, grab the wire. No power in it, no blinding searching flash as five thousand volts arc across your body. I twisted the wire backwards and forwards, backwards and forwards until eventually it snapped. Then I let it hang down to the ground. Its weight would have been too much to hold, anyway, squatting there on the cross trees. I slid down the pole, ran across the ground, and twisted the wire again. When it snapped I had a coil at least fifty metres long. It took me only a couple of minutes to fasten one end of the coil around the trunk of a tree, about four feet from the ground. I dragged the rest of the coil across the road, and hid behind a tree at the other side of the road. After five minutes, a lorry came along the road and I left the wire lying on the ground. Then a car. It was half an hour before a motor-cycle came down the road, accelerating when he was round the first bend, racing along the straight, slowing down for the second bend. By then, I'd fastened the wire around the tree and it stretched across the road, twisted taut, four feet high. I caught the motor-cyclist on his chest, twanged up to his throat and snapped his head backwards as he was thrown off the saddle. The bike carried on away from him, toppling down and sliding along the macadam of the road, sparks screeching from the footrest pedal. The driver was already dead when I got to him, put my arms around his waist and dragged him into the trees. I ran back out, lifted the bike and wheeled that out of sight. His outer clothes fitted me reasonably well, including his helmet and goggles. The bike started first kick. Its tank was full. I left the wire still tied around the trees, and the bike took me three hundred kilometres before it ran out of petrol north of Clermont-Ferrand.

The cross-roads outside Brioude were ahead of me. A sentry was stamping up and down in the cold air, banging his hands beneath his arms, his breath coming from his mouth in a grey airy balloon. His motor-cycle was parked beside the cross-roads on its stand. Stone walls ran down the side of the road and I slid slowly, silently I hoped, along the ground behind one. Village down the road a kilometre away. Army camp behind me, two kilometres away. No farms, no animals in the field, no people, other than this one cold sentry, guarding a cross-roads from nowhere to nowhere, alone and miles from home.

Easy does it, slide forward along the stones. Now I have a pistol, a clumsy Sauer self-loading 7.65 mm, with seven rounds. I have four grenades, all taken from the motor-cyclist. I creep closer. Silent, like a cat. He walks up and down. He stops, leans against the wall, scrapes a match on a box, lights a cigarette. I smell the pungent acrid odour of both the match and the cigarette. Form a loop of the wire I've brought with me. Hug the wall, behind him. Loop wide, swing up, pull back, twist, twist. His hands scrabble up and the cigarette, forgotten, drops in a shower of sparks. Tin hat pushed forward by the top of the stone wall so I can't see his face when I stand up straight. Fingers scrabbling at the wire in a brief agony, but already I've let go of the twisted ends, knowing he can't get rid of it, knowing he's dying, fast, and not caring because he's one of them and his boots are flaying the stone wall and his machine pistol is banging against the stones, but already he's twisting round and down and for him it'll soon be over and I don't give a damn, I just don't give a damn because all I can see are those bullets pumping into Solange's body and that flame reaching out for Max's throat as if it had a will of its own. And he clatters down.

That motor-cycle was only half full, but it was a 750cc model and it took me quickly south to Le Puy.

FIFTY

They were doing it so badly that I winced as I watched. It had nothing to do with me, of course, and I had no intention of becoming involved. But they were making concealment difficult for me, attracting attention. She was in her early thirties, I would say. He was a slip of a boy, no more than twenty-one or two. Still wearing his flying jacket and his flying boots. And, unbelievably, a white silk scarf wrapped round his throat that flashed like the arse end of a rabbit. Four Germans were lying in wait in the bottom of the hedge. Doing nothing, needing to do nothing, since they could see that this inexperienced French girl and this lumbering lad with her, would walk straight into the trap they had set at the end of the field. A small copse behind the Germans, but I couldn't make my way through it so long as they were there. I couldn't go back to the main road behind me, with its stream of traffic. I didn't want to go left into the Loire. That left only the copse. I resigned myself to wait.

The Germans were as bad as their quarry. Nervous, I imagine. When the boy and girl were fifty metres away they began to shoot. The boy was quick and disappeared into the bottom of the hedge-row where he should have been all the time. The girl ran across the open field. Two Germans broke cover and ran alongside the hedge where she could see them. The two who remained in the bottom of the hedge stopped firing. The girl might have made it if she hadn't tripped and sprawled full length on the springy turf. The two Germans grabbed her, pulled her to her feet and pushed her to where their two companions were waiting. The RAF boy broke cover, little Prince Charming and Sir Galahad, all in one. One of the Germans turned, touched the trigger of his machine pistol and stopped the RAF boy in his tracks. He sank to his knees, pitched on his face, and stayed there. The German was about to spray him with another machine pistol

238

burst when one of his companions muttered something to him. They stood still, listening. Nothing, no echo of the shots he'd fired. One of them walked to the RAF boy, flipped him over, bent down, and I saw the silver flash of a wrist watch before he put it into his pocket. The other three were crowding the girl into the copse. I followed, since that was my only route out. About twenty yards inside the trees, one of the Germans hit the girl behind her knees. She sprawled kneeling on the ground. The man dropped his machine pistol, reached over her from behind, caught her dress at the neckline and ripped it to her waist, uncovering her white shoulders. He went round in front of her. The man on his left put the muzzle of his machine pistol against the girl's ear and, grinning, the first man unbuttoned his trousers. He put his hand behind her head as she kneeled before him and slowly pulled her forward. The other man jabbed her ear gently with his machine pistol and her mouth opened. The first man grunted with pleasure, his eyes gleaming, sweat pouring down his forehead.

The first of the motor-cyclist's grenades killed those two Germans and the French girl. The second one killed the other two.

The RAF boy was not dead, only stunned by one shot that had creased his forehead without even breaking the skin. The sound of the grenade explosions must have brought him round and he sat up. 'Come on,' I said disgustedly. I'd have preferred to leave him there.

We walked and ran away from that place, keeping in the hedges, concealing ourselves in every furrow of ground. Why the hell didn't they teach these poor bastards a bit of fieldcraft to use if ever they were shot down? He had no idea of how to cross ground and several times I had to chop him down to prevent him giving both of us away. After an hour of cross country travel, I felt safe enough to take a breather. He was wheezing like a grandfather, anyway. I gave him a swig of water from the motor-cyclist's water bottle. He grimaced at the tinny taste.

'What happened to Yvonne?' he asked me.

'She died.'

'How?'

'Don't ask questions when the answers don't concern you.'

'But I need to know. She was good to me. She helped me.'

'And she died. Isn't that enough?'

'I'd feel better if I knew how she died . . .'

'You'd do better to ask "why" she died, not "how". She died because she was helping you, and didn't know enough to do it properly. She died because they forgot, when they were pinning wings on your manly chest, that one day, you might be caught out here on the ground, with no *jolly good show* to help you, and it wouldn't be a *wizard prang*, it would be a bloody, gut-spilling, mess.' I pointed my hand south by south-west. 'Down there if you manage to keep going long enough, you'll find Spain. If you get over the Pyrenees. If the Spaniards don't split your throat or turn you in, you'll find Portugal. And in Lisbon, if you queue up outside the Embassy with all the other wizard prangs, they'll arrange to fly you back to England.'

'You're British, too, aren't you? We're in this together, aren't we? I mean, we should stick together, help each other get through.'

Marlborough? Winchester? Eton or Harrow? It didn't matter too much. 'That's your way,' I said, 'but for Christ's sake, stay off the skyline. And avoid them all, the French and the Germans and other wizard prangs as inept as yourself.'

'There's no need to be offensive,' he said.

And then I realised I had to take him with me. At least part of the way. Because I realised that if I didn't, he would be caught before he'd gone fifty kilometres. And they'd assume he'd been the one with the wire. I didn't want that. They had to work out that *I* was the one with the wire, that I'd been the one to cause the deaths of the motor-cyclists. My survival depended on that.

We found an isolated gun position outside Vallon-Pont d'Arc

on the Ardeche. I slipped a loop of wire round the neck of the single sentry and we went in. The rest of them were in a hut, and I lobbed two grenades through a window after wiring the doorhandle shut. When we went into the hut two of them were still alive and blood and bone were everywhere. I wound wire round the necks of the two still kicking in agony on the floor. The RAF lad puked his guts up, but ran when I told him to. I had pâté, bread, two cooked chickens in a pot, two bottles of white wine and the gun would never fire again.

'You didn't need to kill them all,' he said, refusing the food. I was gorging myself on the pâté, smearing it liberally over the crisp French bread with my fingers, since I'd forgotten to grab a knife and fork. Or a napkin, come to think of it. I ignored him, but he wouldn't let himself be silent. He grabbed my shoulder and shook it petulantly. 'You didn't need to kill them with that disgusting wire,' he said, pressing his face close to mine, his mouth working in pain, rage, and frustration. Three more with that wire round their throats. That makes five in all, five bodies, lying in a straight line that points to Marseille, each with a wire round its throat.

I let him shake me, though it made chewing the pâté difficult and spilled breadcrumbs into my lap. He saw it was useless to continue and sat sullenly back. I waited and then handed him a slab of bread and pâté. He took it and ate it slowly, chewing each mouthful as doubtless he had been taught by some starched matron. I knocked the neck off one of the bottles, spilling little of the wine. The edge of the glass had broken cleanly. It's a trick you learn, part of the survival package that decides if you'll live or die. He gulped down the wine and I let him.

The gun position had its own lorry parked under the trees. A Mercedes with a concertina bonnet and five gears. I was still wearing the motor-cyclist's uniform. With the food, I'd grabbed a pair of mechanics overalls and gave them to him to wear. They hid the fur of his flying boots, but he had to discard his woollen flying jacket. I made him put it back on, over the overalls, determined not to let him leave it anywhere near that camp. We got into the lorry which started first time, after I had shorted the electrics, and we drove along the valley of the river Ardeche through the long pale glowing evening. Peter – I soon discovered that was his name in one of those typically British 'I suppose we'd better introduce ourselves since we're in this thing together' sessions – talked incessantly. All the John Bull stuff. All the half-formed ideals. 'I suppose you had to make certain they were dead, but to strangle them with a wire . . .' 'If we behave as badly as they do, what's the difference between us . . .?' Down through the golden twilight, the sun low over the hills to our right, the water gleaming like a lacquered ribbon to our left and ahead of us, the wastes of the Camargue, Avignon with its Papal memories, and ultimately Marseille, where I'd dump him. I had felt my strength returning to me along the way south, fed by my bitter memories, the dreams that, whenever I slept, came jostling into my mind, the knowledge of the death of Solange, so easy to remember but so hard to accept. And, listening to Peter, a growing feeling of frustration. Asking myself, what was it all about, knowing he would never understand anything beyond a simplistic Us and Them, Good and Bad, the God and the Devil. Then, miraculously, we found a petrol bowser at the side of the road, temporarily untended while the driver and the crew of one took a piss in a nearby wood. We pulled up cautiously and waited. 'Don't you say a word,' I instructed him and, for once, he was content to cower back in the passenger seat of the Mercedes. I swung out and down, walked across to the bowser, then into the edge of the wood. They came out incautiously, talking together. Two throw-outs from the Supply Corps, two southerners, to judge by their accents, with no feeling for the war, for security, for military preparedness. I shot them both from behind, then twisted a loop of wire round each one's neck, my calling card. The bowser carried its own pump. I filled the tank of the Mercedes and three jerry cans, then left the pump running. With one of the jerry cans I laid a line of petrol down the side of the road about a hundred metres, then tossed a lighted match in the trail as we drove past. When the bowser blew we were already a half mile away

242

and could watch the jet of flame rise to fifty feet before it was extinguished by its own pall of thick black smoke.

We found the first road-block just outside Chateaurenard. We'd skirted Avignon during the night, working our way southwards and eastwards, crossing the Rhone in a leaking boat we found tied to the west bank, rowing sluggishly with two planks of wood. Peter was a University Blue, but you couldn't tell it from the way he handled the plank. The night was so dark, with black heavy clouds, that we couldn't even see the opposite bank until we were almost on it. We heard a dog bark somewhere, a ferocious angry sound with no target except the dog's own frustration. A train came along the railway lines, spitting sparks from the bad fuel. Lorries ran along the road showing only thin jets of blue light. The water smelled of dank weed, acid like last year's wine barrels. A dead cat floated past us as we drew close to the shore and Peter, not recognising what it was and not being trained well enough to leave it, tried to pull it out of the water before recoiling in horror at its disgusting bloated body. We crossed the countryside rapidly once we'd abandoned the boat, hugging hedgerows. My feet and the bottoms of my trousers were soaking wet and the cold seemed to seep through the marrow of my bones. The motor-cyclist's boots had been made of cardboard, not designed for the treatment I was giving them.

Near the road I saw three lorries stop, then move slowly forward, then stop again. Then the first one steered round an S-bend and we saw its lights flash in the trees.

We crawled, now, despite the dew soaked grass in the bottom of the hedge. I was frozen and in a lousy temper but perked up when I saw the small detachment and the oil drums spread along the road. I left Peter under a tree and went closer. When the third lorry arrived at the two rows of oil-drums around which he'd have to negotiate the S-bend, the driver leaned out.

'What are you looking for?' he asked as he handed them his papers.

'An Englishman. In German uniform. A murderer.'

'Aren't they all?' the driver said, looking into the light of the torch without blinking. It was something to say. They compared his papers with those of his vehicle. Asked him questions about his name, his unit, where he was from, where he was going. He answered them all laconically, obviously bored by the whole proceedings. Finally, when they could think of no more questions to ask him, they waved him on. He didn't bother to say goodbye, slammed the door of his lorry, and slowly wrestled the wheel past the oil-drum obstacles, banging the end one with the back of his lorry as he turned round it. He drove off without stopping.

When I got back to the tree, Peter was chattering with cold. 'I think I'm catching 'flu,' he said, sorry for himself.

'Don't worry; I'll sweat it out of you.'

We set off in a shambling jog-trot parallel with the road but about half a kilometre from it, heading south in the direction taken by the lorries. In the two hours before dawn, we covered well over eight kilometres, and I heard no more about influenza. I knew that soon, we'd have to stop for food, if only to provide energy to carry on. Now I knew I'd attained my first objective; they had the road-blocks out and were looking for me. I was anxious to get to my destination as soon as possible.

They caught us on the other side of the Berre Etang. By rotten bad luck. I'd knocked off a motor-cycle combination and had hidden him in the side-car, crouched out of sight. I was bowling along the road when I came past a Gestapo staff car, with a blown tyre, skewed across the road. I had to slow down to walking pace to get past. The Gestapo Major stopped me. 'Drive me into the city,' he commanded, reaching for the handle of the side-car. Trapped! I couldn't go forward since the staff car was blocking the roadway, and on the side was a sheer drop into a dyke. The co-driver guard of the staff car, no doubt because of the presence of the Major, had his Schmeisser held at the ready. The Major looked

244

down into the side-car, saw Peter's boots. He pulled his gun faster than Buffalo Bill. I had no option.

He beckoned at me with the gun. 'Off!' he said. I climbed off the saddle of the motor-bicycle.

He flung open the side-car door. 'Out!' he said.

Off and out. Just that. Knife down my sleeve, into my hand. Motor-cycle between me and the Major. He's watching Peter climb stiffly out of the side car but then he moves to the left, past the front wheel, no doubt thinking the guard with the Schmeisser is watching me. But he isn't. Too damned curious to see what comes out of the side-car, bends to his right putting himself off balance. Now the Major's clear of the wheel of the motor-cycle. Move fast. Knife out. Left hand grabs the Major. Knife in, up, and under the ribs. Hold his body for a count of one, two, while the guard presses his trigger in nervous reflex and starts to swing the Schmeisser to the left spraying the ground, across the side-car, coming towards the Major and with one gigantic heave that contains all my strength, all my frustration at allowing myself to be caught so simply, all my anger at my carelessness, I throw the Major from me on to the barrel of the Schmeisser and the rounds thump into him as he and the guard go down in a heap.

I darted in quick. It was easier to grab the Major's pistol than to get out mine. One shot for the driver already scrambling for the protection of the other side of the staff car, one shot for the guard who's struggling to disentangle his gun from the Major's belt and himself from the bloody mess of his superior officer. The Mauser swings left and I miss. The second shot blows a hole in his face.

Peter had been pitched half out of the side-car, three holes in his chest.

'Believe me, Peter, you're better off dead.'

Too many ideals. Too many honourable thoughts. You'd have taken all they could give you rather than soften that stiff, stiff, upper lip and they'd have killed you for it, the slow painful screaming way.

His eyes opened, already glazing like the eyes of old fish.

He couldn't speak. He didn't need to. He died, hating me worse than the Germans because I was British, and ought to have known better.

As I went into the cafe, two men dressed in fishing clothes got up to leave. If my instincts hadn't been so finely tuned I'd have missed the gesture of the man behind the counter, the lifted hand that said, 'warning, stay!'

'Let's have another drink, let's have a last one, before we go,' one of them said. They sat down again, this time between me and the door. I walked slowly across to the bar, feeling prickles along my spine that told me I was being watched and assessed. The barman looked at me, dispassionately. I knew I *looked* all right. I'd had a stroke of good fortune on the outskirts of Marseille when an old man, wobbling along on a bicycle, had accidentally brushed the leg of a German, walking along the road. The German had swung his rifle at the old man, who fell sideways on the road, his thin skull doubtless crushed. The German had dragged the old man off the road into a wood, the same wood in which I was hiding. I left the German and the old man lying together in there, both dead, but I stripped the old man and took his clothing and his bicycle. Both fitted me perfectly, both got me into Marseille without challenge.

'A wine, please.'

'Any special kind? White, red?' Routine question, asked a million times for a routine answer. But I was different.

'Do you have *a vin de Salses?*'

'How do you like it?'

'Mixed with Porrier water . . .'

'None left . . .'

'*Ah, l'absence est le plus grand des maux.*' With that, I'd gone through stages one and two. But he still hadn't accepted me. He poured me a glass of wine. Poured one for himself. Poured one each for the two men sitting near the door. I took his glass and my glass, and walked to the two men with them. I put the two glasses on the table, felt the escape of

246

tension, like air hissing from a bottle. They picked up the glasses and scrambled to the bar. 'Quick, who are you?' the barman said, in French.

'I'm the man they're chasing, the man who escaped from prison in Paris.'

'*Merde*, you've done a marvellous thing getting through.' The barman was looking at me with a different brand of appraisal, an admiration. After all, in the past five weeks I'd killed well over fifty Boches in such a way the local cells could not be blamed or taken for reprisals.

'Everybody's talking about you,' he said.

'I hoped they would be. That way, you won't be asking for references from my previous employer.'

'How were they killed?' It was a loaded question. I reached into my pocket, drew out what was left of the telegraph wire, laid it on the counter in front of him.

'With that,' I said, 'and if you check the places on a map you'll find they head straight to Marseille.'

'That was a dangerous thing to do,' one of the fishermen grumbled, 'to point them straight towards us . . .'

'But, at least, it made sure you'd accept me when I arrived with an out-of-date code. There's nothing more suspicious than yesterday's password . . .'

'I still think it was dangerous . . .'

The patron silenced him with a wave of his hand. 'What do you care,' he said. 'He killed more Boches than any man in our section, hein? I can't see a provocateur doing that? And all with a length of telephone wire.'

'And a few grenades, a gun or two, some petrol.'

'You're an inventive man, that's for sure.'

'Inventive in killing, yes.' I saw Peter's eyes again, felt the reproach of his unspoken words.

I felt the draught on my back as the door opened. In the mirror behind the bar I could see the Germans as they looked in. I raised my glass and drank. They peered myopically around the dark interior, but then went out without saying a word.

'They've brought five battalions into Marseille,' the patron

247

said. 'All looking for you. You should take that as a compliment.'

I wasn't interested in compliments. I'd come here because I knew he had a radio transmitter, hooked into the aerial of the Customs House next door, where the German Direction Finder squads couldn't identify it. I'd come here because he was an old hand, known and trusted in London. And because he had the instinct of survival.

'We can find you a job,' he said. 'We need men like you, inventive men. We're getting stale, here.'

'I don't want a job.'

'Pity. We could make great use of you.'

'The Germans already did. I've had enough . . .'

'And you want to get back?'

'Yes, as soon as possible.'

'We can broadcast but I'm not certain they'll listen.'

'When? How soon?'

'In an hour.'

It was nearer two hours when he came to get me from the guest bedroom in which I'd fought sleep, fearing the return of the nightmare. The water-tank in the attic was on wheels, its connections made of rubber pipe painted to look like lead. Behind the tank was a door into a small space in the eaves in which was a bed, some books. The bed was hinged. Beneath it was his transmitter. One meter on it intrigued me. The needle was perking rapidly, even though he hadn't switched on.

'I can only transmit at certain times,' he said. 'That meter tells me when it's safe.'

'I.e. when the customs house next door is transmitting?'

'You know too much,' he said, his earlier suspicion returning. 'That could be dangerous for me, if you're taken.'

I opened my mouth. 'I used to have teeth,' I said, 'not these broken stumps. And you're still operating.'

'Everybody can be broken, one way or another.'

'I've been tried, by experts,' I said.

'So I'd heard. It's still dangerous!'

248

'Then it's all the more important for you to get me away,' I said. He had to agree with that.

UK came on the air, sending smooth and cold. He identified and they acknowledged. He sent the group that meant, *I have a problem*. They said, *wait*. No doubt they'd be alerting the officer charged with looking after such problems. He was on the air in two minutes. *Here we go gathering nuts in May.* The guys who think up these things have a curious sense of humour. We were in a hurry. 'I have Ted Cork,' he said in clear. Then a number that would tell Nuts-in-May to translate into French. Ted Cork in French, Edouard Bouchon, as near as dammit is to swearing.

The rest was in code which I didn't have, but I could guess what they were saying.

'Really? *The* Ted Cork? Have you checked him? Is he the real thing? Or a substitution?'

I'd been prepared for this, had written a potted biography in the latest code I could remember. 'Send this,' I said, 'and tell them to verify with Major Why at Queen Anne's Gate. Case number 72/456.'

He sent it and closed down the set.

An hour later he opened up again. The Customs House needle was still performing its dance, so the D/Fs wouldn't spot us. He started confidently. 'Apprentice to Buds-in-May . . .'

Buds-in-May sent a short group.

When Apprentice turned towards me, the pistol that had been in the pocket in his leg was in his hand.

'They don't know you,' he said. 'There's no Major Why at Queen Anne's Gate. There never has been.'

That was just downright bloody crude, and he knew it. Okay, what were they afraid of. Either I wasn't who I said I was, the man they'd sent out as Moulin-Bas, alias, Patrice Morgat, alias Edouard Bouchon, or I was. If I wasn't, then I must have obtained the information from the man who was. Which made me a substitute. But surely, even as a substitute, I would have made damned certain I'd got the correct information *before* I'd venture into the cafe in Marseille. If I *was* who I said I was, I could see there was a risk I'd been *doubled* by the Germans. That I'd become a traitor. It would be the perfect way to infiltrate a man into the British Special Services. That, however, was why I had made my journey down through France so blatant, so obvious. And why I'd killed so many Boches on the way down. Not even a *double* would wilfully kill fifty people to establish a false identity. In either case, I'd know about Major Why. Queen Anne's Gate. 72/456. I composed another message. Several sentences I could remember him saying to me. Sentences with no military significance, things an interrogator would be unlikely to ask about. Phrases, barely remembered, like '*Do I look like a medical wallah? If you need a truss, we've left it a bit late, h'm?*'

When he had finished sending it, I clipped him behind the ear, took his gun from him. When he came round, I was sitting in front of him with the gun pointing between his eyes. He quickly looked around. The radio had a self destruct button on it and I felt his urge to tap it, to blow us both to hell.

I reversed the gun and handed it back to him. He checked it was still loaded, turned his puzzled eyes back to me. 'Just in case you were having any doubts yourself,' I said. 'I could have strangled you quite silently. But I didn't, did I? Now, open up the radio again. They've had enough time to digest that little lot.' I had a mental picture of Major Why, sitting with a telephone in his hand. The bastard. Asking himself, am I genuine or false. Better not take a chance old man, eh what, h'm. Better not bring him back. Write him off. Human life's expendable. Train another one to replace him. And then, putting down the telephone getting into his Burberry, setting out for the club and a bottle brought up from the cellar. He'd need that, wouldn't he? He'd need to forget, if only for one bottle, that he'd just condemned a man to death.

'*Buds-in-May...*'

'*Apprentice...?*'

'Abort...'

He closed down the set. Now it comes. How will he do it? He must have some signal to the two men, doubtless waiting downstairs. They'd take me, or try to, on the way out. Knife and thuggee garotte. Silent. Then throw me, weighted, into the harbour as a contribution to next week's bouillabaisse. The gun came up. I flinched. No room to do anything but sit there and take it. Somehow, I didn't care any more. Images floated past my mind. Major Why, walking along the corridor, Solange falling slowly down the side of that wall, Max arcing his body away from the blow torch. Maurice, la Mouche, a lock of hair.

He gave the gun back to me, reversed.

'I know where there's a fishing boat you can take,' he said. 'It even has a gaff rig, for when the fuel runs out. Keep near the coast, about five miles out. Once you get off Spain, you'll need to go further off shore. With luck, you might make Gibraltar.'

We crawled out of the attic and slipped into the kitchen. I made a move to leave. The patron touched my arm, grinned and winked. 'Wait,' he said.

I waited.

He pointed to the cauldron beside the stove. It was three-quarters filled with soup, dumplings floating in it.

'A speciality of the house,' he said. 'Served only to my best customers, the Boches.'

'So?' I said.

'You could show your appreciation,' he said.

'How?'

'Piss in it!'

I hesitated.

'Go on,' he said. 'Every one of you who comes through here does. Those pigs in *there* never know the difference.'

I added my contribution, and went out into the night.